BREE McCREADY
AND THE
FLAME OF IRENUS

HAZEL ALLAN

WWW.STRIDENTPUBLISHING.CO.UK

Published by
Strident Publishing Ltd
22 Strathwhillan Drive
The Orchard, Hairmyres
East Kilbride G75 8GT

Tel: +44 (0)1355 220588
info@stridentpublishing.co.uk
breemccready@googlemail.com
www.stridentpublishing.co.uk

A catalogue record for this book is available from the British Library.

ISBN 978-1-905537-17-4

The publisher acknowledges subsidy from the Scottish Arts Council towards the publication of this volume.

Typeset in Book Antiqua
Designed by Sallie Moffat

For Sandra – because sisters are special.

ACKNOWLEDGEMENTS

Once again, thank you to everyone at Strident Publishing, in particular Alison Stroak and Graham Watson who came along when I needed them most.

Massive thanks to Lawrence Mann who came up with yet another incredible cover design.

Love to my amazing Mum and Dad whose arms must ache from holding me up. You are simply the best.

A big shout out to my friends, who have provided encouragement and laughter every step of the way.

Much love to Laurie, who brings a touch of magic to my every day and makes even the bumpy times worthwhile. Without his endless supply of cuddles and inspiration none of this would have been possible.

Thanks to Stuart Smart from Low Port Primary School in Linlithgow who came up with the name 'Guinessberry Heights'.

Last—but not least—a huge thank you to everyone who read *Bree McCready and the Half-Heart Locket* and gave me such wonderful feedback about it. Without you there would be no *Flame of Irenus*.

'The hues of the opal, the light of the diamond are not to be seen if the eye is too near.'

Ralph Waldo Emerson

'Is solace anywhere more comforting than in the arms of a sister?'

Alice Walker

PROLOGUE

Mimi had not meant to pry. She had only been bored. And her sister Honey's drawer was already half-open. Considering the mess in it a little rearranging should have gone unnoticed. A shaft of morning sunlight had drawn her eye towards something small and golden shining out from the clutter. It was one half of a heart-shaped locket. She had never seen it before and picking it up she had to squint to read the tiny inscription down the jagged edge:

LOOK

ON

SHELF

FOR

BOOK

SEVEN

It sounded like an order. Mimi thought about putting the half-heart back, but then again, Honey would never know she had taken it. Besides, it would serve Honey right for leaving her out of all the exciting stuff she did with Bree and Sandy…

Mimi ran outside into the warmth of the morning with the half-heart cold and sharp in her pocket. She felt she was finally allowed in on a special secret. The thrill made her giggle as she ran towards Rockwell Housing Estate.

1.

MEET THE GEEKS

Under a high August sun Bree McCready and her best friends Sandy Greenfield and Honey Pizazz were trying to enjoy the last days of the school holidays. But even though it was early morning Bree's rooftop garden was already baking. Looking up at the flawless sky Bree found it hard to imagine anyone being unhappy on a day like this.

'Make it stop! I'm melting…' groaned Sandy, taking off his glasses and wiping his brow. 'This has to be the hottest summer in history!'

He flailed around on the sun-lounger in shorts and a t-shirt, his ragged, raven-coloured fringe falling over his pale face.

Honey laughed and shielded her eyes. 'Stop moving, Sandy! Your legs are giving me snow blindness!'

'It's not my fault I don't tan,' Sandy grumbled, and slurped a cold drink sulkily. 'We can't all be perfect.'

Honey giggled and chewed on her gum. Wisps of her golden hair blew in the breeze and her blue eyes dazzled. Anyone who said there was nothing in a name had obviously never seen Honey Pizazz.

'We shouldn't moan,' Bree sighed from the only

patch of shade. 'We'll be stuck in a classroom this time next week.' Beside her was a box of photographs and letters spilling out across the rug. She picked one up and fanned herself with it.

Honey stretched like a cat and lay down beside her. 'At least it's going to be nice for Annie's party tonight,' she smiled as she fiddled with the ring on her middle finger.

Annie was Sandy's grandmother. Bree had suggested they celebrate her birthday up here on the roof garden.

Or *her* roof garden as Bree liked to think of it.

It could only be reached by a ladder from her flat and was particularly special at this time of the year when the pot plants and flowers were in bloom. Weaving around the perimeter walls between roses and honeysuckle were wild gatherings of fragrant clematis. This high up the wind was little more than a whisper scented with sun-baked flowers. You could see into Guinessberry Heights – the tower block opposite – and beyond, across the city, to a miniature world of winding roads and tiny people.

Turning onto her front, Honey swung her bare feet in the air and held her ring up to the sun to let the light glint off the dark blue stone. 'My mood ring is telling me I'm happy and calm,' she grinned, and blew a gigantic pink bubble.

Sandy threw down his graphic novel. 'How on earth can a ring know what you're feeling?'

Honey cleared her throat in the way only she

could and recited: 'It has been told, in legend old, when the mood ring changes tone, that thoughts concealed are now revealed, and emotions will be known.'

Sandy raised his eyebrows.

'Where did you learn that?' asked Bree.

'It was on a leaflet that came with the ring.' Honey held her hand out so Bree could see it. 'You can't get better than purple,' she continued. 'Purple means you're as happy as can be. Black is not good though. You really don't want the stone to turn black.'

'Pah. They'll sell folk any old rubbish,' frowned Sandy, reaching for his drink.

'Lighten up, Granddad!' laughed Honey. 'You don't have to dismiss everything you don't understand.' She sat up, crossed her legs and turned her attention to Bree's box of pictures. 'Found anything interesting?'

Bree lifted out a heap and dropped it into her lap. 'Just my swimming certificates, some old report cards and photos,' she shrugged. 'Mum asked if I could sort them out.'

Honey rummaged through the pile until something caught her eye. 'Who're these two?' she asked, holding up a dog-eared photo of a pair of smiling young women with matching pushchairs.

Bree smiled fondly. 'That's me and Sandy when we were babies, with our mums.'

'Give us a look,' Sandy said, reaching out.

Honey passed it over. 'I've never seen your mum before,' she said, pointing to the dark-haired woman with the bright smile and laughing eyes. Sandy had a quick look and nodded solemnly before he handed it back without a word.

'It's really cute that you and Bree have known each other for…well, forever.'

'Mad isn't it?' said Bree. 'We know all of each other's secrets, don't we Sandy?'

Sandy smiled then looked away. Bree pulled out a Polaroid from the jumbled mountain of memories. 'Oh look, here's my mum and dad together,' she said sadly, 'when they were still young and in love.'

Bree's mum had an enormous bump under her dress. Her father had his hand on it and smiled proudly, showing off the little dimples in his cheeks. She turned it over and read the faded scribble on the back:

'Taken by Jane Greenfield – June 28th. Any time now!'

'This must have been only a few days before he died.' Bree stared at the image and tried to see anything that foretold her father's terrible fate. Instead she saw an ordinary young man excited about the birth of his first child. Her mother beamed with happiness. Her hair was different, curly and darker, but otherwise she looked the same. It was hard for Bree to imagine that the beach ball under her mum's dress was her.

Honey thrust a more recent photograph under

Bree's nose, pulling her away from her thoughts. Mrs McCready had taken it a few weeks ago on the first day of the holidays. In it, Sandy stood between Bree and Honey, with Mimi in front of him, her gap-toothed smile framed by her strawberry blonde hair.

'I like this one,' said Honey. 'Look, Sandy.'

Sandy pulled his gaze away from his book to glance idly at the photograph. 'Yeah, that was a cool day,' he nodded with a lopsided smile. 'Wait, let me see that!'

In the picture Honey was making rabbit ears behind his head.

'You pest!' he laughed and gave her a shove. Honey shoved him back, stabbing her tongue into her bubblegum and making it snap. 'At least that time it wasn't Mimi being her usual annoying self.'

'Don't be so mean,' scolded Bree. 'I'd have loved a kid sister.'

'Take mine. Please! Can I keep the pic?'

'Sure,' Bree nodded. 'Look! Here's one of my dad's school photos.'

Honey ran her finger over the glossy surface, searching the rows of serious faces. She stopped at the last boy on the front row. Sandwiched between a thin red-haired girl and a plump boy wearing wire-rimmed glasses was Richard McCready.

'He's so handsome,' Honey sighed, swooning theatrically.

'He's so young!' laughed Bree. 'Probably not much older than we are now. It's funny to think of him as my age.'

Sometimes everything about her dad's death came back to Bree in a dizzying rush. Although she had moved on in the last few months there was always a feeling of sadness at the back of her mind. It was like having tiny splinters of glass buried beneath her skin. Even though the wound of losing him had healed into a barely visible scar, there wasn't a day that she didn't wish he was still around. Old photographs helped a little but at the same time they also made her desperately sad; she was looking at fragments of a life story that was not allowed to reach its proper conclusion.

'And who's this pretty face?' interrupted Honey, pointing out a shy-looking girl in the back row.

'That's my mum,' said Bree.

'I didn't know they went to school together!'

'Yes, they met at school. It was chemistry.'

'Oh boy,' grinned Honey. 'When the chemicals kick in nothing can stop love!'

'No – they fell in love during chemistry. They had it first period on a Monday.'

As if on cue, Bree's mother climbed up the ladder to the roof garden, bearing a jug of homemade lemonade. 'Anyone for a top up?'

'Yes please, Mrs M.' Sandy held his glass up in the air.

Madeleine laughed and climbed the last few rungs of the ladder. She wore a loose, raspberry-coloured tracksuit and had pulled her ponytail through the gap at the back of a baseball cap. 'Heavens, Sandy, don't get up. I'll come to you.'

Once Sandy's glass was refilled he gave a thumbs-up to thank her. She ruffled his hair affectionately and made her way over to the girls.

'Look at this lot! I have far too much stuff,' she sighed at the avalanche of photographs, cards and letters. 'I ought to sort it out so your memories make a bit more sense.'

'They're fine as they are, Mum,' replied Bree. 'It doesn't matter to me if they're a bit jumbled.'

'Now, who's this?' asked Honey, holding up the school photograph again to point out a boy in the front row with a serious expression.

Madeleine tilted her head and peered short-sightedly. Almost immediately a flicker of distaste crossed her face. 'Hmm. That's Tomas Deanheart. He was only at our school for a few weeks. Bit of a strange lad.'

'And him?' asked Honey, moving her finger to the left.

Madeleine smiled. 'Harry Montague. Bree's dad and Harry played on the hockey team together.'

Something inside Bree clenched. Her dad liked hockey. That was something else her mother had forgotten to tell her about him.

Honey squealed. 'He's gorgeous!'

'You think every boy is gorgeous,' Sandy muttered.

'Only because a lot of them are, Sandy,' Honey smirked with an indignant flick of her hair.

'To be fair Sandy, Honey is right. He *was* gorgeous,' said Madeleine with a wink. 'But I only had eyes for one boy.'

'Your one and only?' said Honey breathlessly. 'Tell all right *now!* I want to know the first thing you noticed about him.'

'I remember that like it was yesterday—' Madeleine began, when she noticed Mimi had appeared at the top of the ladder. Mimi squinted in the sunlight, crinkling her nose until her freckles touched. 'Oh, hello sweetheart!' Madeleine chirped. 'Come up and have some lemonade.'

Honey scowled. Mimi smiled broadly, showing off the gap in her front teeth. She jumped onto the rooftop and made a beeline for Sandy. 'Hi!' she cooed, shyly playing with the string of beads around her neck.

'Hi Mimi,' Sandy replied flatly, without lifting his head from his graphic novel.

Bree smiled. It was clear to everyone except Sandy that Honey's little sister had the biggest crush on him.

Honey put the photograph back in the pile. 'She always butts in at the best bits. What do you want, shrimp?'

'None of your business. And stop calling me shrimp!'

'I'll bet mum doesn't know you're here, shrimp,' Honey's jaws clicked as she chewed her gum.

'So what if she doesn't? I'm not a baby.'

'That's debatable,' mumbled Honey lying back on the blanket and closing her eyes.

'Shut up,' Mimi hissed under her breath.

'Please go away, brat,' sighed Honey.

Mimi folded her arms. 'Sandy wants me to stay. Don't you Sandy?'

He was too engrossed in his book to get dragged into it. He moved his legs along to make a space for her on the lounger.

'You really shouldn't talk to her like that, Honey,' whispered Madeleine, raising an eyebrow in mock judgement. Honey pursed her lips but kept her eyes closed. Bree knew from experience that the tension would only get worse if the two sisters hung around together. She had an idea. 'Mum, are you going into the library today?'

Madeleine McCready had become Ramthorpe Junior's school librarian at the beginning of the year. It was a job she had always wanted and she was already miles more popular with the pupils than the previous librarian, the terrifying Mrs Oxter. Nobody seemed to have thought it strange that old Mrs Oxter suddenly disappeared during the Christmas holidays but Bree was relieved no-one was asking questions about it.

Realising Bree was trying to break the atmosphere, Madeleine put the jug of lemonade down and said, 'Mimi, why don't you come to the school library for a little while? I need a helper to get it ready for the start of term.'

Mimi jumped up from the sun-lounger and clapped her hands excitedly. 'I'd love to!'

'Result,' said Honey, folding her arms tightly across her chest.

Mimi's eyes filled with tears. 'Stop it!' she spat.

Honey sat up. '*You* stop it. These aren't even *your* friends, they're mine.'

'I hate you!' yelled Mimi, stamping her foot in frustration.

'Elephant shoe,' Honey sang with a taunting grin. Mimi turned away and pouted.

'What the heck is an elephant shoe?' asked Sandy.

'Just a family thing,' shrugged Honey. 'It's sort of a way of saying I love you without actually saying it. Your mouth makes the same movements.'

Sandy looked puzzled for a moment as he rolled the words around his mouth like they were polished pebbles.

'Why don't we *all* go to the library?' tried Madeleine.

'But it's too hot!' Bree wafted her face.

'Oh come on,' her mother persisted as she took Mimi to the ladder. 'It would do you all some good to get a change of scene.'

Sandy got up from the sun-lounger and stretched his arms. 'I'm up for a walk,' he yawned. Mimi squealed with delight. Honey tutted.

'You really shouldn't be so horrible to Mimi,' Bree chided quietly. 'Sisters are supposed to be special.'

'You're just saying that because you're an only child,' snapped Honey, shoving a tube of sunscreen into her satchel and making her way towards the ladder. Bree was shocked. Sandy stayed silent but raised his eyebrows at Bree in sympathy.

• • •

The lift was being fixed so they had to walk down the eight flights of stairs. On the ground floor they found an assortment of boxes and suitcases, stacked one on top of the other. Passing the open front door of flat 1A Bree could hear laughter and the murmur of conversation.

'Some new people must be moving in today,' she whispered as her mother guided Mimi round a pile of clothes. As they did, a tall man carrying a bunch of flowers came out and bumped into Madeleine. She was startled at first then gasped. 'Harry? Oh how funny—we were just talking about you upstairs.'

'Madeleine! I hope you were saying nice things about me,' the man laughed. 'I heard you lived here.' He wiped his free hand down his jeans and extended it, smiling. 'Small world, eh?'

Madeleine shook his hand then self-consciously removed her baseball cap, smoothing down her hair. She suddenly remembered her manners. 'This is my daughter Bree, and her friends, Sandy, Honey and Mimi.'

Harry nodded politely in their direction as they all chorused their hellos.

'Sweet peas,' Madeleine looked down at the bouquet. 'They used to be my favourite flowers.'

'Used to be?' Harry enquired with a direct stare.

Madeleine shrugged. 'They are beautiful but they don't live for long. I can't bear to have something so wonderful for such a short time.'

'Better not to know what you're missing?' replied Harry, with a glint of understanding. 'I was so sorry to hear about Richard,' he added.

'Thank you. It happened such a long time ago now,' said Madeleine, catching Bree's eye. 'Are the flowers for someone special?'

It never ceased to amaze Bree how good her mother was at changing the subject.

'They're for Susan,' Harry replied, 'I thought they would freshen up the flat, make her feel more at home.'

Madeleine took a step backwards. 'Is Susan moving into the building?'

Harry smiled until the corners of his eyes crinkled like crushed linen. 'Yes, I thought you would be pleased.'

Madeleine shook her head incredulously. 'Well, it really is a small world.'

Mimi, who had been dancing on the spot for the last five minutes, tugged on Madeleine's sleeve. She was finding it difficult to conceal her boredom for another second longer.

'Anyway, we should be going,' said Madeleine. 'I have a brood of restless children to entertain.'

'I'm sure we'll see each other again,' Harry nodded.

'I hope so,' replied Madeleine. Bree could tell she meant it.

As they walked towards the front door, Madeleine whispered out the side of her mouth, 'Is my hair a total disaster?' It sat straight, parted in the middle, and was tucked neatly behind her ears.

'No mum, it's fine.' Bree rolled her eyes. 'Should he have been flirting with you like that if he has a wife?'

Madeleine looked puzzled until the penny dropped. 'A wife? Oh, you mean Susan. Susan's not his wife. She's his sister.'

Bree held the door open for everyone to step out into the delicious blue and white morning.

'Besides,' Madeleine added with a flush cherrying her cheeks. 'He wasn't flirting, he was only being friendly.'

'Sure!' said Bree, raising a dubious eyebrow. Sandy chuckled, prompting Honey to elbow him in the ribs. Before she left Bree turned around in time to see Harry Montague slipping inside flat 1A, leaving the scent of sweet peas and cologne behind him.

•••

The gates to Ramthorpe Junior were open when they arrived. Bree supposed the school janitor Mr Flangelberry was doing some last minute maintenance before everyone came back to start the new term. Everyone but them, that is. Next term Bree, Sandy and Honey would be going to high school.

While Bree sought out a bit of shade, Madeleine headed to the main entrance. 'Aren't you coming in?' she asked.

'I think we'll wait out here,' replied Bree, letting Mimi skip up the stairs before she sat down. The bottom step was blissfully cold beneath her legs.

'We'll carry on the sunbathing Mrs M,' said Sandy, sitting beside Bree and stretching his legs into a block of sun.

'You need all the sun you can get,' said Honey, eyeing his pasty pins.

'Leave him alone!' cried Mimi defensively. 'You're always teasing Sandy!'

'I'm allowed to. Because he's *my* friend, shrimp, not yours,' said Honey, her expression darkening for a moment.

Madeleine held the door open wide for Mimi. 'Come on,' she laughed, trying to keep the mood light. 'There are biscuits in my office.'

Mimi turned on the top step and glared down at Honey. She put her hand into the pocket of her shorts and blinked away hot, angry tears. 'Anyway, I know something you don't!' she snapped and marched into the school, slamming the door behind her like a thunderclap.

Honey shook her head and sat down with Bree and Sandy as an explosion of music erupted from her satchel. Honey dug around inside and fished out a string of candy beads. 'Here, hold this,' she said, plonking it into Bree's hands. She rummaged around a bit more and pulled out a half-eaten chocolate bar. 'It's a bit old and melted,' she shrugged apologetically as she handed it to Sandy, 'but if you pick off the fluff I'm sure it'll be fine…'

'What exactly do you have in there?' he asked, trying to see inside the bag as the music got louder.

'Everything a girl could need,' replied Honey. 'Perfume, gum, purse, umbrella. And my phone.'

She flipped it open and pressed it to her ear. 'Hi mum.' She uncapped a tube of strawberry lip-gloss and casually offered it to Bree (who screwed up her face) then applied some as she spoke. 'Yeah, we're all fine. *She's* with Mrs M.'

Saffron Pizazz sounded distant and high-pitched but Bree could tell she was dishing out instructions.

'Yep, I promise, mum. I won't take my eyes off her,' said Honey, rolling her eyes and feigning a yawn. She snapped the phone shut and tossed it back in her satchel.

'Anything else in there for eating?' asked Sandy, scrunching up the gold foil.

A cloak of morning shadow settled across the playground, making them grateful for a break from the sunshine.

'I might actually miss this place when we go to high school,' said Sandy, surveying the empty playground.

'I won't,' said Bree firmly. 'It's time for a change. And time to leave some things behind.' She had never quite understood the secret languages, rival cliques and hierarchies that formed in school. She had not said anything about it to Sandy and Honey, but she hoped she would fit in better at Rockwell High.

'Pity we won't be leaving Princess Renshaw behind,' snorted Honey.

Just then two people turned the corner.

'Oh, speak of the devil…' muttered Sandy as he locked eyes with Alice Renshaw.

'…And she appears,' finished Honey.

In the red corner! Alice Renshaw: all bright lipstick, designer bags and catty comments. Despite being pretty and privileged, Alice was burnt up with bitterness; inside her was a smouldering fire that nothing could quench.

In the blue corner! Bree McCready: well-balanced, nice, smart beyond her years. Alice used to make Bree feel like a square peg trying to fit in the round hole of life. But the events of last Christmas changed all that. With the aid of the Half-Heart Locket, Bree had, for a moment, seen life through Alice's eyes. It was so awful she couldn't wait to get back into her own body.

Alice was shrieking with laughter and tossing her hair around even more than usual.

'She'll have someone's eye out with those extensions,' said Honey, as Alice and the boy came through the gates and into the playground.

'Who's that she's with?' asked Sandy, straightening his glasses.

'I don't recognise him,' replied Bree. From a distance all she could see of him was his floppy fringe and lopsided smile. A shot of unfamiliar emotion spread through her body. She suddenly felt shy and hoped they would walk past without noticing them. No such luck. They were heading straight for the steps.

'This should be fun,' smiled Honey, relishing the prospect of a confrontation.

'Yeah, sure,' groaned Sandy, 'about as much fun as an angry wasp.'

Honey slapped her hand on his leg. 'Then get ready for some pest control.'

Alice and the boy stopped about ten feet away from them. Alice folded her arms. 'And this is Ramthorpe Junior. Oh my God, it's a complete dump. I don't even know why my parents sent me here. Maybe it was some kind of experiment.' She pretended not to have noticed them. 'I'm *so* glad I'm not coming back after the holidays! It's totally full of nobodies.'

'What's happened to her voice?' whispered Sandy. 'It's gone all...syrupy.'

'Hi sweetie!' called Honey. Alice shot her a venomous glare. Everyone knew that the two girls were not the best of friends. 'I wish you wouldn't do that,' said Bree, hoping the ground would swallow her up. 'Why not?' blurted Honey, 'Miss Prissy-pants shouldn't get away with being rude to people.'

Most days Alice Renshaw's mood-o-meter went from 'sulky' to 'seething'. Today the needle seemed to have stuck at 'irked'. She smoothed her already perfect hair in a way that made Bree feel even more self-conscious about her own wiry tangle. From beneath her long lashes Alice's blue eyes were chilly. Bree held her gaze until her own eyes nipped. Alice's cheeks hollowed as she sucked in air.

'And to prove my point,' she said to the boy. 'Meet the geeks.'

The boy smiled down at Bree, revealing a row of perfectly polished teeth. 'Hi. I'm Adam Eastbough.'

Bree felt herself blush from the soles of her feet to the crown of her head but she did her best to smile back. 'Hi, I-I'm Bree.' She was now not only painfully aware of her mouse-brown hair but also of her useless tongue, which suddenly felt all lumpy and heavy.

'I just moved to the area,' Adam explained. 'So Alice is showing me all the places she knows.'

'That shouldn't take long,' said Honey with a smile. 'We don't have too many shoe shops round here.'

Alice threw her a dirty look and Bree knew her mood-o-meter had swung into the red zone. She waited for Adam to turn round and notice Honey. As soon he did she could be certain he would forget he had ever met Bree McCready.

'These are my friends, Honey and Sandy,' she offered, hoping to shift the focus for a moment. Adam turned and acknowledged them courteously. Honey waved enthusiastically, clattering her bangles. Sandy nodded indifferently then gave Adam a quick once-over when he turned back to Bree.

'Maybe if you guys are at a loose end you could join us?' Adam suggested with a disarming smile.

Alice shuddered exaggeratedly and stepped forward. 'Adam. I'm sure The Geeks are busy with library time and role-playing games and stuff.'

'Thanks, but we do have plans today,' Bree apologised, her mouth dry as dust.

'Looks like it's just you and me then,' Alice whooped as she made puppy-dog eyes at Adam.

'*Just* you and Adam?' Honey asked. 'What happened to the missing link, Alice?'

'If you mean Perpetua Andulus,' sniffed Alice, 'she's at netball practice. And anyway, Adam, she's not even really my friend.'

'Perpetua must be smarter than she looks.'

Alice was smouldering but she managed to compose herself. She turned to Adam. 'I'm having a party at my house tonight,' she cooed. 'Everyone who's anyone will be there. I'd especially love it if you came along.'

'We can't make it.' Honey gave her a sideways look. 'We have our own party to go to.'

Alice's lips pursed in amusement. 'Sorry but only cool people are invited.'

'If your plans change, just drop me a text,' Adam nodded to Bree. 'Shall I give you my number?'

'I don't have a pen or paper,' Bree answered, patting her pockets.

'Me neither,' Sandy added hastily.

'Anyway, we should be going,' said Alice impatiently with a thin and poisonous smile.

'Here,' said Honey, pulling something out of her satchel. 'Stick your number in here and we'll text you later.' She handed her phone to Adam.

'Cool, thanks,' he said as he tapped it in.

Alice's blemish-free complexion seemed to have taken on a green pallor.

'Hurry up, Adam. Alice has given you an order,' teased Honey, loving every second of Alice's fury.

Alice's nostrils flared. 'My God, totally ancient phone…'

Adam handed it back to Honey and nodded at Bree again. 'Buzz me if you change your mind.'

Bree smiled. She didn't trust herself to speak. Alice threw a sulky glare at Honey then spun dramatically on her heels and strutted away.

'It was nice meeting you all,' smiled Adam, holding Bree's gaze a little longer than she was comfortable with. Sandy cleared his throat.

'See you guys,' Adam waved to Sandy and Honey. He turned and ran to catch up with Alice. When he was out of earshot Honey nudged Bree. 'He *so* likes you!'

'He does not,' Bree laughed. 'He was only being nice.'

Honey said, 'You're starting to sound like your mum.'

Sandy looked despondent. 'It looks like Ruthless Renshaw has got her claws into him anyway.'

'Not a chance!' Honey replied. 'He's way too smart for that airhead. Believe me, he's not interested in her at all.'

As Bree watched Alice and Adam walk off down the road together, she was surprised to find herself hoping Honey was right.

2.

Annie Helps Out Again

Madeleine McCready flipped the light switch, flickering the fluorescent tubes into harsh yellow brightness. Having been sealed up for weeks the library smelled of warm plastic and hot dust. Mimi skipped over to the window where she stood on tip-toes to look out. By craning her neck she could see her sister, Bree and Sandy talking to another boy and girl down in the playground.

'Why don't you have a wander around while I sort out the office?' Madeleine told her. 'I won't be long.'

Mimi listened for Mrs McCready filling the kettle and once she was sure she wasn't looking she dug around inside her pocket until she found the gold half-heart. Mimi held it up to the light and read the inscription again. Maybe the book in question was somewhere in this library? She trailed her finger across the spines that lined aisle 139 in closely-packed rows. The letters quickly blurred and all the books started to look alike. She hoped that wherever 'Book Seven' was it would jump out at her soon.

Halfway along aisle 142 Mimi began to feel colder. She looked around to see where the draught was coming from but there were no gaps in the windows or open air vents. She rubbed away the goose bumps on her arms and continued to look along the army of spines. She had been holding the half-heart so tightly that it had left a jagged imprint on her palm.

The light above her blinked on and off as the hairs rose on her neck. An icy chill travelled all the way through to her bones and for a second she thought she saw a little puff of white breath. As she went to put the half-heart back in her shorts she heard a strange noise, like stone being scraped. A tremor rumbled across the floor and made her turn around. Mimi stared as the wall behind aisle 142 started to tear open. The shelves split apart and the bricks moved away from each other, one by one to reveal a bright light behind them. Mimi shielded her eyes, rooted to the spot with a mixture of fear and awe. A cold misty light seeped out of the crack and curled through the air towards her. Although it was very beautiful an instinct told her she should run. Before she could move tendrils of light wrapped around her ankles sending a sensation through her body like the vibration of a plucked string. The light roped around her legs, pulling tighter and lifting her off the floor until she was floating a few inches above the carpet.

She tried to scream for Mrs McCready but no sound came out of her mouth. The light spread up over her stomach and towards her throat. She could feel fingers of icy light cover her mouth, tight and freezing against her lips.

The last thing Mimi saw as she was pulled through the split in the wall was the glint of the half-heart on the floor. Then, the library melted away and everything went dark.

The two sides of the wall heaved back together, brick interlocking with brick. The paint melted back like the skin of a healing wound and the shelves welded, the books rearranging themselves neatly. Lastly, a blue light washed over the scar in the wall leaving no trace of Mimi behind.

'Here's your biscuit, sweetheart.' Madeleine popped her head around the tall metal bookcase. 'I've just remembered. There was a book I used to love when I was your age. You could help me try and find it then maybe you'll want to read it…' A cold shiver ran up her spine and she pulled her tracksuit top a little tighter. 'Mimi?'

Madeleine looked in the other aisles, calmly at first but then with increased urgency. Mimi was nowhere to be seen. She was alone in the library. She tossed the biscuit into the wastepaper bin and ran into the corridor. She looked left and right but the corridors were empty and quiet. Madeleine started to feel the edges of her mind unfurl. Her heart was pounding wildly in her chest.

'Mimi!' she yelled. The single desperate word shot up the long corridor and disappeared.

•••

Bree spun around to see her mother running out of the school building, shouting Mimi's name. Her voice echoed across the deserted playground.

'Are you okay, Mrs M?' asked Sandy, jumping to his feet.

'Kids, have you seen Mimi? Did she come out this way?'

Bree could feel the waves of panic radiating from her mother. Her furrowed brows creased deep lines into her forehead.

'No, we thought she was with you,' replied Bree.

Madeleine bounded down the steps two at a time and over to the gate. She looked down the street, her eyes large with fear.

The colour drained from Honey's face as her eyes darted between Bree and Madeleine. 'Something bad has happened,' she muttered, dropping the candy necklace. It shattered on the stone steps.

Madeleine ran back, holding out her hand. 'Honey, give me your phone!' Her voice was an octave away from hysteria. 'Your sister has gone missing. I need to phone your mother.'

• • •

They left Madeleine with the janitor in case Mimi turned up, and made their way to Honey's house, where her parents would be waiting. After Madeleine had spoken to them she had called the police. The urgency in her voice chilled Bree's blood.

'She can't have gone far,' tried Sandy. 'She might not even have left the school. She could be hiding in a classroom.'

'They're all locked over the summer,' said Bree.

Honey shook her head pensively. 'It's just not like Meems to run away.'

'I bet she's hiding at home. She's doing this to get back at you,' Bree offered with an unconvincing smile. She was trying to reassure herself but a terrible dread had already settled in the pit of her stomach.

'She's done something stupid, I know it,' said Honey, her eyes brimming with tears. 'I think I've really upset her this time.'

Sandy said, 'Don't be daft. She's used to you being mean to her all the time.'

It was Honey's turn to look wounded. Bree shot Sandy a warning glance to let him know he wasn't helping. He winced.

They passed Gillespie Gardens and within minutes were a world away from Rockwell's concrete tower blocks, graffiti and smog. In Freesia Lane, tall crisply painted villas stood half-hidden behind ivy and wisteria in manicured gardens. Sprinklers revolved quietly. The air was heavy with the scent of flowers. Sandy pulled out a handkerchief and sneezed.

'Spatangalam,' said Honey, but not in her usual upbeat manner.

As they approached her house the heat rose up from the pavement in shimmering waves.

Although it was the hottest day Bree could remember, the mounting anxiety was making her tremble. Honey stopped in her tracks when she saw the police car parked outside.

'It's routine,' said Bree. 'It doesn't mean anything.'

Freesia House stood at the top of a long gravel drive. It was usually a welcome sight but today Bree, Honey and Sandy trudged to the front door. As they went inside they listened out for Mimi. Other voices broke through from the living room but none of them were hers. Honey's father, Mort, appeared in the hallway with hope in his eyes.

'She's not here either?' gasped Honey.

Her father's expression crumpled and he shook his head. Honey ran to him with open arms and they embraced. Bree's stomach twisted. She had been certain Mimi would be here.

In the living room the police were with Honey's mother. Bree's knees started to feel wobbly. A tall policeman, grey-faced and serious, stood by the door while a policewoman sat on the edge of the sofa. She took off her hat and offered the children a weak smile.

Usually Saffron Pizazz exuded an energy that seemed to make the air around her tingle, but today she looked puffy and broken. The circles under her eyes were as dark as the cold coffee by her side. Her tie-dyed T-shirt was snug over the ball of her heavily pregnant belly. When she saw Honey standing in the doorway she shifted.

'Is your sister with you?' asked the policewoman as she got to her feet.

'Does it look like it?' said Honey.

'Darling, don't snap!' Saffron chastened, her voice choked with angst. Bree searched the policewoman's face for clues as to what was going on, but the policewoman stared back vacantly. The police radio in her top pocket sprung to life and she turned away to speak into it. 'Charlie, Bravo, Proceed.' A tinny voice crackled back: 'Eleven years old, last seen wearing a pink t-shirt, white shorts, a beaded necklace…' Between the clicks and hisses, the words were sharp and jagged.

Saffron let out a moan and held her head in her hands. At that moment Madeleine, her face pale and drawn, burst into the room. She sat beside Saffron and put an arm around her. 'There now, try and stay calm,' she said softly. 'This is not good for your baby.'

'But what about my other baby, Maddie?' cried Saffron. She looked desperate. 'What's happened to her?'

'We'll find her,' replied Madeleine helplessly. 'I promise. Everything is going to be okay…'

Saffron tried to wipe the tears from her face but they still flowed. Mort paced the room, every muscle in his neck pulled taut. Nothing felt certain any more. Honey's solid family had been shattered. Bree sensed that everything was not going to be all right and that her mother's promise was empty. She watched as Honey wrapped her arms around

Saffron's neck. As she did Bree noticed the little stone on Honey's mood ring had turned the shade of wet cement.

•••

They could not help anyone at Freesia House so Bree and Sandy took Honey back to Rockwell while Madeleine gave a statement to the police. Before they left, Honey made her mum promise to phone her the minute they heard anything.

'I can't imagine where she is,' she said as they climbed the stairs to Sandy's flat. She stared at the photograph she had taken from the pile earlier. Mimi smiled out at her. How could they have known then that something like this was going to happen?

'Everything was normal and now everything's crazy,' said Honey. 'I sometimes wish I could see these things coming.'

'Like Sandy's gran?' said Bree. 'Wait a minute. Maybe Annie can help us?' Honey nodded and seemed reassured by just the thought of a visit to Annie Hooten's.

•••

The door to Flat 7B was ajar when they got there, and they could hear Annie singing tunelessly from somewhere inside. The heavy smell of incense floated out.

'Go through and see Gran. I'm going to change out of these shorts,' said Sandy as he disappeared into his bedroom.

'It's only us Mrs Hooten!' Bree called as she and Honey made their way down a hallway crammed with the trophies of a lifetime's travels: polished artefacts and exotic souvenirs were everywhere. Bree knew Annie recently had a hearing aid fitted so didn't like to creep up on her in case it was switched off. She and Honey followed Annie's singing to the little kitchen, where Bree pulled back a long beaded curtain across the doorway. Annie was standing at the sink, drying dishes. Her brindled hair stuck out in tufts and wisps like straw from a scarecrow's head. She wore a long multi-coloured silk robe and painted clogs. Her flamboyance had always seemed a little out of place in drab old Rockwell so it never failed to bring a smile to Bree's face. Annie wore a huge plastic badge on her lapel saying 'Birthday Girl'.

'I know that look!' she said to Bree with a devilish smile. 'You want something, don't you?'

Annie Hooten had a silvery voice, full of magic, adventure and secrets. She was the most mysterious person Bree had ever known. Annie switched her hearing aid on, creating a piercing whine that made the girls grimace. 'That's better,' she smiled, 'I can hear you now.'

Honey got straight to the point. 'We've lost Mimi.'

'Lost?' Annie queried with an arch of her

painted-on eyebrows.

Bree nodded sombrely. 'She was with my mum at the school library and the next thing she had just…disappeared.'

'Oh dear,' Annie scratched her chin. 'That is not good. Have your mum and dad been told, Honey?'

Honey nodded. Her bottom lip quivered and a single tear dripped onto her cheek. 'The police are with them now.'

'Oh my goodness! The police?'

Annie plucked out a tissue from a box and dabbed Honey's cheek with it. She put her arm around her and took her into the living room.

'We were hoping you could help us find out what's happened to her,' said Bree.

Annie flopped down onto the settee and patted the cushion beside her. 'I don't know about that. I'm not sure I'm up for another one of my woozy episodes, sugar plum,' she said.

Honey sat next to her and looked at her with pleading eyes. 'Please Mrs Hooten, you're our only hope.'

'There's no guarantee I'll get anything you know…' Annie warned. 'The frequencies come and go.'

'Anything that will give us a clue will be a massive help,' said Bree. 'Because right now we've got nothing to go on. And neither have the police.'

'I'll see what I can do. Do you have something that belongs to Mimi?' Annie asked.

Honey bit down on her bottom lip. 'Not with me. I only have this.' She pulled out the photograph.

Annie stared at it, her wrinkled face framed by a corona of carrot-coloured hair. Her pencilled eyebrows went up a notch and she smiled. 'Yes. Normally it has to be a watch or an item of jewellery, but this will do nicely,' she said. 'It's such a lovely picture, you all look so happy.'

This made Honey cry again. Bree sat down and hugged her. She had never seen Honey this upset before.

'Come now, Pumpkin,' soothed Annie. 'You must try and stay strong.'

'You don't understand!' blurted Honey. 'The last thing I said to her was really horrible!'

'Listen to me, before Sandy's mother went missing I had two daughters,' said Annie firmly. 'I know how sisters fight. And I know what it is like when one of them vanishes. You can say sorry the next time you see her.'

'But what if I never see my sister again?' cried Honey.

'We have to believe that's not going to happen.'

'It happened to you. Sandy's mother has never been found.' Honey regretted the words the second she said them. Sandy stood in the doorway. He glared at her, shocked and hurt.

'Bigmouth strikes again,' said Honey, wiping her wet face with the back of her hand. 'I can't say anything right today.'

Annie winked at Sandy and gestured for him to sit opposite them. 'There, there,' she said, patting Honey's hand. 'We all say things we don't mean when we're upset.'

Annie never talked about Sandy's parents and Bree thought better than to ask. She knew that Jane and Michael Greenfield disappeared when Sandy was little and although they had lived in this flat and been good friends with her parents, Bree had been too young to remember them. She had blurry recollections of her mother and Jane laughing together, and of Madeleine crying when she disappeared. Annie moving in to look after her grandson was difficult to forget: she arrived on a motorbike with a sidecar stacked with masks and spears and books tied up with twine. Over the years she introduced Rockwell to psychic readings and all manner of strange foods and intriguing pastimes, not to mention barefoot jogging. But the neighbours still remembered how Annie had rescued Sandy when he was left alone. The other option for him – as far as she was concerned – did not bear thinking about.

Honey sniffed and asked Annie the question Bree had never had the courage to ask: 'So, why didn't you use your powers to find Sandy's parents?'

It hung as heavy as smoke for a moment or two. Sandy looked down at the carpet but Annie held her head high and inhaled deeply. Everyone had tiptoed around the mystery for so long that for a split second it looked like she was relieved to be asked. The hurt in her eyes softened and was replaced by something like resignation.

'I tried,' she began, 'but it never worked. It was always as though I was a poorly tuned radio, or had crossed phone lines. The messages were jumbled, meaningless. Only static and the odd word now and again that meant something.'

Her eyes misted over. 'It exhausted me to keep trying and my eldest daughter eventually persuaded me to stop.'

'Your other daughter?' said Honey. 'What's her name?'

'Val.' Annie spat out the word like it would leave a nasty taste in her mouth if it stayed there a moment longer.

'Vile more like,' Sandy shuddered.

'Now, now,' Annie smirked. 'She may not have been around much but she is your mother's sister. And that's reason enough to respect her.'

Sandy looked sheepish and shifted uncomfortably in his chair. Bree preferred to stay out of it. Her own memories of his Auntie Val were not particularly pleasant and her mother had always said her name with a lick of distaste. Bree also got the impression that Annie was finding it difficult to be loyal. Her face betrayed her true feelings about her daughter.

'So, you don't see much of her?' said Honey, twisting the tissue round in her hand.

'Auntie Val and Uncle Norrie come to visit once in a blue moon,' said Sandy. 'And it's about as much fun as a trip to the dentist.'

Annie's left eyebrow flew up. 'They're an acquired taste, Sandy. Let's leave it at that.'

Annie gave Honey's hand another quick pat. 'Now. Let me see if I'm any better at finding that sister of yours.'

Honey managed a smile. 'Thank you Mrs Hooten.'

'Call me Annie. I've been saying the same thing to Bree over there for years.' Annie cracked a knuckle but didn't prize her stare away from the photograph. She turned to her grandson. 'Sandy, I need a glass of water and some fresh air.'

He jumped up from the chair and opened the balcony door, before disappearing through the beaded curtain. Despite the heat there was still enough of a breeze to spin the dream catchers. Annie shuffled around in her seat until she was comfortable. The curtain rattled again and Sandy reappeared holding a glass of water. He handed it to Annie and she took a sip, puckered her lips and said, 'Right! Let's get on with this.' Frowning, she touched the picture of Mimi. Her breathing slowed down, measured into heavy breaths. Her body relaxed and began to rock back and forth. She closed her eyes.

'Is she doing it?' Honey whispered.

'Shh!' hissed Sandy. He sat down and peered at his Gran. After a few seconds Annie's skin turned luminous. Her features convulsed in a frown of terrible concentration and as she puckered her lips tiny furrows appeared around her mouth like cracks in marble. Sweat glistened in the creases of her forehead. Her eyes darted feverishly underneath their lids and her arms and legs turned rigid. Her fingers locked into claws and her left hand held the photograph tight against her chest, so tight that her knuckles strained through her skin. For a few seconds Annie sat completely still and stiff, her face ashen. Bree hardly dared to breathe. Honey watched with an open mouth. Sandy leaned forward with a pen and paper. Suddenly Annie's body went slack and she let out a heavy sigh. The photograph fell from her hand and fluttered onto her lap. Annie spoke in a voice that did not belong to her:

'A sister lost, a world away –
Go find her soon, do not delay.
She's frightened now, "It's dark in here...
There is so much for me to fear."
Go back to where a secret lies,
And seven wishes will advise.
This place, well known with paper and spines,
A wall that splits, a light that shines.
And glinting metal on the ground,
Will bring back memories when it's found.'

The hairs stirred on the nape of Bree's neck. Her hand shot up to the hollow of her throat where her half-heart rested on its chain. Surely Annie was wrong...She was talking about the library.

And the magic book they found there. And the seven wishes it granted. Bree felt the room tilt.

Annie slumped in the settee, exhausted from the efforts of the trance. Sandy bent over her but she shooed him away with an impatient flick of the wrist.

'Mimi is in real trouble, isn't she?' breathed Honey, pale and worried.

Bree nodded gravely. 'It's got something to do with *the book*.' Dread rippled over her skin like icy water.

'I think so too,' said Sandy as he removed his glasses and wiped the lenses with the hem of his T-shirt. 'Do you think Mimi found it?'

'Even if she has, it's useless without the two halves of the locket,' Bree said firmly, holding up her half.

Annie stirred. 'Was I any help?' she groaned, her lips almost creaking with the effort of speech.

'You were wonderful, Birthday Girl.' Honey leaned over and planted a kiss on Annie's cheek. She picked up the photograph from Annie's lap as Annie drew a shallow, shuddery breath. Sandy felt her forehead. 'You need to rest now Gran.'

'Oh, I'll be fine. I can't miss my party tonight,' Annie smiled thinly, 'I've got new shoes to show off to you girls...' Sandy plumped her cushion and placed it gently behind her head. Annie's eyelids fluttered and twitched.

'I think she's already asleep,' whispered Bree. 'Let's go—'

She was interrupted by a stifled scream. Bree and Sandy spun round to see Honey staring down at the photograph. 'Stop it! Someone stop it…' she sobbed.

'What's the matter?' asked Bree, jumping to her side. Honey thrust the picture in her face. Sandy looked over her shoulder. 'What?' he said. 'I don't see anything.'

'Look closer,' said Bree.

Everything in the photo was as it had been, except for one thing. Mimi was missing her legs from the knees down.

'Impossible,' he gulped.

A fuzzy white blur was creeping up Mimi's legs and the rest of her body was starting to fade.

'My sister is being wiped out…' cried Honey, the realisation turning her face from pink to white.

3.

Up, Up and Away

As soon as they burst out into the street Bree grabbed Sandy and Honey, her eyes flashing with an idea. 'Hang on,' she said, running back indoors, 'I need to fetch something!'

Sandy thrust his hands into his pockets and looked up towards the end of the road. He seemed preoccupied with something. 'I wonder where Alice went?'

'She's probably showing Adam round her collection of false nails,' Honey said sourly, pulling her hair back into a long, swingy ponytail.

'Maybe Bree's gone up there to text him,' Sandy said.

'And you'd like to know because…?'

'Because Bree is my best friend.'

'And you don't want anyone to come between you, right?'

'Who'd come between us? Adam? I wouldn't let that happen. Anyway, we can't let him get involved with Ruthless Renshaw. He's far too nice for her.'

Honey smiled. 'Yeah, he did seem nice, didn't he? But a boy that good looking can have anyone he wants.'

'I didn't really notice how good looking he is…' shrugged Sandy. 'Anyone?'

'*Anyone...*' said Honey with a smile.

Bree crashed out of the front door looking flustered. Sandy spun around. 'What were you doing up there?'

Bree caught her breath. 'Remember this?' She held up a polished silver key.

'Whoa!' he beamed, slack jawed. 'Don Daines's magic key.'

'Cool.' Honey's bright blue eyes popped wide. 'The one that opens all doors...'

Bree pursed her lips and nodded. 'We're going to need it to get into the school. Come on!'

Sandy and Honey had to run to catch up with her.

•••

First, they made it past Mr Flangelberry's office. He had been too engrossed in the *Rockwell Gazette* to see them diving past his door. Bree's mother had obviously left the library in a hurry: the lights were still on and her mug and biscuits were still on the counter where she had left them. Apart from that nothing was out of place. There were no signs that anything unusual had happened, only the same cloying smell of musty paper, and the loud tick of the clock above the door.

'So far, so normal,' said Honey.

'Don't let that fool you,' Bree replied. 'After all, there was no trace of what happened to us here last Christmas with old Mrs Oxter. Let's look around.'

'I'll check Aisle 142.' Sandy disappeared around the high metal bookcases.

'Oh no. Bree look,' Honey was staring at the photograph. 'It's getting worse.' She sobbed, holding it up. Now most of Mimi's legs had now disappeared, leaving her torso floating in mid air. 'She's slipping away...'

Bree went to a window to look down to the playground. When she pressed her forehead on the sun-heated glass the only sign of life she saw was a defenceless baby bird cheeping and fluttering its wings. Bree watched as a dark shadow passed across it. She shielded her eyes against the glare and looked again, but the bird was gone.

'Over here!' Sandy's shout made her jump. Bree and Honey ran to Aisle 142 where Sandy was pointing at something gleaming on the carpet. 'Where did this come from?' he frowned.

Honey picked it up.

'Just as I thought,' Sandy nodded, nudging his glasses up his nose. 'A half-heart locket.'

'It's not just any half-heart locket,' said Honey. 'It's *mine*. You know what this means?'

'Mimi must've dropped it?' said Bree.

'It means she's been in my drawer!' Honey's nostrils flared.

'Let's look on the bright side,' Bree said. 'At least Mimi doesn't have it with her, wherever she is. Without both halves of the locket the book is useless.'

'And it saves us a trip back to your house to get it,' Sandy smiled.

Honey's shoulders sagged and she groaned. 'I can't believe Mimi would take something that belonged to me,' she muttered, half to herself.

'Try not to think about that right now,' said Bree. 'Wherever she is, Mimi has probably learned her lesson.'

Honey nodded gravely.

'We have to find her and bring her home,' Bree continued.

'We'll need the book,' said Sandy mysteriously. He nodded up at the top shelf. None of them had expected to see the magical book again, after they hid it here last Christmas. The anticipation of what was about to happen hung heavy in the air.

'I'll get the ladders,' said Bree.

'What if someone catches us?' whispered Honey, her eyes darting between the bookcase and the door.

'They won't, so stop worrying,' Bree replied. With the ladder in the right spot she climbed the steps with trepidation. Bringing the book and the two pieces of the locket back together would unleash a set of cryptic instructions ('Like clues or wishes,' Bree had once said) that had led them into terrible danger in the past. Once the first had been accepted there was no way back.

The ladder wobbled when Bree reached the top, so she grabbed the edge of a shelf to stop herself from falling. 'We've got you!' Honey said as she and Sandy held the bottom of the ladder. Bree steadied herself and looked up. Above her, sticking out a fraction more than the others was a tattered copy of *Origami: A Beginner's Guide*. Knowing what was hidden behind it made Bree's throat tight with fear.

'Get a move on!' hissed Sandy from down below.

Bree stretched up and nudged the other books along, working the origami book free until it fell into her hand. Tucking it under her arm, she strained on her toes as she peered into the dark space. There lay the book, like a mummy in its tomb. Carefully, she slid it out and replaced the others.

Bree climbed down and jumped off the last two steps. She brushed the dust from her t-shirt and held the book out to Honey and Sandy. They studied the cracked leather cover and the spiral spine without saying a word. The heart-shaped cavity in the centre of the cover was empty, the screen cold and glassy, and the pages were stuck together.

'It won't open,' said Bree, trying to prize the covers apart.

'It didn't open last time until after it had given us the first wish,' said Sandy.

Bree remembered when they found the book last Christmas, and how the cover finally opened to reveal the six delicate pages. Agora Burton's voice echoed in her mind: *'Once you accept the first you have no choice but to take the others too. If you cannot do this, then you must return the book to where you found it and forget it ever existed.'*

Bree's stomach lurched. This time it was different: they had no choice. Mimi's life depended on them accepting the first wish and the six others that followed. She felt her half of the locket at her neck, warm and smooth and as familiar as a tooth. With a deep breath she handed Sandy the book and unclasped the chain.

'Are you ready?' she asked, the first half of the locket poised above the heart-shaped indentation in the cover.

Honey and Sandy nodded. Bree pushed the half-heart into the slot, excitement and fear coursing through her veins in a fiery rush. Honey peeled her half of the locket from her clammy palm and gave it to Bree. With shaky fingers, Bree aligned the jagged edges, and pressed the locket into place. The zigzag line down the middle vanished.

'There's no turning back now,' said Sandy without taking his eyes off the screen on the cover of the book. No sooner had he spoken than the locket started to glow with an orange light. It grew brighter, turning red and pulsing so loudly that it seemed to resonate in their chests. Bree's hands were trembling but she forced them to stay still. 'Keep looking at the screen,' she said, mesmerised. A blue mist appeared on it, starting at the corners and working its way to the centre where it swirled then faded to reveal a few lines of text. Bree read them aloud:

'A NEW WORLD LIES BEYOND THESE BRICKS,
THIS FIRST WISH GRANTED, LEAVES YOU SIX.
PLUCK A BOOK FROM THE SECOND ROW
BREATHE IN DEEPLY, LET IT GO
SHORTLY AFTER YOU HAVE BLOWN,
SHIFTING METAL, CRACKING STONE.
ONE BY ONE YOU MUST STEP THROUGH
PREPARE YOURSELF FOR A BIRD'S EYE VIEW.'

'Not more flying,' Sandy groaned, slapping his forehead.

'If we want to get Mimi back we have to do exactly as it says,' said Bree.

'I agree,' added Honey. 'So, which book do we take from the second row?'

'It doesn't say. I guess any one will do.'

Honey kneeled and slid out a tattered paperback from the middle of the second row. She placed it on the floor and peered into the thin, dark space that it had left.

'There's nothing behind it. Only the wall,' she said, making a face. She stood up and chewed the inside of her cheek, deliberating. The light from the locket was dimming now and the throb was weaker. Bree put the book in her pocket and knelt down to look into the gap. She filled her lungs and blew into the hole. There was a puff of dust but nothing else.

'We did what the wish told us to do,' she shrugged.

'Let's try another book.' Sandy reached out. As he did a gust of freezing air poured over him, raising goose bumps on his arm. The tall metal bookcases started to rattle. The fluorescent strips on the ceiling flickered on and off.

'Something's happening,' he breathed, 'something is definitely happening...'

With a deafening crash of wrenching metal and splintering wood the shelves on the wall behind them cracked apart, sending books flying. The floor rumbled as the shelves parted to reveal a bright spot on the wall.

'It's just like the last time,' cried Honey, grabbing Bree's arm.

How could Bree forget: the last time this happened she met her dad.

A crack tore down the wall like ice fracturing a frozen pond. It spread and deepened until a long, irregular crevice split the wall down the middle. A halo of white light blossomed around the rupture, flooding Bree, Sandy and Honey with cold air. Bree's bare arms stung as she pulled the others closer. She shielded her eyes to see what was inside but the blinding whiteness made it impossible to look for too long.

'We have to go through,' she shouted above the rumbling. 'The wish told us to!'

Turning sideways, she edged into the crack. At first she couldn't see anything other than the dazzling white light, but through her thin-soled trainers she felt she was walking onto soft ground. Honey jumped in behind her, and looking over her shoulder Bree saw Sandy holding the crack open long enough to slide through. For a moment she saw the book-strewn carpet of aisle 142 under the soupy, yellow glow of the library lights. As the locket pulsed to the rhythm of Bree's heart, she had a sudden urge to run back through the gap into the safety of the school. She willed herself to stay put.

'I can't see Mimi anywhere,' yelled Honey over the vibration of bending metal.

'Me neither,' shouted Bree.

'You don't suppose this is a trick do you?'

The ground rumbled under their feet as warping metal grated together and the gap closed behind them like the doors of a lift. The jagged edges met and the tremor ceased with a judder that shook the air. With that the crack disappeared and the locket stopped throbbing. Silence fell and the dazzling white light lifted.

'Where are we?' asked Honey, rubbing her eyes. Bree blinked and looked around. They seemed to be standing in a grassy meadow surrounded by undulating hills. The sky was bright with the odd puffy white cloud breaking the blue.

'I don't know, but it looks pretty nice,' Sandy sniffed.

'Looks can be deceiving.' Bree glanced around.

'This can't be the right place,' said Honey. 'Annie's riddle said Mimi was somewhere dark.'

It looked normal enough but the stillness unsettled Bree. She looked up at the sun, shining like a gold coin in the powder-blue sky. Honey was right; it was anything but dark and frightening.

'Let's follow that path,' she said, pointing to a trail uncoiling towards the brow of a hill.

Once they reached the top, the sight below made them gasp. In the valley, bordered by a line of dense trees, floated what looked like a giant ball.

'No way – a hot air balloon,' laughed Sandy, relieved it was nothing more sinister. Honey broke into a run down the hill. 'Last one down to it is a smelly old sock.' Bree and Sandy chased after her, giggling and relishing the rush of cool air on their faces.

The balloon dominated the sky like a huge fallen moon. Underneath was an empty wicker basket roped to a peg in the grass. It creaked as the massive balloon strained skywards.

Bree looked at the ladder hanging over the side. 'Who would leave this lying around?'

'Someone who is reading my mind!' said Honey. 'I've always wanted to go up in one of these.'

'It looks like you're about to,' laughed Sandy, standing on tiptoes to peer into the basket.

As sudden as a thunder-clap, an earth-shaking rumble knocked them off their feet and made the balloon bob. 'What was that?' cried Honey, looking at the others. The rumbling came again: louder this time, and chased by a screaming, tearing sound that echoed all around them.

'Maybe the crack in the library wall is opening again?' suggested Sandy as he helped Bree up.

'No, it sounds much bigger this time. It's something else…' she replied.

The hollow rumble became so loud it made their eardrums rattle.

'Whatever it is, I don't think we should stay on the ground. Let's get into the basket,' he said.

Bree nodded just as another seismic jolt made their legs buckle. Sandy pulled Honey onto the ladder and started to untie the anchoring rope. Honey raced up the rungs and threw herself into the basket then leaned over to help Bree. As she lowered herself in, Bree caught sight of a movement at the top of the hill. A deep crevasse had wrenched the hill in half and was zig-zagging across the valley. Earth and grass collapsed into the fissure, throwing up clouds of dirt and debris, as it swallowed everything in its path.

'Hurry, Sandy!' screamed Bree.

'I can't untie it,' he said.

'Leave it and just get in,' cried Honey, stretching out to him.

Sandy looked up to see the crevasse tearing towards him. The knot freed itself under his trembling fingers and he vaulted onto the ladder just as the balloon started to lift. The ground below ripped apart, sending clods of earth into the abyss. He lost his footing on the ladder and clung on, tipping the basket. Bree pulled at his t-shirt: 'Just don't look down, Sandy…' Honey stretched over and grabbed his waistband. 'Don't mind me,' she winked. Together they dragged him aboard and he fell at their feet, glasses askew.

'Oh Sandy – you just had two girls tearing at your clothes…' laughed Bree.

Honey ruffled his hair. 'Unlucky for you.'

'Yeah, thanks guys,' he said, sitting up.

Bree and Honey looked over the side into the yawning chasm. The crack was ripping into a patch of trees. They keeled over like dominoes, smashing in an explosion of branches and leaves before being sucked down into the gorge. The balloon rose, sweeping across the meadows.

'I don't mean to sound like a dweeb, but will this thing just keep going up until it bursts or something?' said Honey.

Sandy stood up, straightened his glasses and tucked in his t-shirt. 'Well, I can answer that! Hot air balloons are an ingenious application of basic scientific principles…'

'Yep, *yawn*. How do we steer this thing, Professor Greenfield?'

Sandy looked up into the core of the balloon and fiddled with a metal lever. 'Warm air rises into cooler air because it's lighter.'

'So?'

'So we need to keep firing this burner to make

sure the balloon stays in the air.' He turned another lever which opened a valve and sent up a giant flame.

The balloon brushed the treetops before it rose higher and higher. Bree watched as their shadow grew smaller on the land. The ground was insignificant now: around them was the wide dome of the sky. They drifted above a patchwork of green woods and amber fields marked by narrow paths and impassable rivers.

'I don't believe it. Look over there,' Honey said.

Bree followed her finger to the horizon where the lush forest stopped dead at an irregular outcrop of grey and black rock. A jagged mountain stretched out of the silhouettes of twisted trees towards brooding sulphurous clouds.

'Castle Zarcalat…' said Sandy. The colour drained from his face.

'The balloon is taking us back…' breathed Bree, her voice as brittle as broken glass.

A wind picked up as the air trembled with the rumble of distant thunder. The black clouds above the castle crackled with lightning.

'Do you think Mimi is in there somewhere?' Honey's voice cracked with emotion. She rummaged inside her satchel for the photograph. 'I-I can't bear to look at it anyway…'

Bree took it from her. Sure enough Mimi had faded further. Now there was nothing left of her body from the waist down. Honey clutched the picture to her chest and stared out at the black mountain in the distance. 'They better not have hurt her,' she said firmly, her chin raised.

When another rumble seemed to make the sky quiver Sandy stiffened. 'What is that? I thought it was thunder but it's starting to sound like something else.'

Across the tent of sky a dark line grew out of the dark cowl of clouds over Castle Zarcalat. Bree, Sandy and Honey watched it weave and dip like an approaching tornado, expand and collapse.

'Are those b-birds?' asked Honey, her voice shaking with every syllable.

'Birds don't buzz. Listen,' Sandy replied, his lip quivering.

The dark mass grew and the buzz became louder, angrier, like the hum of machinery. It built like pressure in their ears. As the dark cloud shifted into focus Bree felt the fast prick of panic. It was a swarm of giant wasps, with black and yellow armour and deadly-looking tails. Her thoughts raced, nightmarish and disconnected. This could not be happening! The noise of the massive insects tore open the sky as they circled the balloon.

'There's so many of them!' shrieked Honey, ducking down in the basket.

'Stay still,' said Sandy. 'They might go away...'

'I don't think the normal rules apply to giant wasps, Sandy!' cried Bree.

As they circled the balloon, the wasps seemed to merge together until they formed a whining wall of sound.

'Get us out of here, Sandy,' Honey screeched, holding her satchel over her face.

'I don't have a steering wheel, it's not that easy,' he yelled back, turning a lever and tugging on a cord. The flame instantly disappeared. Now the only sound was the terrible angry drone and the chafing of wings. Honey pulled her umbrella out of her satchel and started waving it around in the air but this only made the wasps angrier. They started to curl their bodies and stab at the air with their giant stings.

'Okay, we're starting to sink; it shouldn't be too long 'til we land,' Sandy said.

Honey pulled Bree down beside her and they huddled together under the umbrella, frightened and helpless. The balloon had started its slow descent but it wasn't quick enough to escape the aggressive swarm.

'I can't control the balloon any longer,' cried Sandy, his white face vivid against the dark mass behind him. 'There's too many of them.'

He fell to his knees and threw his hands over his ears as something burst above his head. The three of them watched in horror as the wasps attacked the balloon, lancing it with their stings. The wasps dived and tore at the fabric until it was shredded, and in a single movement the swarm spun away.

The basket plummeted, spinning wildly, whistling through nothingness. Sandy gritted his teeth, closed his eyes and gripped Bree and Honey's hands. Honey screamed as her hair whipped about her head. Terror surged within Bree. She was breathing too fast to think clearly. Too frightened to move or speak they tried to hold on to each other as the basket bobbed and spun. Bree's blood turned to ice as she watched the world tilt until it was above them, bearing down in a dizzying flash. She squeezed her eyes shut until she saw stars under her lids. There was an immense thud followed by a sensation like fireworks going off inside her skull. Blinding pain shot through her body before everything went dark.

4.

MORE HELP FROM A FRIEND

The throb inside Bree's skull made thinking impossible. But at least she knew she was not dead. Being dead would not hurt like this. Every part of her body felt bruised.

When she opened her eyes bright yellow pinpricks of light danced before them. Something firm and rough was pressed against her cheek. She was lying on her side on hard ground. She realised she must have been thrown clear of the basket, that lay nearby in a wrecked heap, the wicker ripped and spiking out at dangerous angles. From where she was lying she could not see Honey or Sandy but Bree did not have the strength to look for them. She heard the flapping of material in the breeze, the chirping of invisible birds, the pulse of the earth beneath her. Footsteps...Footsteps! Bree felt the sliding ache of panic. Her shoulder smarted but despite the pain she planted her palms on the dusty ground and got into a sitting position. She tried to focus on a pair of sandaled feet but they moved, lifted, blurred. Her eye sockets throbbed and her head banged. Was there one pair of feet or two?

'She was right, Anando,' said a deep voice.

Someone loomed in and out of her vision: a tall, solidly built man with silver hair framing his face like a steel halo. His features were as vague as shadows on smoke. Bree's head stopped spinning long enough for her to make out that he was on his own. Her hand jumped to her pocket: the book was still there. She heard someone cough.

'Is everyone okay?' It was Honey's voice.

Relief washed away some of Bree's fear as she watched Honey crawl out from under the tattered remains of the balloon. Her hair was tousled, her face streaked with mud and her satchel was askew but otherwise she looked unhurt. She stood up and brushed herself down, stopping in her tracks when she saw the man standing over Bree. Shock and fear made her eyes pop wide.

'You have nothing to fear,' said the man, raising his hands in submission.

Honey was not convinced. 'W-where's Sandy?'

'I'm in here,' a muffled voice came from inside what was left of the basket.

Keeping one eye on the stranger, Honey reached in and helped Sandy out. He staggered and groaned, his glasses dangling from one ear. A shiny pink bump had swollen above his right eyebrow. He straightened up and touched it tentatively, grimacing. Honey leaned over to take a look but he dismissed her with a flick of his wrist and straightened his glasses.

'At least these aren't broken,' he said. 'Though I'm not sure about the rest of me...'

'And what about you?' The man thrust his hand towards Bree and helped her to her feet in one swift motion. His hands felt calloused, his knuckles raw. His tanned arms were criss-crossed with old scars and roped with prominent veins. 'My name is Dunubas,' he said with a nod. His weather-beaten skin gathered into wrinkles around eyes that glinted like chips of grey slate.

'I'm Bree. This is Sandy and Honey.' Bree combed her tangled hair with her fingers.

Sandy limped over with Honey supporting him the best she could.

'You are a long way from home,' said Dunubas, shielding his eyes from the blazing sun. Bree nodded even though it had been more of a statement than a question.

'We're trying to find someone,' said Honey, eyeing Dunubas suspiciously.

'And you think you'll find them here?'

'Not exactly,' shrugged Sandy. 'We were on our way somewhere else when...this happened.' He pointed to the ripped, deflated balloon. 'And we would have got there if it hadn't been for those giant wasps.'

'Don't worry,' said Dunubas, 'they won't come back.'

'It's typical. Sometimes I can't believe our luck,' Sandy grumbled, kicking the dry earth with the toe of his shoe.

'Don't be so cynical. It could have been worse,' said Bree, scanning the arid landscape for signs of life.

'Sandy, we fell out of the sky and *survived.* That's pretty lucky don't you think?' Honey said, brushing the dust off Sandy's back. 'And it's just as well. I can't lose anyone else today.'

'Then you better get me a drink. I'm gasping,' said Bree, clicking her tongue against the roof of her mouth to demonstrate.

'Me too. It must be all this dust.'

'Come with me, none of you have broken any bones,' Dunubas told them.

'How would you know?' Sandy frowned, rubbing the angry lump on his head.

'Trust me,' he smiled, 'I've seen enough broken bones to know what I'm talking about.'

Sandy eyed him shrewdly, his eyes settling on the faded scars on his arms.

Dunubas turned to walk away. 'Come. You can drink at my house.'

Having no other choice, they followed him over the dry, cracked earth until it became patched with random clumps of grass. A little further ahead the patches spread wider, until eventually the dusty plain ended in a lawn. On it stood a little weather-beaten cottage under the shade of an ancient tree that had a trunk as thick as three men.

'Welcome to my home,' said Dunubas as he climbed the steps to the porch.

The house looked tired and thirsty for paint. Sun-blistered window shutters creaked half open, and on the veranda fiery geraniums sagged over the railings. Purple bushes clustered next to them.

'This looks like lavender.' Sandy plucked a bud from a stem. He rubbed it between his fingers until the blossom crumbled. He sniffed his fingers and raised his eyebrows approvingly. Honey brushed her fingertips along the pastel heads making them bob on their long stems. The movement threw up even more perfume into the air. 'Yep, it's lavender all right,' she said, breaking a stem and popping it into her satchel. 'I'd know that smell anywhere. Dad has this in our garden to keep away unwanted insects.'

'But it smells so lovely,' said Bree, tugging at some of the fragrant purple flowers and putting them in her pocket.

'Not if you're a bug,' smiled Honey, following Dunubas up the steps. 'And it doesn't just smell good. You can use it for all kinds of stuff. Burns, insomnia, head lice…' Sandy automatically scratched his head.

Creepers on the veranda cast wavering fingers of shadow across a splintered and bleached door. Dunubas pushed on it until it creaked open. The scent of warm pastry made Bree's stomach growl. Inside there was only one room. It had two beds at one end and a stove at the other, with a table in the middle. Bunches of lavender and herbs hung from the ceiling. At the window, gauzy curtains wafted in the warm breeze, sucking in and billowing out. The draft brought with it the scent of wild nettle to overpower the aroma of cooking. Sun splashed a patchwork of gold onto the far wall and, as the shadows lifted, Bree noticed a woman in the corner, leaning over a basket. Her loose, waist-length hair was dark blonde, veined with white. She wore a long dress, a vague shade of beige that echoed the colour of her hair. She was slender but there was a curve in the area of her stomach. She turned and smiled disarmingly, her lips blossoming like a wild rose against the whiteness of her skin. 'Hello,' she said quietly.

'This is my twin sister,' said Dunubas, making his way over to the sink where he pumped a long handle until water flooded out. He filled three cups until they overflowed, then placed them on the table next to a candlestick spattered with wax. The woman came over, her hand outstretched. 'My name is Nevidas,' she smiled warmly. Bree shook her hand and introduced Honey and Sandy who were already drinking from their dripping cups.

'And this is Winrad…' said Nevidas as a sleepy dog click-clicked over the bare floor. He was a brownish tan colour with creamy paws that looked like boots. Dunubas bent down to pet him, murmuring in his ear. The dog responded with an enthusiastic wag and a lick. Bree held out her hand for the dog to sniff. His rough tongue rasped her palm and her laughter only seemed to encourage him. Winrad spun around excitedly before bolting past Sandy. 'I'm usually not bad with dogs,' Sandy sniffed as Honey handed him a tissue from her satchel. 'As long as they're not as hairy as him...'

Dunubas clapped his hands together making everyone jump. 'Enough, Winrad!' He pointed to the stove. The dog padded over and lay down beside it, resting his chin on his huge paws, eyebrows twitching. Dunubas pulled out a chair at the table and gestured for Bree to sit opposite.

'I've been meaning to ask you,' she said, sitting down. 'Where are we?'

Dunubas lowered his eyebrows and thought carefully. It seemed like an age before he replied. 'You could say this is a pocket of peace,' he said eventually, his grey eyes returning Bree's gaze with a steady intensity. 'The last place unscarred by the war.'

Sandy shifted from one foot to the other and peered out of the small window. 'The war? It doesn't look like there's a war going on out there.'

Dunubas scratched his stubbly chin. 'There's danger not far from here, over a boundary which should never be crossed.'

'Would it take us to Castle Zarcalat?' asked Bree, searching Dunubas's face for a reaction. He looked shocked and started to stammer. 'H-how did y-you know about Z-Zarcalat?'

Honey stepped forward. 'We think that's where my little sister, Mimi, is being held prisoner.'

'I hope you're not thinking of going there?' said Dunubas disapprovingly. 'It is far too dangerous.'

'But we need to get her back!' cried Honey, her big eyes filling with tears.

Bree took a deep breath and bit down on her bottom lip. She looked directly into Dunubas's grey eyes.

'We know what to expect. We've been there before,' she said solemnly.

Dunubas's craggy face crumpled and his eyebrows dipped until they met in the middle. Nevidas came over to Bree. Bending over, she spoke softly into her ear. 'Did you meet anyone when you were there?' she asked, her eyes full of concern.

Bree nodded. A gurgle came from a basket in the corner and Nevidas smiled automatically. 'Come and meet Pamela,' she whispered. Bree stood up and followed Nevidas to the basket standing in a rectangle of yellow light. Lying inside on a white blanket was a baby with eyes as dark as a midnight sky. Her mop of black curls was as unlike Nevidas's burnished gold as Bree could have imagined.

'This is my beautiful daughter.' Nevidas picked up the baby and nuzzled into her neck. She stood at the window where the sunlight reflected off the strands of white in her hair. She gently rocked her baby, her lips parting as she sang a lullaby:

'When you look back upon your life,
I hope that you can say,
'I felt the warmth of love and saw,

The wonder of each day'.
A snowflake melting on your tongue,
The blossom on the trees,
Autumn leaves that turn to red,
And float down on the breeze.
So what you must remember,
When the distant voices call,
It truly was a miracle,
That you were born at all.'

'What a lovely song,' said Bree. The baby responded with a chorus of contented gurgles.

Nevidas handed Pamela to Bree. 'Take her. I need to check on the Marziplum Tart.'

Although she had never held a baby before Bree soon got used to the wriggly body in her arms. She pressed her nose into the velvety curve of Pamela's neck. It smelled warm and faintly sweet. She marvelled at the baby's rosebud lips and tiny, perfectly formed fingernails.

'*So* cute,' cooed Honey.

'She won't be when she's puking on you,' mumbled Sandy.

'You better get used to this, mister,' Honey smiled impishly. 'You'll be holding my baby brother or sister soon.'

But Sandy was already looking away. Nevidas had placed a bubbling golden tart on the table and was slicing it up into five wedges. The delicious smell of warm pastry made Bree's stomach flare with hunger. 'Can I do anything to help?'

she asked. Nevidas laid the plates, stopping briefly to kiss Pamela on the nose. 'You already are,' she smiled.

'Will her dad be joining us?' Bree asked. She instantly regretted it when she saw the expression on Nevidas's face. Bree looked at Honey who shook her head to confirm she had made a terrible blunder. Lifting Pamela from Bree's arms, Nevidas kissed the baby's plump cheek. 'Her father is no longer with us,' she said sadly. 'But let's not think of the past. Come now, tuck in. You'll need your strength.' She laid Pamela back in the basket and let the baby kick her legs contentedly.

The sweetness of the plums and the marzipan complemented the crispness of the pastry and it did not take long for Bree, Honey and Sandy to finish every last crumb on their plate.

'That was amazing,' grunted Sandy.

'It's good to see someone with a healthy appetite,' Nevidas laughed.

'You can say that again,' Honey rolled her eyes.

Sandy smiled sheepishly and wiped his mouth.

'And I've got some other things that you can take with you on your journey,' Nevidas said, standing up and placing her hands on Dunubas's wide shoulders.

'*My* journey?' he queried, his eyebrows knitting together.

'Surely you're not going to let these children go there alone, are you?' she said.

'Of course. Unless you are suggesting that I

take them over Strangledoor?'

Nevidas looked at Bree with narrowed eyes. 'You say you have been to Zarcalat before?'

Bree nodded, her hand feeling for the book in her pocket.

'Then, I say you can do it again,' Nevidas winked. 'With the help of a friend of course.' She rested her chin on Dunubas's shoulder and he slumped in his chair.

'What is Strangledoor?' asked Sandy.

Dunubas swallowed and sat back in his chair. He wrestled silently with something for a few seconds then made a small gesture that indicated he was about to tell them something important.

'Many years ago our land, Geldoss, was a utopia. But it was torn apart by hatred and intolerance. Back then we had one spirit and we spoke one language. Until the forces at Zarcalat divided us. They told us they had a revelation that would change our lives. They showed us the Flame of Irenus, and told us it carried immense power over us all. Many people fell down to worship it, others were sceptical. Soon factions formed and those who believed in it took arms against those who did not. Geldoss was divided into two states: Swarnbideah and Calvaria. They are kept apart by the border of Strangledoor. No one is allowed to cross from one state to another. Anyone who tries risks being killed.'

Dunubas allowed a moment for the words to sink in before he continued.

'For the citizens of Swarnbideah, the Flame of Irenus symbolises hope. They believe that it is the source of all peace and think that anyone who disagrees is their enemy. If you ask me their minds have been poisoned. The Flame of Irenus keeps the fire of hatred alive and this is exactly what those at Zarcalat intended. They thrive on darkness and misery. As long as the Flame burns there will be division, war and death.'

'What about the people who live in Calvaria?' Bree asked.

Dunubas sighed. 'The conflict has gone on so long that most people have forgotten what they are fighting for. The people of Swarnbideah are taught to believe that we in Calvaria are the evil ones for not trusting the Flame. Their children are not encouraged to ask questions or seek the truth. It is not their fault, they are victims too.'

Nevidas sighed gently and spoke: 'They feel the comfort the Flame of Irenus brings makes up for the evil done in its name. Our rejection of the Flame is seen by them as a reason to kill us.'

'They blame us when there are floods and if crops fail,' Dunubas continued. 'Diseases are seen as judgement; punishments for our lack of faith. The people of Swarnbideah cannot explain them in any other way. Everyone's lives have been poisoned by lies, hatred and violence. We live under the same sun, the same stars and yet we speak a different language! We have all lost somebody in this war, some have died, others have chosen to join the other side…'

Dunubas let the strands of his tale fade. Nevidas took his hand and nodded as if giving her brother permission to carry on.

'So, if there is to be any chance of a reconciliation between the two sides the Flame of Irenus must be extinguished. Only then can our people come back together.'

'How do we extinguish the Flame?' asked Honey.

A frown puckered Dunubas's forehead and he shook his head fervently. 'It is impossible.'

'Nothing is impossible!' shot back Honey, thrusting her shoulders back in a defiant stance.

Dunubas snorted. 'I admire your courage, but pity your naivety.'

'Oi! I'm not the one who's afraid of fire.'

Bree decided to interrupt. 'My mum has a saying. Every path has its puddle.'

Dunubas looked puzzled.

'It means that life is full of problems,' she explained, 'but there are always ways round them.'

Dunubas thought about this for a moment. 'You have a very wise mother,' he smiled.

Bree nodded. Dunubas's eyes narrowed. 'I have been told there is an opal dagger somewhere in the castle. It fits a slot in the dome that protects the Flame. That is all I know.'

'Doesn't sound impossible,' Sandy said.

'It's not that simple. There are many obstacles between here and the Flame,' said Dunubas with a solemn shake of his head. 'Anando tried once but–'

Something inside Bree's mind cracked open and a memory began to seep through. 'Anando?' she said. 'You said something about Anando when you found us.'

Dunubas steepled his fingers and rested his chin on top. He seemed to be controlling a difficult emotion. 'Anando was my friend,' he started, his eyes becoming moist. 'Well, he was so much more than that. We grew up together and he became a brother to me.'

Bree nodded and smiled at Sandy.

'When Anando and Nevidas fell in love I could not have imagined a better man for my sister. We were all so happy.'

Nevidas sat down next to them, her eyes brimming with sadness. 'He was the world to me, but I was naïve. Love can do that to a person.' She smiled an empty, bitter smile that did not reach her eyes. 'I thought nothing could come between us but I underestimated the power of hatred and war. When we fought side by side I was so sure our love would win over all else. I still believe that if we had stayed together Anando would have been here to see his daughter.'

'You cannot keep blaming yourself Nevidas!' Dunubas slammed his hand down on the table. Anger tightened his face. Bree was startled. The dog whined and covered his face with a paw. Dunubas slumped back in his chair and shook his head wearily, his twisted features relaxing again. 'Pregnant women cannot go into battle.'

'Nobody else knew I was expecting a baby.' Nevidas shook her head. 'I could have gone with him that day.'

'And what if you had been taken too? Or killed? I would have no one left.' Dunubas's eyes seemed filled with unspoken thoughts. Nevidas paused, then took a deep breath and continued while her brother composed himself. 'We have all lost loved ones, on both sides. Many children are growing up without parents…' Her voice wavered and tears suddenly filled her eyes.

Bree understood her pain only too well. She saw the same expression on her mother's face every day. A single tear ran down Nevidas's cheek. She wiped it away angrily and composed herself, her jaw clenched with honour. 'I live with the hope that one day we will be reunited.'

Dunubas seemed ready to continue. 'Anando's great-grandmother had a vision when she was a little girl. We call it the Yahala Prophecy. She saw our country being torn apart by two-legged snakes that spat words instead of venom. The land would be poisoned and divided and everyone would live in fear. The snakes would draw strength from the vulnerable and feed off hatred. But they would fear one thing: three wingless birds falling from the sky. Between them they will carry a scroll. Then the Flame of Irenus will falter.'

'And what happens to these birds in the end?' Sandy asked nervously.

Don shook his head solemnly. 'Terrible destruction. Little Yahala saw raging infernos and terrible floods. She saw horses with serpent tails, plagues of giant insects and many deaths.'

'Oh. I was hoping for a happy ending,' Sandy said grimly.

'We're *all* hoping for that,' chastised Honey.

'Sometimes things have to get worse before they get better,' Dunubas sighed.

Something occurred to Bree. 'Wait. We fell from the sky. Do you think *we* are the wingless birds?'

Honey thought about this for a moment. 'Mimi is vulnerable.'

'And we've already seen some giant insects,' added Sandy.

Bree pulled the book out of her pocket and laid it on the table. Nevidas gasped. Dunubas stared at it in disbelief. He reached over to touch it but something stopped him and he pulled back.

'Could this be the scroll carried by the three birds?' Bree asked.

A heavy silence hung between them before Dunubas eventually spoke. 'I can't b-believe it,' he choked in a hoarse whisper. 'I heard stories about this but I never thought I would ever see it.'

Nevidas hesitantly touched the cover then put her fingers to her lips, her face filled with dread. 'This is sought by the dark side,' she said, her eyes darting between Bree and the book. 'They must *never* get it.'

'Yep, we know,' said Honey, 'we've done all that.'

Bree picked up the book and put it back in her pocket. 'When we first found it, something terrible came after us. We kept it safe. We'll do it again.'

Nevidas started to speak but stopped; her mouth closed around the unspoken words. Something had agitated her. She went to the window and looked out, caught up in her thoughts.

Dunubas watched her for a moment. 'Many people thought Yahala was crazy but it looks like there might have been some truth in her prediction.'

'Look, we're not here to fulfil any predictions, all right?' Honey said. 'We think my kid sister is being held in that castle. Can you take us there?'

Dunubas looked solemn. 'I can show you the way but I cannot come inside with you. You have to make that journey yourselves. Be careful and alert at all times. The Flame is well guarded. Use your minds, guard that book and stay together.'

'Always,' said Bree with a confident nod to Sandy and Honey.

'I cannot tell you everything you need to know but I can warn you that there are things in the castle—terrible things—that will hinder your quest.'

Cold dread trickled over Bree's scalp. Nevidas had rummaged in the box on the windowsill and held something to her chest, a piece of paper covered with writing. A shiver tiptoed up Bree's spine.

'I think this was left for you,' Nevidas said.

Bree took it, her hands shaking. The thick parchment was covered in elaborate, spidery calligraphy. As soon as Bree saw the handwriting her breath caught in her throat. She had seen it before – the last terrifying time she was in Castle Zarcalat...

5.

Words from the Past

The tense silence made it feel like the room was holding its breath. Bree held the letter in her quivering hand.

'A little while ago there was a raid on Castle Zarcalat,' Nevidas explained. 'Some things were brought back here to Calvaria.'

Bree could not stop staring at the page. Nevidas put a hand on her shoulder.

'They brought some letters and notes by a man called Donald Daines…'

Bree felt the room sway at the mention of his name. Sandy's eyebrows raised and Honey's mouth fell open.

'I believe you know him?' Nevidas said.

Bree steadied herself and shook her head. 'We *knew* him.'

Nevidas tilted her head and nodded sadly. 'I see. He wrote about the war. His writings contained important information about the Flame of Irenus that could help us extinguish it.' She gently took the letter from Bree's hands. 'I kept this one aside. It was obviously part of a larger bundle, but I felt it was special.'

Nevidas walked into a long slice of golden sunlight, cleared her throat and began to read:

'There will be no victors in this war, only those who have manufactured this terrible lie for their own ends. They fear the only thing they have no power over. Death. For this they will seek the spirit of youth. They search for a child, one pure of heart, an innocent who symbolises eternal life.'

Nevidas paused and glanced at the basket in the corner. She looked back at the letter. *'I have seen the Flame of Irenus with my own eyes, and held the Opal Dagger that opens the glass dome that protects it. The Flame is fragile; it may be extinguished by a waft of wisdom, a whiff of common sense. And for that reason it is well-guarded. Few have made it past the first obstacle, and none have made it past the Magnentity, a fearsome creature which guards the final door.'*

Nevidas turned the page over and continued to read. Bree chewed the inside of her cheek as she listened closely.

'Darkness will always pursue light, and evil is cunning. Since time began the forces of evil have fought the forces of good to destroy the world. Hidden from both, legend tells, is a certain book. At its centre is the key to freedom and peace; a beating heart. Across the generations this book has changed hands from one guardian to another. But those from Castle Zarcalat are trying everything in their power to find it, and if they ever do, their evil will reign supreme.'

Nevidas stopped and touched Bree's shoulder. She flattened the letter in front of her. A note was scribbled at the bottom:

Dearest Bree,

You are one of the bravest people I have ever met.

I don't have time to tell you everything, just that the door to your heart can only be opened from the inside. Remember my name when it won't open. Trust in the goodness of humanity. Find your own light, my angel.

Your good friend,
Don.

Bree stared at the note through a blur of tears. Don had obviously written it in his last moments. A pang of remorse tore through her as she recalled his hurry to write something before Tanas Theramonde burst into his room. Did Don know he was going to die? She tried to remember his face – his bushy eyebrows, his kind hazel eyes – but his features fell away like the last grains of sand in an hourglass. Tears pricked her eyes. She read the message again. The sound of Pamela gurgling in her basket reminded Bree of Don's lost child, and her heart gave way. Tears made tracks down her cheeks and landed on the table. After a while she felt Dunubas's warm hand pat her own.

'I'm all right, thanks,' she said, trying to control her trembling voice.

Dunubas said gently: 'He was a brave man. One of the best Calvaria ever knew.'

Bree nodded and took a couple of deep breaths.

'Not just Calvaria,' she said.

'So, this child who is pure of heart. That'd be Mimi?' said Honey, as she searched for a tissue in her satchel. 'That's why they've taken her, right?'

Nevidas looked grim. 'Possibly, but let's remember they also want Bree's book.'

'Mimi is bait,' muttered Sandy. 'They're using her to lure us to the castle.'

Bree said, 'That's good, in a way. It means they won't do anything to her until they have what they want.'

Honey looked doubtful.

'And we have to ensure they won't get what they want,' said Dunubas. 'There's no time to waste. Let's go.' Winrad jumped up in anticipation.

While Sandy and Honey helped Nevidas pack a rucksack with food and water Bree peered into Pamela's basket. The baby's tiny lip curled with recognition. 'Goodbye little one,' she whispered. Pamela chuckled and gave Bree a gummy smile. For a second her black eyes seemed to fill with a strange intensity.

Nevidas saw them all to the door. 'Be careful, be brave,' she smiled as she waved her goodbyes. She caught Bree's hand and pulled her close. 'And make sure I get my brother back in one piece.'

•••

As they made their way down a narrow street they heard the clamour of a large crowd up ahead. Honey's eyes clouded with alarm. Dunubas said, 'Don't be afraid. They are my friends.'

He led them round a corner into a marketplace. Men and women with baskets over their arms or on their heads jostled between the cluttered stalls, while others sold spices and perfumes from carts. Dozens of eyes turned to study them; three unfamiliar, strangely-dressed 13 year olds. People side-stepped them and smiled or nodded a greeting to Dunubas as he led them through the crowd. Some of the men snatched off their caps and bowed their heads.

'Why are they doing that?' whispered Bree, suddenly self-conscious.

Dunubas smiled. 'Everyone is talking about the brave warriors who fell to the ground like shooting stars!'

'Ha! How is that bump on your head, Sandy?' asked Honey, smiling back at the curious onlookers.

'It doesn't make me feel very brave,' he grumbled.

Dunubas laughed. 'You've brought these people hope for a new beginning.'

'Oh great. No pressure then?' Sandy gulped, adjusting his glasses.

Dunubas guided them past a butcher's stall hung with raw meat buzzing with flies (Honey made a face and pulled her t-shirt up over her mouth), one laden with waxy oranges and ripe plums, and another stacked with trays of sweets and pastries. A beautiful young woman stood behind it calling out to passersby. She smiled broadly at Bree, revealing a mouth filled with rotten teeth. 'Wanna try thum?' she drawled.

'I know she's not the best advert for sweets,' whispered Sandy. 'But still...'

Bree elbowed him in the ribs as he snatched a couple of peppermint creams. Bree took a rock of honeycomb that fizzed and melted on her tongue. She nodded gratefully as Honey squealed, 'Coconut ice – my favourite!'

Dunubas led them through crooked alleys, into the gloom between buildings so tall that only a thin strip of sky could be seen above. Halfway down one, they jumped when a gnarled hand reached out of the shadows. Sandy staggered, tripped over his own feet and fell face first into the gutter. When Bree picked him up, she noticed he had cut his forehead.

Irritated, Honey thrust her hands on to her hips and glared at the figure in the doorway. There cowered an old woman with a shawl around her shoulders.

'We didn't see you...' said Bree, as Sandy looked at the blood on his fingers.

The woman turned in Bree's direction and opened her milky eyes. From the way they rolled without fixing on anything, Bree knew the old woman was blind.

'Seeing is done with more than eyes,' croaked the old woman.

Bree turned to Dunubas and whispered out the side of her mouth. 'She *can't* see me – can she?'

'I can see you have a lion's heart,' the old woman laughed before Dunubas had a chance to reply. Bree could hear her breath rattling in her chest. The old woman coughed and thumped her chest with a fist.

'Aren't you cold, sitting here?' Bree said, kneeling down beside her. 'Can I help you up?'

The woman's smile slipped and her forehead creased. She pulled her shawl tighter and closed her parchment lids, her eyes moving around underneath.

'No! Stay back…' she cried, holding up her hand. 'I will not go with you. You lead all to their doom. Beware, the rest of you, of dangerous angels!'

Sandy shifted, and tapped Dunubas on the shoulder. 'Can we get out of here?' Dunubas nodded and started walking ahead, with Winrad at his heel.

'Bree is far from angelic,' Honey tried to joke, but the old woman gripped Bree's t-shirt and pulled her down until her ear was level with her lips. 'Only the eye of the day will save you from them.' She let go and Bree stumbled backwards.

'Come on,' said Honey, helping Bree to her feet. Shocked and confused they tore off after the others. Behind them, unseeing and yet seeing, the old woman shrank back into the shadows.

• • •

Honey caught up with Sandy as they approached a green field.

'Are you all right?' she said, putting her arm around his waist.

'What do you think she meant by dangerous angels?' he asked, watching Bree walk ahead with Dunubas and his dog.

Honey laughed. 'Back there? She was just a batty old bag. She probably ate something from that meat stall!'

Not far away, across the smooth blanket of grass, a large tent stood in the shadow of a giant tree.

'There's somebody I would like you to meet,' Dunubas said as he led them towards it. 'Her name is Witch Hammamalis.'

'A witch?' groaned Sandy. 'Just our luck!' His shoulders sagged with reluctance as Dunubas drew back the tent flap and gestured for them to enter. Honey followed Bree inside. Dunubas laughed heartily and slapped Sandy on the shoulder. 'Don't worry, my boy, I know you'll get on very well with her.'

Inside the air was balmy and thick, the darkness blurred by candlelight. As they waited for their eyes to adjust, the flap lifted in the breeze, allowing the sun to lay tiger stripes across the dusty floor. A large red and orange rug was spread at their feet and above them hung banners of flaming crimsons, vivid tangerines and blazing yellows.

'So, where is this old witch?' Honey hissed.

A woman stepped out from behind a curtain. She wore a plum-coloured dress, gold glitter on her eyelashes and clusters of irises in her long hair, as black as crow feathers.

'She's here,' she breathed in a deep voice. 'I'm Witch Hammamalis. Welcome.'

'Hi!' Bree and Honey smiled. They liked her straight away. She was nothing like the dried-up old stick Bree had expected. On the contrary, she was very beautiful. She came towards them with her arms opened and wrapped Bree and Honey in an extravagant embrace. She smelled of cloves and something earthy.

'Come on now shy boy. Your turn,' she smiled at Sandy and opened her arms to him too. He blushed and stepped forward, and as he did she noticed the cut on his forehead. 'Oh you poor child,' she said. 'I know the very thing that will help!' She gestured for him to sit on a chair while she went to a set of drawers and pulled out the top one. She ran a long purple fingernail along a row of bottles until she found a horn-shaped phial and removed its cork.

'Here we are,' she smiled as she dripped a clear liquid onto her fingertips and touched the cut.

'It's gone numb,' he said.

'Once it stops, your head will be as good as new,' smiled Hammamalis. She held up a round mirror and Sandy stared at his reflection. The cut had changed colour from furious red to purple and then to yellow before it disappeared altogether.

'Some kind of…healing water?' he said.

Hammamalis broke into a smile. 'In a sense. It's a bottle of Akeso tears.'

'Does it heal everything?' Sandy asked pointing to the bump he got from falling out of the hot air balloon.

Hammamalis shook her head. 'Akeso tears are only effective if used quickly. If too much time has passed since the injury, they'll be no good.'

She lit a stick of incense with a candle. Tendrils of smoke wreathed up, filling the tent with a citrus scent.

'Can we have it?' asked Honey, taking the bottle from Sandy and shaking it so that the contents sloshed against the glass. The incense was curling around Hammamalis's head like an aura. 'There is very little left in there but you are welcome to keep it.'

Honey smiled and dropped the bottle into her satchel.

'Have you got anything else really cool?' asked Sandy. Hammamalis smiled mysteriously. 'Just for you…' she said. She reached into another drawer and pulled out a small blue bottle. She pulled out the rubber stopper and poured some grey powder into the palm of her hand.

'What does it do?' Sandy asked.

'Watch closely.' Hammamalis blew the powder

into the air, where it formed a glittering cloud above their heads. The flecks merged together until a large globule, fat and heavy bobbed in the air.

'Looks like the inside of my dad's lava lamp,' said Honey.

Immediately, Sandy's arm started to jerk. 'Argh! Something's got me!'

'What's happening to him?' asked Bree.

'Nothing. It wants that thing around your wrist,' laughed Hammamalis, her gold eyelashes glinting in the candlelight.

Sandy's arm twitched and waved around as he desperately tried to reach his wrist. Quickly, Bree took hold of his forearm and loosened the strap. Before she could unfasten it, the watch tore off Sandy's wrists and shot upwards, where it attached itself to the floating bubble.

'Ah—it's magnetic?' he smiled, impressed. Hammamalis nodded and handed him the blue bottle. Sandy took off the lid and sniffed, instantly letting out a deafening sneeze. Bree rolled her eyes. 'Let me see it,' she said and poured some powder into her hand.

'Think of the fun we could have with that!' Honey squealed, a mischievous glint in her eye.

Hammamalis shot her a stern look. 'Use everything I give you wisely,' she warned. Honey looked disappointed. Bree tentatively poked the pile of powder before tipping it into her pocket.

'What if I want my watch back?' asked Sandy.

'The spell doesn't last long,' replied Hammamalis. 'But if you're in a hurry all you have to do is this.' She clapped her hands together twice and the globule exploded back into particles of dust, sending the watch flying to the floor. Sandy caught it and inspected it closely. 'Amazing,' he breathed.

Bree glanced round the tent, curious about what else was hidden in the shadows. She spotted something gleaming not far away. 'You have a crystal ball!' she squealed, running over to a small round table.

'That's the Ball of Secrets,' smiled Hammamalis. 'In this you can see the deepest thoughts of those you love.'

Bree's face changed and she shuddered. 'I don't know if I would want to see that.'

'I do!' Honey shrieked as she dived over and peered into the glass sphere.

'You have to relax and focus on the person you love,' advised Hammamalis.

'Something is happening...' said Sandy, coming closer for a better look. Bree noticed a white swirl of mist clearing inside the crystal ball. Hammamalis smiled. 'Ah. I see someone has a boy on their mind.'

'It must be one of you two,' Sandy said quickly.

Bree averted her eyes. 'Well, it's not me,' she mumbled, her cheeks reddening.

'But wait. Something else is emerging,' said Hammamalis. Her tone made Bree feel uneasy.

Honey pulled her hair back from her face as

Bree joined her. The mist cleared to reveal three hooded figures cloaked in white. The ends of their sleeves were crimson with red feathers around the cuffs. Even though the image was distorted, the figures seemed to be drifting above the ground between trees. Bree could not see their faces beneath their hoods but the huge swords they carried turned her blood to ice. Hammamalis gasped and beneath her gold lashes her eyes flashed with dread.

'You recognise them?' Bree asked.

Honey was unable to pull her gaze away. 'What are they?'

'The Phasmitis,' whispered Hammamalis, peering into the ball. 'They're terrible warrior spirits who haunt the forest.'

'I thought this was supposed to be fun,' frowned Sandy.

'And I thought I was supposed to see the thoughts of someone I love,' said Honey.

'That's the problem. I think you are…' said Hammamalis. 'Your loved one must be asleep. We are seeing their nightmare.'

'That's even worse! We've got to do something,' cried Honey.

'Were you thinking of Mimi?' Bree forced herself to watch the scene inside the Ball of Secrets.

'Take comfort from the fact that this is merely a dream,' offered Hammamalis. 'A terrible dream, but a dream nonetheless. Nobody has ever been harmed by a nightmare.'

'But don't you see?' cried Honey. 'Mimi didn't make them up, did she? You know what they are. If she is dreaming about those things she must have seen them somewhere.'

Hammamalis sighed and pursed her purple lips. 'You've seen enough,' she said and draped a gaudy cloth over the ball.

Honey turned to Bree and Sandy, 'Right, we need to get to her quickly. I'm going.' She made for the tent flap and Bree and Sandy followed.

'Wait!' shouted Hammamalis, reaching into the drawers again. 'I have one more thing for you.' She opened her fist and there, lying in the centre of her palm were two small spheres, transparent, with the perfect fragility of bubbles. Inside swirled a dark blue fog. They reminded Bree of the time her Granddad had blown a mouthful of his pipe smoke into a bubble. She stared in wonder at the little balls in Hammamalis's hand. The churning blue smoke struggled to penetrate the thin exterior of the globe but somehow it remained trapped inside the oily walls. 'They're beautiful,' she sighed, reaching out to touch one.

'Be careful not to break them.' Hammamalis pulled back her hand. 'These are Slumber Buds.'

'What do they do?' asked Sandy, looking closer.

'I use them to cure people tormented by their thoughts. They bring on a deep sleep and when they wake their bad memories have evaporated like smoke on the breeze.'

'That sounds nice,' Bree said wistfully.

Hammamalis smiled. 'It is. But you have no time for heavy lids.' She handed the Slumber Buds to Honey, who carefully wrapped them in a tissue and put them in her satchel.

'We have to give you something in return,' said Bree, although she was not sure what she could offer. Hammamalis waved her hand dismissively. Honey rummaged through her satchel. 'Try this,' she said snapping off a square of chocolate and handing it to Hammamalis. She inspected it for a moment and hesitantly popped it into her mouth.

'Where we come from chocolate is used to uplift the spirit,' Honey grinned cheekily.

'And it tastes pretty good too!' added Sandy.

Hammamalis's skin flushed with pleasure. 'It really does. You must give me the potion. This… chocolate is like our Slumber Buds then? It wipes away the bad memories?' said Hammamalis, rolling the word around her mouth with the melting square.

'Not permanently,' answered Bree, wishing that could be true.

'You do have something for that though?'

Bree gave this some thought before answering. 'Only time.'

One by one they said their farewells before Honey pushed aside the tent flap. Stepping out into the warmth, they found Dunubas sitting cross-legged on the ground. Winrad wagged his tail as he bounded over to Bree.

'We should get going. We have a long journey ahead,' Dunubas said as he stood up. He patted his thigh and Winrad ran to his side.

'Time to bring back my sister,' said Honey.

'Try not to worry. After all, it takes a lot to stop us,' Bree tried to smile as she clasped Honey's hand. Just then a veil of cloud passed over the sun and for a moment the land went dark and chilled the air. Bree looked up at the sky. A low growl of cloud had gathered overhead.

6.

STRANGLEDOOR

Ahead of them, the dusty expanse stretched towards a horizon that dissolved in wobbling colours. There were no trees or bushes for as far as the eye could see, as the baked ground was cracked into fissures that gaped like thirsty mouths.

Bree had never seen so much space before, or so much sky that was not interrupted by rooftops, chimneys and aerials. A haze bleared the searing sun until it shimmered like a coin under water.

'How much further?' panted Honey, her cheeks flushed with heat and exertion.

'Not long now,' said Dunubas, scuffing before them in the parched dirt. 'If we follow this path.' He pointed to a track that wound off into the distance, narrowing and widening over the contours of the rising land.

'You said that an hour ago,' grumbled Sandy, his hair sticking up in sweaty spikes from his forehead.

Dunubas puffed, 'I promise. We'll rest on the other side of those hills.'

Bree noticed he was looking at a spot on the horizon that seemed to shimmer in the heat. Far in the distance a cluster of green hills rose up, mottled by the shadows of drifting clouds. She did not think her legs would carry her that far. A stitch jabbed at her ribs and her calf muscles tugged. The dry air scorched her nostrils and the top of her head felt fried.

They stopped to catch their breaths as the path steepened, and looked back at how far they had walked. The only marks on the landscape were the straight tracks made by their four pairs of feet, and the irregular prints of Winrad's four paws. He ran on ahead to the brow of the hill, where he stopped and wagged his tail. He barked excitedly as though encouraging them to keep going.

'What's he fussing about?' wheezed Sandy.

'You'll see in a minute,' said Dunubas.

When Bree reached the peak of the hill she gasped. The dusty earth ended abruptly at the foot of the hill and beyond it a carpet of daisy-covered grass rolled past a forest with a river running though it. The sight was so unexpected that for a moment she wondered if it was a mirage. Surely the heat was making her delirious, and her mind was playing tricks on her? 'It's beautiful,' Bree sighed, wiping the sweat from her forehead.

Honey agreed. 'Wow. This view is well worth the trek.'

'Sure it is,' said Sandy ruefully. 'I can't wait to do it all again on the way back.'

'We'll rest down there,' said Dunubas, pointing out a shape made formless by the warping heat.

A downhill hike took them to a large boulder that had been worn smooth by the dusty winds.

They sat with their backs against it and waited for Dunubas to unload the bag Nevidas had packed with food and water.

'This might be our last meal for a while,' he said, unfolding a napkin to reveal a pile of oat-cakes. He gave them two each and brought out a pot of fruit and onion chutney to share.

'We'll be fine, thanks. I'm not even that hungry,' said Bree.

Sandy's stomach growled as he ran his finger around the inside of the chutney pot. 'Speak for yourself. I'm always starving.'

Honey absently plucked some daisies and started to make a chain. 'I'm too worried to eat anything. I mean, guys, what if we're too late to save Mimi? What if she's already…' At that moment a scarlet butterfly landed on her leg. When it folded its wings they saw its orange and inky black underside.

'It's a good thing you like colourful friends,' smiled Sandy, trying to lift Honey's mood.

Dunubas nodded. 'Some people believe butterflies are the souls of the dead coming back to visit those they love.'

'What? You mean this could be Mimi?'

'No. That's not what he's saying,' said Bree quickly.

'Are you saying my sister is already dead and now she's turned into an insect?'

Sandy said, 'He only means that in some cultures butterflies are a symbol of rebirth. They're a symbol of hope when everything else seems hopeless…' He did not need Bree's glare to shut him up. They all saw the tears in Honey's eyes when she silently got to her feet and trudged down the hill.

•••

'We're nearly there,' Dunubas said flatly a little later.

A few miles beyond the forest towered the jagged mountain of Castle Zarcalat, cloaked in a broiling grey thundercloud. Dunubas looked concerned.

'Is it weird that I feel like turning back?' Honey sighed, placing the daisy chain around her neck like a wreath.

Bree took her hand and gave it a comforting pat. 'You have to stay strong. Your sister needs that.'

Honey's eyes filled with tears again. 'Listen, what I said to you earlier on the roof garden about you being an only child. I'm sorry. I wish I hadn't said it. Bree, what if I'm an only child now too?'

'They won't have done anything to the girl yet,' Dunubas said with certainty. 'After all, they need something to barter with.'

Bree was not sure if that helped. She realised that once they exchanged Mimi for the book they still had to get out of the castle alive—and if they were leaving the book, they would have to do it without any magical protection. They barely escaped last time, even with its help.

They looked across the valley to a cluster of houses that clung to the hillside like limpets to a rock. From here it looked like a model village, a mosaic of rooftops crowded around a labyrinth of miniature streets.

'And this, I'm sorry to say, is Swarnbideah,' said Dunubas sombrely.

'You're sorry? But it's so pretty,' said Bree, taken aback.

Dunubas nodded. 'At first glance. But take a closer look.'

The grey towers of Castle Zarcalat dwarfed the village, drowning everything in its pitch-black shadow. Smoke rose in quivering plumes from the countless spindly chimneys.

'There's no noise. There's no-one on the streets,' said Sandy, scanning the landscape. 'It's dead. And yet people must be home because all the smoking chimneys means their fires are lit.'

'And what else?' asked Dunubas.

Bree noticed it first. 'The shutters on all the windows are closed.'

Dunubas nodded. All the houses with the pinched roofs and narrow gables seemed to shrink and cower and close their eyes under the menacing glare of the castle. It was as though the heart of the village had ceased to beat.

'So, where are all the people?' asked Honey.

'They're hiding indoors,' Dunubas replied. 'All of them are too terrified of Castle Zarcalat to leave their homes.'

Sandy gulped. 'And we're headed back there, aren't we? The place that's so scary the locals won't even look at it. Great!'

'Sandy, it's that or we go home without Mimi,' warned Bree. 'Come on. There's no turning back now.'

Dunubas pointed to a fringe of tall trees at the foot of the hill. 'That's the forest of Strangledoor. That's where we are heading first.'

'And that's the border?' asked Honey, fiddling with her daisy chain.

He nodded. 'Once we cross it into Swarnbideah it's not far to Castle Zarcalat.' He swung his bag onto his shoulder and set off. Winrad took this as a signal to run beside him down the hill.

As they watched the man and his dog get smaller and smaller until they disappeared into Strangledoor forest, Honey spoke. 'I suppose this is it. Look, Mimi is my sister. And it's my fault that we're here so if you want to hang back I'll understand.' Bree and Sandy looked at each other the way best friends do, when words are not needed to decide something important. 'I can go with Dunubas on my own,' Honey continued. 'And hopefully I'll meet you back here. Bree? Sandy! Wait for me!'

They were already running ahead, down the hillside towards the trees.

• • •

As they walked through the forest Bree commented on how peaceful it was. Other than the distant birdsong high up in the impenetrable canopy of leaves, there was absolutely no noise. The ground was cushioned with moss and ferns and the shadows of the leaves swam to and fro as the high branches swayed in the breeze.

'It's not too bad,' said Sandy. 'I thought it would be much scarier.'

Dunubas gave him a sideways glance. 'We're still in Calvaria. It doesn't get dangerous until we cross Strangledoor.'

Bree was about to reply when she realised Winrad was frantically searching the forest floor. The dog stopped in his tracks and sniffed the air. He lowered his ears and started to whine. Overhead the sky turned grey and a wind suddenly came from several directions at once, stirring up leaves and twigs from the forest floor and sending them spiralling around their ankles.

'Something's coming,' Honey shivered, rubbing her bare arms.

Bree turned to Dunubas. 'What's happening?' she asked.

'We've arrived at the border,' he said, patting the dog as it cowered at his feet.

Sandy looked around. 'How can you tell? I don't see any border.'

Dunubas squatted and brushed aside heaps of

leaves and pine needles. Something started to emerge from underneath: a plait of roots running in a straight line through the undergrowth.

'The border is a twisted tree root that stretches across the forest,' he explained, kicking away more leaves. 'This is all that separates the two countries.'

As the wind rose, the roots twisted out of the mouldering earth, thick and tangled.

'So that's Swarnbideah over there?' said Bree. 'It doesn't look any different to Calvaria.'

Dunubas clenched his jaw. 'Many travellers have been fooled. But look at the sky.'

They all looked up through the swaying branches. Despite the wind, the sky above the Calvaria side of the border was blue. Yet on the other side it was brooding with sombre clouds. The trees were different too in Swarnbideah. Their branches were bare and shook in the wind like petrified fingers, while just above their heads the leaves spread thick and green. Winrad yelped and a chill crawled up Bree's spine. She knew what was coming next.

'Are you all ready?' asked Dunubas.

'Not really,' replied Bree. 'But Mimi needs us.'

Together they stepped over the boundary and in an instant it felt as though summer had changed to autumn. The warmth and the birdsong vanished as a cold gale blasted from between the angular trees. As they crept cautiously over a forest floor black with rotten ferns, Bree felt dozens of unseen eyes watching her from the shadows. Above them, a frown of dark cloud crossed the sun and chilled the air even further. Goose bumps prickled on Bree's arms.

Dunubas picked up speed. 'The rain isn't far away. And that means we're getting closer to Zarcalat.'

Bree glanced over her shoulder. She could still see the border of Strangledoor and the green glade of Calvaria. Not for the first time that day she had to fight down the urge to make a break for freedom.

'What's that?' asked Sandy, pointing to a tree a few feet ahead. Something on the trunk was flapping around in the wind like a panicked bird. As they got closer they could see it was a scroll of paper nailed to the trunk. Dunubas removed it with the tip of his dagger and read it out:

'Swine heard hating. Numerate fascinatedly shrivels confusably idolatrize penitence. Toughest, hollow hearted scorn now clean thrifty keen. Arouse weedy of radiate roundhead or tasty blooding. Win Evil one ulcerates narrowly. Low minded farewell if hate. Fortuitous, tender elaboration, venomously seduced as breakably…'

'It doesn't make sense,' said Honey. 'It's just gibberish. Isn't it?'

As soon as the last word had been read, tiny pinpoints of black mould appeared all over the paper. They grew and merged until all the words were blotted out. The scroll turned completely black and started to burn at the centre. Dunubas dropped it and as it fell to the forest floor a brief flash of fire completely destroyed it, leaving behind only a plume of smoke. Winrad cocked his head at the ground and barked once. Dunubas absentmindedly patted him on the head as he viewed the forest with a gimlet eye.

'It didn't sound too friendly, that's for sure,' said Sandy.

'Dunubas, what did it mean?' asked Bree. 'Tell us!'

The gathering wind sent huge clouds across the sky casting shadows into the forest. A distant roll of thunder shook the earth.

Dunubas stared pensively through the trees. 'It was a warning that we shouldn't go any further,' he said.

• • •

The sky darkened. Ash-coloured clouds massed overhead as a chilly fog smothered the forest, dampening their skin with droplets. All colour seemed to have been bled from the world, leaving only shadows and whiteness. Crows argued high in the jagged trees, then scattered like twists of black paper. There was silence. Without warning, Winrad froze. His tail went rigid, and the fur on his neck bristled. Dunubas signalled for them to stop as he stared ahead.

'What is it?' whispered Honey.

Bree couldn't see anything. Nevertheless, a cold breath shuddered up her spine. She was about to speak when out of the corner of her eye she caught a flurry of grey. A few feet away, there it was: a sinister silhouette in the mist. It looked like a wolf, only much larger.

'A Cleptathorn,' Bree murmured. She had seen them before and knew that if you ever ran into one you must never look it in the eye or it would absorb all the energy from your body. Dunubas took a few steps back but she could not move. She felt as though her bones had crumbled under her skin. The Cleptathorn turned. Its grey coat was matted with filth and dried blood. A deep ragged scar ran across its shoulder to a point where a hint of white bone glistened around its blood-spattered neck. This Cleptathorn was wounded. Before Bree had a chance to look away it locked its amber eyes onto her and let out a guttural snarl. A rush of fear clawed at her skin.

'Don't move a muscle,' whispered Dunubas as he felt for his dagger. Honey and Sandy froze. The Cleptathorn stalked towards them, panting gruffly. The smell of stale blood soured Bree's throat as froth dripped from its wet black tongue. Winrad's growl grew louder. The Cleptathorn bared its vicious teeth without taking its eyes off Bree. She tried to look away but for some reason could not do it. Staring into its unblinking glare made her head feel fuzzy and her limbs go heavy.

'D-Don't look in its eyes…' she managed to

warn the others seconds before it leapt. Out of the fog sprang a mass of grey fur, and a glint of fang and claw. In a flash, Winrad pounced at its throat, knocking it sideways. Dunubas grabbed Bree's shirt and dragged her backwards. Honey and Sandy dived behind a fallen tree when Bree crashed to her knees beside them. Sandy put his hand on Bree's shoulder. 'It was looking into me,' she shuddered, covering her face. 'It was inside my head.'

The air was filled with violence; snarling, barking, flying limbs, tearing fur and spurts of blood. Hideous wailing came from the knot of bodies and no-one was sure which creature was making the worst noise. As soon as Sandy put his arms around Bree and Honey they buried their heads against his chest. Honey covered her ears against the awful yelping and Bree could not bear to look up. The squealing and snarling abruptly stopped and there was silence. Bree broke away to peer around the edge of the log, terrified of what she would see. Through the fog she could not tell where the Cleptathorn ended and the dog began. They lay in a tangle of bloodied and unmoving fur. She looked at Dunubas with searching eyes but he stared ahead desolately. 'Winrad?' he said in a cracked whisper. Something in the pile moved. Bree jumped in fright. It reared onto its legs and bounded towards them.

'Get up,' he told Bree, Honey and Sandy. 'Get up and run!'

As they clambered to their feet they saw him thrust out his dagger. The fog parted and Winrad leaped up against Dunubas, wagging his tail. He dropped his dagger and threw his arms around the dog. 'It's all right. It's over now,' he laughed.

'Is that thing dead?' said Sandy, pointing to the ruined mass of hair and blood.

Dunubas nodded distractedly. 'Just as well it was already injured or we wouldn't have stood a chance.'

'Dunubas, let me see your hands,' said Bree coming closer. They were smeared with bright, fresh blood. 'Look!' she gasped, pointing at the dog. Blood welled from four deep bites on his neck. Winrad cowered in pain as Dunubas tried to look. 'He's badly hurt,' he said.

'Poor Winrad,' Honey sighed as she stroked his back. 'If it hadn't been for him that thing would've killed us all.'

'He is going to be all right though, isn't he?' said Bree. Dunubas shook his head, his eyes welling up.

'Hang on. What about the Akeso tears that Hammamalis gave us?' said Sandy. 'We could try that.'

Dunubas frowned. 'No, I can't let you use them up, they're precious. You never know when you'll need them. And after all, he's…he's only a dog. Aren't you, boy?' Winrad whined and flicked his tail. Dunubas's voice sounded choked and he looked at the ground so they would not see him crying.

Honey pulled out the horn-shaped bottle from her satchel and held it out to him. 'He's only a dog – but you never know when we'll need *him*.'

Dunubas looked at her with clouded eyes.

'Only *some* things can be replaced,' she said. 'Others, you've got to hold on to.'

Taking the bottle from her he removed the stopper and poured a few drops onto his blood-stained fingertips. While she replaced the stopper Dunubas held Winrad firmly, and rubbed the gaping wounds in his neck. The dog whimpered and trembled. Dunubas stroked his ears as they waited to see what would happen. Almost immediately the flow of blood stopped and reversed. The torn skin knitted back together and the missing fur grew back, leaving behind no trace of Winrad's terrible wounds.

'It worked!' cried Honey, spinning around and laughing. The tiny amount of Akeso tears sloshed around inside the bottle as she punched the air.

'Woah! Careful with that!' warned Sandy and made to snatch the bottle from her.

Even the dog's blood on Dunubas's hands faded away until there was nothing left to show that Winrad had been hurt at all. The dog sprung up from the forest floor and shook himself.

'As good as new and ready to get going,' Bree giggled, as she tried to dodge his exuberant tail.

'Yes,' said Dunubas, picking up his dagger, 'as I

suppose we should too. We've lost time already. Let's go.'

As they passed the dead Cleptathorn Winrad lowered his muzzle and growled. Bree tried not to look at it. She knew they were used by guards at the Castle to detect intruders and hunt down anyone who tried to escape. She decided not to say anything to Honey or Sandy but she wondered what lay ahead.

As the wind increased the fog disappeared and thick, black clouds rolled above them, turning everything in the forest to shadows.

'Are we near the castle?' asked Honey, her ponytail flicking around her face in the wind. Dunubas looked up through the skeletal branches as they whipped and swayed above their heads. 'Not far now.'

They continued on through the forest, avoiding hidden tree roots and hillocks until they reached a clearing. A shaft of murky light slid through the trees and lit up a corner of the glade to reveal a row of strange-looking plants with tall, cylindrical stems and large frilly crimson heads. Dunubas stopped in his tracks. 'You must be very quiet,' he whispered. 'These are Crimboids.'

'Crim-whats?' Sandy peered nervously at the plants.

'Crimboids,' repeated Dunubas as he took out his dagger. 'They are very dangerous, so we don't want to wake them.'

'What should we do?' whispered Bree.

'The only thing they are scared of is fire, but we'll have to make do with this.' He held up his dagger. 'Stay close to me, and whatever happens don't make a noise!'

They nodded and started to tiptoe past the line of plants. No-one dared breathe, and even Winrad was quiet. As Bree, Honey and Sandy edged past them their stems bent and flexed, as though they were stirring in their sleep and their thick crimson lips pulsed like sea anemones. Bree had no idea what would happen if they woke but judging from Dunubas's terrified expression it was best they never found out.

They'd almost reached the end of the row when Honey tripped over a tree root. She tumbled to the ground and for a moment everybody stood still. Honey lay motionless, panting with fear until Dunubas signalled for her to stand up slowly, which she did, all the time eyeing the long whiskery stems that swayed sluggishly from side to side. One of the large flower heads opened above her head and puffed out a cloud of yellow-brown vapour. It dispersed into the air leaving behind the most dreadful smell. Honey gagged and covered her nose and Bree put her hand over her mouth to try and stop the acid rising in her throat. Sandy gasped for air, his eyes wide and panicked. When Winrad ran off, Dunubas mouthed the words 'Come on!' but the terrible smell had wiped every other thought from Bree's head. All of a sudden Sandy let out a deafening sneeze that echoed around the entire forest. The Crimboids jolted and twitched their tube-like stems and started to open and close their terrible frilly heads. Small shoots appeared all over them and grew into crawling tentacles, as thick as a man's arm. They waved and lashed around like angry serpents while the purple frills opened wide to reveal deadly looking barbs.

'Hurry up!' yelled Dunubas, knowing it was too late to stay quiet.

Honey bolted over to him but staggered and fell. Sandy grabbed her, pulling her clear as one of the tentacles greedily wound itself around her ankle. She screamed and kicked her leg. Dunubas dived and plunged his dagger into the rubbery arm forcing a vile green slime to spurt out. It let go and shrunk back, leaving behind a trail of bloodied goo. Honey jumped to her feet and threw herself at Sandy.

'Quickly, Bree!' yelled Dunubas.

Honey screamed, 'Run while you've still got a chance!' But Bree was immobilised with fear. She had been surrounded by an army of waving vines. All around her the terrible creepers were growing and searching, moving across the forest floor like serpents. Each way she turned the tendrils coiled around her wrists and ankles. She could feel them crawling up her legs until they were tight around her waist. They jerked and bound her until she was helpless to do anything but collapse to the ground. The vines tightened like ropes around her legs and started to drag her through the dirt and pine needles. She watched in horror as the stems bowed their purple heads to the ground and opened wide to reveal rows and rows of gnashing teeth.

'Bree!' cried Sandy. She turned to see her friends watching helplessly as she was pulled feet first towards the gaping mouth.

'Hold on!' shouted Honey. She broke out of Sandy's grip and darted forward. Dunubas tried to stop her but she was too quick. She dodged the tentacles that whipped the air around her head and pulled her umbrella out of her satchel. Swinging it like a baseball bat she pounded them until they flinched and drew back. It only stopped them for a moment for within seconds she too was wrapped up in vines.

Terror swooped over Bree as she frantically dug her heels into the earth to slow the pull of the Crimboids but nothing stalled them. She turned her head and saw her fear mirrored in Honey's eyes.

In that moment all her hope turned to black.

7.

THE SHRILLFLITTERS

Bree was inches away from the gnashing teeth when she felt something buzzing in her pocket. 'Honey, the locket must be glowing!' she cried.

'Can you reach it?' Honey screamed back. Bree tried to struggle free but it was no use. Her arms were completely pinned to her sides. 'I... can't...move.'

Honey puffed and grunted as she wriggled across the ground like a caterpillar. With all the effort she could muster Honey lifted the top half of her body and dropped down onto Bree's chest, knocking the wind from her lungs. Bree was helpless to do anything. Her mind was fuzzy with terror, her thoughts jumbled. All she could feel was Honey's hair fanning out across her face and the terrible tightening of the vines around her throat. The locket continued to pulse but Bree knew it could stop at any second and their chance of escape would be over.

'Turn your head away,' Honey hissed then sunk her teeth into one of the thicker tentacles that had wound itself around Bree's torso. There was a hideous, high-pitched scream followed by an explosion of foul sticky slime that spattered the ground like spilled paint. Honey tore through the tentacle until it slithered away in pain and shock. That was enough to free Bree's left arm. She wasted no time. Thrusting her hand into her pocket she pulled out the book and squinted down at the throbbing locket. The little screen had sprung to life with three words:

PLEASE OPEN ME.

Bree prised open the leather cover. It creaked loudly and revealed the first thick, yellow page of the book.

'What's happening?' shouted Sandy, as Dunubas held him back.

Bree and Honey flipped and twisted as more vines wrapped themselves around their limbs. A few inches away the lethal purple heads snapped the air in anticipation.

Bree felt the sticky slither of more tentacles creeping through her hair like worms across her scalp. They tightened their grip until she was pinned to the ground, barely able to breathe. Out of the corner of her eyes she could see a page of the open book turning transparent until it looked like glass.

Honey bobbed her head one way and another as she dodged the lunging flower heads. 'Can you see it? What does it say?' she screamed.

'Only just,' Bree managed to say.

A white mist had started to churn in the centre of the clear page and was quickly followed by the blurry outline of some words. Bree strained to read them:

FROM MY CENTRE FLAMES WILL RISE
AND TAKE THESE CREATURES BY SURPRISE.
A BURST OF HEAT, A FLASH OF LIGHT
ENOUGH TO GIVE THEM ALL A FRIGHT
BUT ONLY FOR A LITTLE WHILE
SO TAKE YOUR CHANCE TO RUN A MILE.

With shoots already curling around her free arm, Bree held the opened book out as far as she could. It began with a spiral of smoke that curled up from the page, followed by a spit and a crackle like a sparkler. Then a tongue of yellow fire rose so suddenly Bree felt heat on the side of her face. Honey yelped in fright when a fountain of red and orange flames blasted out of the little black book. The Crimboids blanched and their tangle of vines slackened. Some shrivelled and dried up immediately, others screamed and lashed against the rising heat.

'Hurry!' yelled Honey ripping the dead vines from her chest and scrambling to her feet. Bree kicked and struggled free, then slammed the book shut, extinguishing the flames in a puff of blue smoke. 'Run,' she cried, grabbing Honey by the hand and dragging her past the Crimboids.

'Uh-oh. Wait,' said Honey. 'I dropped my umbrella!'

As Honey lunged at it a tentacle lashed out and wound around the handle. As though it was a whip it yanked her back towards to the salivating flower heads.

'My turn to rescue you!' cried Bree and she bit into the vine. It immediately let go and without thinking she pushed Honey towards Sandy and Dunubas.

'Let's get out of here,' Sandy yelled in horror as the tentacles crept across the forest floor. The frilly Crimboid heads turned and the plants started to writhe and twist as if trying to pull their roots from the soil and give chase.

With Winrad nipping ahead they bounded through the bushes and between the trees. Overhanging branches forced them to duck and swerve but they pushed through a dark curtain of foliage and dashed for a clearing.

Only when they were sure they had left enough distance between themselves and the Crimboids did they stop to catch their breaths. Bree strained her ears but she could hear nothing but her own breath and the quiet rush of wind through the bare branches. Honey wiped a splodge of slime from her face and pushed the umbrella back in her satchel.

'Thank you,' puffed Honey, throwing her arms around Bree. 'You have perfect timing.'

'Not to mention a killer bite!' added Sandy, clearly impressed.

'I learned from the best,' laughed Bree, gnashing her teeth at Honey.

Bree looked down at the book and turned it over slowly, half expecting to see scorch marks but there were none. The locket lay lifeless, the page had changed back to paper and the words were gone.

'Quite amazing,' said Dunubas, staring down at the book with raised eyebrows.

Bree nodded and stroked the locket. 'A good friend of ours told us that in times of trouble the book would help us find a way forwards.'

'Well that certainly was a time of trouble!' replied Sandy, wiping his glasses with his t-shirt.

'I never believed I would ever see the book at all,' said Dunubas. 'But to actually see it use its power. It's it's its…' He shook his head incredulously.

'Pretty wicked?' nodded Honey with an impish smile.

'Oh no, not at all wicked,' said Dunubas. 'Unless of course, you're referring to the old stories about the book…?'

'It's just a turn of phrase,' muttered Sandy.

Bree said, 'Wait a minute. What *old* stories?'

She was cut short by a flash of lightning and a rolling growl of thunder in the distance, in the direction of the Castle. Dunubas looked over his shoulder. 'I think we are nearly there,' he said. 'Are we all set to continue?'

'Only if there are no more nasty surprises,' said Sandy, his eyebrows pulling together in a scowl.

Dunubas looked at him sombrely and drew a deep, steadying breath. 'I can't make any promises,' he replied.

In this part of the wood the path petered out

and the trees seemed to close in on them. Except for the rumble of approaching thunder, there was silence. Bree was still too shaken to talk and eyed every branch and twig with a nervous suspicion. She hurried to keep pace with Dunubas, who travelled the path with long, swinging strides.

'We're very close to the Castle now,' he said, looking up at the stain of ebony clouds above them. He pointed to a thick mesh of branches up ahead. 'Through here.'

He held back the branches and Bree heard herself gasp. The hill dropped away beyond the thicket, and out of the valley the jagged mountain soared, filling the sky until it seemed to blot out the rest of the world. It turned dark as the sliver of sun was swallowed by the seething black clouds that trembled with veins of lightning. Stretching up like a claw from the summit stood Castle Zarcalat.

The bitter wind whipped Honey's hair across her face and she tossed her head to shake it free. 'I never thought we'd see it again,' she said, fiddling with her daisy chain.

Sandy stared ahead miserably. 'We barely got out alive the last time.'

After a ground-shaking boom of thunder, the rain began to fall so hard it kicked up the dust. It hissed in the foliage and spilled down from the upper branches overhead. At Dunubas's side Winrad sneezed and shook himself. Bree felt the drips running over her scalp, down her face and over her lips. It tasted warm and metallic. 'The poisoned rain,' she said. 'Remember not to swallow any.'

It lashed the Castle and streaked from the window ledges in long mournful bars. Bree searched for the room where she had found her father, and felt a gnawing knot of sadness tighten inside her.

Dunubas placed his hand on her shoulder. 'Do you know where you're going?'

'There's the courtyard.' Honey pointed at the cobbles glistening in the rain.

'But what's down there?' asked Bree.

The perilous drop down the mountain ended in a dark sea of trees that was being swallowed by fog. Dunubas wiped the raindrops from his face and stared down pensively. 'Around the mountain is The Realm of the Lost.' His voice was weak with an emotion that Bree could not quite fathom. 'No one ever comes back from there.'

They shivered as the thunderclouds massed above them and darkened the forest. Dunubas turned to face Bree with rivulets of rain tickling down his face and into his mouth. Somehow she knew what he was going to say and spoke first. 'Please don't leave us,' she said, trying to stop her voice from breaking with panic. He placed his dark, scarred hands on her shoulders. 'It would be too risky for all of you if I came with you,' he said apologetically. Bree felt crushed. 'But I won't let you down,' he continued. 'I'll be waiting right here for you when you come out.'

Bree shook her head and frowned. '*If* we come out.' She turned to Honey and Sandy and took a steadying breath. 'Right, come on then,' she said, 'let's go and tell them we're back!'

Great forks of lightening ripped the sky as the rain shot the ground at their feet like bullets.

'Let's head for the bridge,' yelled Honey above another boom of thunder.

'Go now! Be safe,' shouted Dunubas from the trees. Winrad barked once as if in agreement and Dunubas ruffled his wet furry head. As they scuffled down the muddy slope Bree glanced back to see Dunubas turning away. His smile had faded as though it had been carried off on the wind.

•••

By the time they reached the bridge the fog had rolled in from the valley and swirled around it like thick white smoke. The bridge stretched out like a jetty, with gaps between the spars and no railings at the side. Before Bree stepped onto it her stomach lurched when she saw the infinite chasm between the planks. She looked at Sandy as the fear welled inside her.

'Guys, wait a minute,' said Honey, and they turned to see her holding up her mobile phone. 'If you stay like that I can get you both and the castle in shot.'

'Is this *really* the time to take a picture?' said Sandy.

'Why not, I can't make a call on it, can I? We're way out of range.'

'You don't say,' laughed Bree.

'I've just thought,' began Sandy, suddenly curious. 'Where does your GPS say we are?'

'Oh come on!' Bree cried, dragging him away. She was first to step into the centre of the swaying bridge. It creaked and sent a ripple along its length.

'Okay, we can do this. Just look straight ahead,' she said, trying not to focus on the fact that there was nothing to stop her from rolling over the edge. 'Or look wherever. Close your eyes even. Just don't look down.'

There was a gap the width of a hand between the planks, and for a moment a break in the fog revealed the yawning abyss below.

A few more paces and Bree felt the bridge wobble as Sandy followed with hesitant steps. 'One at a time, Sandy,' she called out. Her throat felt dry and her skin suddenly prickled when she realised there might be planks missing up ahead. The bridge buckled again as Honey called out, 'I'm on and I'm watching you both. You're both doing great. Just keep moving.'

'It's slippery up here,' Bree warned. Rain sliced the air at an angle and a boom of thunder was quickly followed by a blue flash of lightening.

'Stop. Can we go back?' said Sandy breathlessly.

'You're fine, Sandy,' said Honey. 'Don't stop walking.'

'We're at the halfway point anyway,' said Bree putting her arm out behind her. 'Here, take my hand if it helps.'

He didn't reply.

'Sandy?' She turned around and saw him standing still, frozen with fear. But Bree was seized by a jolt of panic that wiped her mind clear of every other thought.

'Where's Honey?' she cried, the terror swelling in her stomach.

Sandy's eyes swivelled and his face drained of colour. 'S-she was right b-behind me.' Bree looked around, trying not to wobble the bridge. She could still see the start but there was no sign of Honey anywhere. Dread trickled down her spine with the drops of metallic rain. 'Honey!' she screamed.

'She must have slipped,' whimpered Sandy, his small voice lost in the howl of the wind. Bree clutched her head and tried to fight the tidal wave of horror sweeping over her, making her legs melt beneath her. She fell to her knees sobbing, making the bridge swing precariously.

'I'm down here,' came a faint, panicked voice. Sandy dropped to his knees too. 'Over here!' he yelled to Bree. She crawled over to where four multicoloured fingernails gripped the edge. Bree's heart slammed into her throat.

'Help me…' Honey's voice wafted up from below.

'Sandy, jam your feet between the planks,'

commanded Bree. 'Then get a hold of Honey's wrist. Honey, try and reach out to me with your other hand.'

The bridge creaked and swayed in the wind, tilting dangerously as they reached over the edge. Sandy encircled Honey's wrist with his wet fingers and tried not to move in case she lost her grip. Honey's fingertips were slipping away from the wet wood and her waterlogged clothes were pulling her down.

'Guys, I'm going!' she shrieked with angry helplessness as one of her fingers slipped.

'No! We've got you!' cried Bree.

'Just don't look down!' yelled Sandy. 'Look up at us.'

'Listen,' said Honey, her eyes welling with tears. 'Just get Mimi home to mum and dad. Please, promise me you will.'

Only two of Honey's fingers were clinging to the edge now. 'You're not going anywhere! Grab my hand!' Bree screamed through the wind and rain. Just as Honey swung up and grabbed onto Bree's arm her two fingers slipped. Her hand shot out of Sandy's wet grip. She screamed, but Sandy swung over and grabbed Bree's waist as she started to slide towards the edge.

'Please, don't let me go,' Honey whispered.

Honey swung above the bottomless drop, clinging so desperately that Bree thought she heard her bones crack. When another flash of lightening lit the sky Bree saw for a terrible moment the absolute horror in her eyes.

'I won't…' sobbed Bree through gritted teeth. 'I promise!'

Sandy looked around for something to help them, but there was nothing. He held Bree with one arm and tried to reach Honey with the other but Honey's hand was already slipping down Bree's forearm. Soon only their fingers were hooked together. Bree closed her eyes and grimaced through the pain. Just as the sky rumbled again she felt Honey's fingers vanish altogether. Through a blur of tears she saw Honey falling away, her hair blowing up around her face.

'No!' bellowed Sandy. 'Honey! No!'

Bree was too stunned to scream and even as she watched Honey drop through the air until she was swallowed by the lower layers of fog, she still reached out to her.

• • •

Bree crawled back onto the bridge and brought her knees up to her chin. 'I promised her…I promised her…I promised her,' she shivered. Honey's face swam in her brain and soon the tears spilled from her eyes, as her head swooned with shock and grief and horror. The rain lashed around her in glittery ribbons but she didn't feel it anymore.

She lifted her head when the bridge started swaying like a hammock. Sandy was struggling to keep his balance as he tried to remove the stopper from a blue bottle.

'W-what are you doing?' she sniffed.

His fingers were slipping so he used his teeth until the stopper popped out. With a shaking hand he poured a big pile of the grey powder into his palm.

'It's the stuff Witch Hammamalis gave me. This will stop Honey falling and pull her back up. Just as long as…'

'As long as what?'

'It's magnetic. It will only catch her if she's wearing something metal.' He blew the powder into the air with precise and startling violence. The filings floated in the air like leaves on water. Sandy replaced the stopper and shoved the bottle back into his pocket.

'Will it work in the rain?' she said as a pearl of hope started to bloom in her stomach.

Slowly the particles started to merge into a large floating bubble. It changed shape, shifted, grew, contracted. Bree shuffled to the edge of the bridge and peered over.

'It's not going anywhere. Why is nothing happening?' she whispered, her voice strangled with despair.

Sandy shook his head hopelessly and bit down on his lip. '*Was* she wearing anything metal?'

Bree blinked back the tears as she searched her memory. 'I don't think she was.'

'Come on,' whispered Sandy. 'Please…' They waited for what felt like an eternity.

'It's no use. It was our only –'

'Shh!' he said. 'Listen…' Bree strained her ears and shook her head. All she could hear was the rain hammering the planks on the wooden bridge.

'Can't you hear it?' said Sandy.

And there it was.

Bree spoke hesitantly. 'I know it can't be, but it almost sounds like…Like someone cheering far away.' It seemed so strange under the circumstances.

'Ha! Did you hear *that*, just then? It's someone laughing.'

Bree clapped a hand to her mouth. 'Not just someone…' She looked at Sandy and saw that he was smiling. Relief crushed the air from her chest. Leaning over the edge they saw the tiny figure of a blonde-haired girl speeding up towards them like a cork through water.

'Honey!' Bree screamed. 'It's Honey!'

Sandy laughed, 'It worked.'

'You're a genius!' sobbed Bree, throwing her arms around him. Then she added mischievously, 'I don't care what anyone says.'

'Watch it, McCready. We don't have enough left if you accidentally go over,' he smiled, a red flush creeping up his neck.

Honey floated upwards hanging from the strap of her satchel. 'Every good girl needs good friends and a good bag,' she called up to them.

'It was the metal zip,' laughed Sandy. 'That

dodgy metal zip saved her.'

Once she was eye-level with them Honey broke into a wide grin. 'What would I do without this satchel?'

'What would we do without Sandy Greenfield?' smiled Bree, throwing her head back and letting the rain mix with her tears of joy.

Sandy puffed out his chest, savouring the moment. 'Are you okay?' he asked gallantly. Rain sparkled on Honey's hair and eyelashes. 'I thought I was a goner,' she said darkly, 'and I broke two nails. But I'm still in one piece thanks to you, mister. And by the way, that ride back up was *amazing!*'

Anyone would have thought she had been on a fairground ride, not hanging over a bottomless grave. She was still a few feet away when Bree remembered Hammamalis's warning that the spell wouldn't last long.

'Here, give me your hands,' Bree instructed, balancing herself on the precarious treads. 'And don't you *dare* let go of me this time!'

• • •

The rainstorm loosened to a cold grey drizzle. Looming up in the half-light, Castle Zarcalat stood before them, its age-scarred stone glinting black. A foul-smelling mist swirled and blurred their vision as Bree, Honey and Sandy crept between the gates into the deserted courtyard.

'How do we get indoors?' asked Honey.

Bree looked around. 'Last time there was a door left open.'

'The door with the chunk missing from the bottom,' said Sandy, wiping the rain from his glasses.

'It led to that spiral staircase,' said Honey with a shudder.

'But there was another passageway,' continued Bree, trying to sound positive. 'We'll take that one this time.'

The fortifications towered above them like a blackened cliff face, merging like a shadow with the sky. Acidic rainwater poured down the walls in dark rivulets. A large blood-coloured flag slashed with a silver Z snapped in the wind like a whip. They scurried into the shadows and pressed their backs against the slimy stone. In the intermittent flashes of lightning they saw gargoyles grimacing on the lower roofs. For a moment, Bree thought they were turning towards her.

'Over there,' said Honey, pointing to a shield hanging from an arch. 'I saw that last time. The door is just around the corner.'

The shield flashed as a great bolt tore through the sky. They cautiously approached the yawning arch, knowing that once they passed under it, the portcullis would fall and there would be no way back. As it thundered down behind them with a rolling, metallic clang the wind died to a dark whisper.

'There it is,' said Sandy, pointing to the splintered door.

Bree tried not to shake as they approached it. She tugged the heart shaped handle and the hinges squealed like a wounded animal. Her prickling unease was growing by the second.

One by one they stooped into the small dark space. Light from burning torches flickered off the wet flagstones and the sweating walls. Up ahead, Bree could see the first few steps of the staircase they had taken the last time they had been here. A long corridor stretched the other way, so black it seemed to have no end; darkness whispered in the corners.

'It's just as creepy as I remember,' said Sandy.

As Bree looked she shivered. She reached up and pulled a torch from a sconce. 'Keep close by me,' she said as she set off into the blackness. Honey and Sandy followed reluctantly. Through the darkness there came the sound of dripping and scurrying feet. Bree shrank from the putrid liquid that licked at her shoes and struggled to fight a spasm of panic with each step. The airless corridor narrowed and curved, taking them deeper into the unknown.

'What's that up ahead?' gasped Honey, her voice ricocheting off the walls.

Two large black holes appeared before them like empty eye sockets.

'They're underground tunnels,' said Sandy.

Bree held her torch into each of them where it flickered and smoked but revealed nothing except a few feet of curved wall. 'I guess we have to choose one,' she shrugged, her voice echoing back in a swollen wave. She eyed Sandy and Honey. 'Hands up for the one on the right.' No-one spoke. 'Hands up for the one on the left,' she said, a little more impatiently.

'Hands up for neither,' replied Sandy, shuffling from one foot to the other.

'We have to choose one of them.'

Honey rummaged around at the bottom of her satchel until she found a coin. 'Okay. Let's make it easy. Heads we go right, tails we go left.'

Bree and Sandy nodded for Honey to toss the coin. She caught it mid-spin and slapped it onto the back of her hand. 'Tails,' she said firmly, taking the torch from Bree and stepping into the tunnel. Sandy and Bree edged behind her into the dark, silent hole. Inside the air was close and damp; soundless except for their breathing. With their arms outstretched, they felt their way along the rough stone. Bree felt a cobweb brush her cheek and she fought the urge to run.

'Up ahead,' said Sandy, indicating a slash of weak light in the distance. 'It could be a way out.'

Honey pointed the torch in front of them. 'It's not much further.'

'Hang on, look at this,' said Bree. Patches of light were rippling on the tunnel walls; eerie blues and pinks mottled like a moon-filled sea.

Sandy took a closer look and saw a swarm of tiny specs. 'They look like fireflies,' said Sandy.

'*So* pretty,' said Honey.

The splinters of light danced off the walls in the darkness like quivering, fleeting rainbows. They pulsed and glowed as though from hidden currents.

'Something's happening to them,' said Sandy.

They were changing shape. At first they drifted like dandelion seeds, but soon they flew in jerky loops above Bree, Honey and Sandy's heads before flittering away, leaving trails of spectral light. When one flew close to her nose, Bree saw they were tiny human figures with wings. Their faces had no other features except two large black eyes. 'We are Shrillflitters,' it sang.

'They're incredible,' she laughed. As their song grew louder they started to circle her head. Her skin was bathed in their white crystal light and for a moment she felt a feeling of peace wash through her. The Shrillflitters clustered around Bree's arms and legs and gently lifted her off the ground.

'Hey guys,' said Honey, ducking and dodging them as they swarmed the tunnel, 'they're getting a bit weird now…'

Bree heard her, but Honey's words sounded distant. The Shrillflitters swirled around her head like snowflakes, their wings whirring so fast they were almost invisible. Their colours had faded, replaced with a bright white that burned like a million stars. Their singing had become a shrill confusion of mixed frequencies, but Bree, Sandy and Honey caught a few words:

'Dear are the shadows. Sorrow will take you away…'

Bree covered her ears but still the irresistible whispers broke through.

'Death is just a dream…'

As the Shrillflitters lifted her higher she glanced back to see them lifting Sandy up off the floor, his teeth bared in pain. His breath came in ragged, frightened gasps. Honey tried to swat away the Shrillflitters from around his head and mouthed something to Bree. But Bree was unable to move, unable to answer, held ransom by the piercing threads of sound and light. A wall of air pressed down on her, squashing the breath from her lungs. Black and white spots began to dance in front of her eyes and she felt herself slipping away.

8.

SNAKES AND BONES

Only Honey was unaffected by the Shrillflitters. Even though she swiped and batted them away from Sandy not a single one of them landed on her. She fingered the daisy-chain around her neck and swung at the swarm with her umbrella until the Shrillflitters shrank away in waves. A sudden memory seeped into Bree's drowning senses.

'The eye of the day will save you from them.'

The old woman had said this as they left the village. What's the eye of the day? she wondered sleepily. A day's eye...Daisies!

Bree summoned up enough strength to wave to Honey, pointing to her daisy chain. Honey looked confused for a moment, then tugged it off, scattering the little flowers to the ground. She threw the torch to the floor where it hissed and threw flickering shadows up the tunnel walls.

'Here, have some of these!' she yelled. Honey scooped up a handful of daisies and threw them at the Shrillflitters holding Sandy above the ground. With a collective shriek they dispersed and dropped him. He landed in a confused heap with his glasses askew. Honey dived over to Bree and tossed the daisies over her like confetti. The Shrillflitters spun drunkenly into the walls, letting Bree fall to floor. 'Are you all right?' Honey asked, helping her to stand.

'I think so,' replied Bree, as the tiny figures melted back into the stone, leaving only the spluttering torch to light the tunnel. Sandy stood up, straightened his glasses and picked up the torch. It sparked back to life, framing his face with an amber glow.

Bree gathered up a handful of the battered flowers and put them in her pocket. 'We better arm ourselves just in case they come back.'

'Maybe they were the dangerous angels the blind woman warned us about,' said Sandy.

Honey nodded and took a few daisies. 'I guess she wasn't such a batty old bag after all.'

They headed on until they came to a low ceilinged junction where more tunnels spidered of in all directions.

'What do you think they are used for?' said Honey.

'Dunno,' replied Bree. 'Escape tunnels?'

'So, which way now then?' asked Sandy. As soon as he spoke they heard a sound like ice fracturing. 'What the heck is that?'

The three of them froze and exchanged quick glances. Sandy looked down at his feet as a network of cracks appeared. Bree was too surprised to scream when the floor collapsed. They fell feet first into a darkness so thick they could not tell up from down. Bree caught sight of Sandy tumbling through the air next to her, his arms wind-milling and his legs kicking. The air was knocked from her lungs as she slammed against a dirt heap and rolled into an earth tunnel. The sides of the steep, mossy slope flashed past as roots scraped her back and weeds whipped her face. One by one they plunged around the sharp curves until they eventually burst through an opening and crashed onto a rocky ledge high above the ground in a vast, vaulted chamber.

'Ouch…Some escape tunnel!' moaned Sandy as he tried to sit up. He had lost the torch but it didn't matter. Countless candles were set into holes around the walls.

Dizzy and bruised, Bree glanced over her shoulder. 'Don't make any sudden movements,' she warned as she pulled a twig from her hair.

Honey groped back from the edge. She jumped and let out a panicked yelp. 'I've put my hand in something!' she screeched, wiping her hand down her leg. A pile of small white orbs sat stuck together in a moist clutch. Bree crawled over and peered at them through the gloom. They were leathery with no sign of movement within and too many to count. 'They look like eggs,' she said.

'Not just any old eggs,' said Sandy, squinting over his glasses. 'Those are snake eggs.'

Honey's eyes almost popped out of their sockets. 'I put my hand RIGHT ON THEM!'

'What kind of snake lays eggs like that?' asked Bree nervously.

Sandy studied them and scratched the back of his neck. 'Most snakes lay eggs but going by this…' He held up a shrivelled length of discarded skin making Honey pucker her face with disgust. 'It's likely to be a non poisonous corn snake.'

'That's a relief.'

'Corn snakes shed their skin just after they lay their eggs,' continued Sandy.

'And then where does it go?' asked Honey, her eyes darting wildly.

'It's probably hiding. They can be quite shy.'

'Perfect. I won't introduce myself,' muttered Honey.

Bree peered over the ledge. 'The big question is how do we get down from here?'

'It's impossible to jump from this height,' said Sandy.

'Perhaps we have to go up?' suggested Honey, craning her neck.

Keeping her back against the rock face Bree looked around. Holes were spaced out evenly up the walls and not all of them had a candle inside.

'We could use these as foot holds,' she said, putting her hand inside one of the empty cavities. She immediately snatched it back out, as though she had been scalded.

'What happened?' yelped Honey.

'There's something in there.'

'What kind of something?' Sandy asked, turning white. Bree shook her head, mute with fear.

Sandy edged closer and peered into the hole. 'It's clear. I can't see anyth—'

Something bolted out at him and knocked the glasses off his face. He staggered backwards towards the edge. Honey and Bree grabbed him just in time and pulled him back to safety. They looked at the hole and watched in horror as a stocky snake wormed its way out. It was dark grey with a black zigzag down its back. Vertical pupils flickered at either side of an angular head.

'That *is* a corn snake isn't it?' whimpered Honey as it thumped onto the ledge. It held its head steady as it focussed on them, and started to shift nearer exposing its grey belly and vertical slashes.

Sandy shook his head and gulped. 'That's an adder. Or, to give it its Latin name, Vipera Berus.'

Honey shrieked, 'Forget the Latin name! Is it poisonous?'

Sandy nodded frantically and took another step back. They were all dangerously close to the edge now.

'You said the eggs were from a harmless little corn snake!'

'It's not the adder's nest. Adders don't lay eggs.'

'That must mean there's more than one snake up here,' said Bree.

'Just stay really still,' whispered Sandy. 'And whatever you do, don't run.'

Honey looked at him like he had lost his mind. 'Exactly where would we run to?' she asked flatly, indicating the tiny shelf of rock.

'There's no way up and no way down,' snivelled Bree as the adder coiled like a thick rope around Sandy's glasses.

Sandy stared blindly, 'I can't see a bloomin' thing without them.'

'How do you suppose we get them back?' hissed Bree.

The adder raised its head, the tongue flickering gently.

'Snakes have poor vision too,' whispered Sandy. 'It's sensing vibrations with its tongue.' He started to edge towards the snake with cautious steps.

'Be careful!' gasped Bree, hardly able to watch.

'She won't even know I'm here.'

Honey and Bree held onto one another as they watched him reach slowly for his glasses. The adder waved its forked tongue lazily, testing the air. It brushed Sandy's hand as he curled his fingers around the arm of his glasses. He stopped moving. Bree could see beads of sweat forming on his brow, his tongue poked out in concentration.

Thump. Another snake fell beside the nest of eggs, making the adder flick its flat head round. Sandy jumped back, without his glasses, as more snakes started to emerge from the holes in the wall.

'More adders!' cried Bree, as the chamber resounded with hissing and rattling.

They poured out onto the ledge, all shapes and sizes, so tangled together in knots it was impossible to tell where one ended and another began. The snakes spilled towards them, pushing them backwards towards the edge. Bree felt the cold crawl of sweat over her scalp. The coiled adder revealed two sharp fangs and pounced at a smaller snake. Sandy leaped over and snatched his glasses. The adder spun round and lashed at him, missing his arm by a fraction of an inch as he whipped it away. When his eyes focused again he saw Bree and Honey standing in a mire of writhing, iridescent snakes.

'Watch your ankles. They'll bite them!' he warned, wading through the churning, wriggling bodies. Honey pulled her umbrella out of her bag and quickly flicked them away from around their feet. Bree pulled the book from her pocket and batted them back to clear a space for Sandy. A pair of snakes hissed and dived at her, sinking their fangs into the book. Bree screamed and tried to shake them off. 'It's making them worse!'

Honey smacked the two snakes with her umbrella until they let go and dropped into the pile. Bree, Honey and Sandy edged towards the drop as the tide of snakes swelled closer.

'We're going to have to jump,' said Honey firmly.

Sandy said, 'Are you out of your mind? We're about as high as the roof garden back home.'

'Honey's right,' Bree resolved, her voice trembling. 'There's no other way.'

Just then she felt the half-heart locket pulse on the cover of the book. She turned it over to see the locket glowing bright red.

'Open it up. What does it say?' asked Sandy.

'Is it a wish?' asked Honey.

Bree opened the book and found the second page had become transparent, and showed a billowing mist.

'Perfect timing…' said Bree, her body wilting with relief. She stared down as words appeared through the mist:

IN ORDER TO ESCAPE THE ADDERS,
USE THE CREEPING VINES LIKE LADDERS.
YOU MUST INHALE AND HOLD THAT BREATH.
TO KEEP YOU SAFE FROM CERTAIN DEATH,
IF YOU SHOULD FAIL BY TAKING AIR,
THE CLIMBING PLANTS WILL DISAPPEAR.

Bree looked around, confused. 'What creepers?' A small, thin snake slid over her shoe and she kicked it away angrily.

'There must be some around here. The book is never wrong,' said Honey as she used her umbrella like a golf club.

'Down there. Something's moving,' said Sandy, pointing to the foot of the drop. When Bree peered over she saw a mass of green vines had started to grow up the rock-face, faster than her brain could process. The locket pulsed stronger than ever as they crept up and over the ledge.

'The wish says we have to hold our breaths,' said Bree, as the words began to fade from the page.

Sandy nodded at her. 'At least you won't have any bother with that, Flipper!'

Bree smiled. That was the nickname he'd given her when they went swimming because she so good at holding her breath under water. 'You should go down first,' she instructed, with a pat on the back. 'Then Honey can come behind you. And I'll come last.'

Sandy nodded and reached over for the thick creepers. He took a couple of deep breaths and held it on the third. Bree gave him the thumbs up as he fumbled around for his footing and climbed over.

'You next, Honey,' said Bree, gesturing Honey to tiptoe through the carpet of snakes. 'And remember; hold your breath for as long as you can.'

'What about you?'

'Don't worry about me. Just get down there fast.'

Honey took an enormous breath and scrambled down after Sandy. Bree kicked the snakes back a few feet then filled her lungs with as much air as she could. She swung herself over onto the lattice of vines and, looking over her shoulder, saw Sandy struggling to keep holding his breath. Halfway to the ground his face turned beetroot pink and even from the top she could see the whites of his panicked eyes. She willed him to hold on for just another few seconds. Falling now would mean certain death. The breath was already starting to burn in Bree's chest and there was still a considerable way to go but she focused on keeping a secure footing. From far below her, Bree heard Sandy suddenly gasp for air. She froze in fright and closed her eyes, knowing that as he'd broken the wish the vines would disappear.

But instead, he called up breathlessly, 'I'm down.' Bree glanced over her shoulder to see him bent over with his hands on his knees as Honey jumped to his side. Bree would only need to hold on for a few seconds more.

'Come on!' cried Honey. 'You're nearly there...'

With a surge of relief Bree knew she was going to make it. She punched the air with one hand and Sandy and Honey cheered. But as she lifted her foot she felt it snag in a tangle of vines.

'What are you waiting for?' cried Sandy.

Bree pulled her foot again but it wouldn't budge. A wave of adrenalin crashed through her. The vines had wound tightly around her ankle. She was trapped. The blood rushed in her ears and without air she was starting to feel dizzy. Pinpricks of light danced before her and she knew she wasn't going to be able to hold her breath for a second longer.

'Let go and jump!' yelled Honey. 'We'll catch you!'

Bree shook her head. She felt she was drowning. She swallowed, her starving lungs bursting in her chest until she could hold on no longer. Bree threw her head back and gasped, almost in shock. The air flooded her in a rush, making her choke and gag. The instant relief was immediately replaced by terror. Between her fingers the creepers turned brown and dry. Their glossy leaves withered and curled like burning paper. As the roots shrivelled and died, they snapped and tore away from the wall. Bree did not have time to think. Hands clutching at nothing, she tumbled backwards, until she hit something and rolled to the ground. Her head was spinning so much that Sandy's voice seemed distant and garbled at first. 'Blimey Bree, that was a direct hit! Are you both ok?'

Honey was spread-eagled on the ground, hair fanned out behind her. 'Honey, I'm so sorry,' yelped Bree, kneeling beside her and cradling her head. Honey groaned and struggled to sit up. 'I did say I'd catch you, didn't I?' she mumbled, rubbing the back of her head.

Above them the creepers had disappeared, leaving behind only rough rock. The book stopped throbbing and now lay inert in Bree's pocket against her thigh. Bree helped Honey to her feet and they looked around. The damp walls of the cave glistened in the light of a single torch, and somewhere nearby water was dripping. Bree took down the torch and swung it in a wide arc around the walls. Everywhere the shadows seemed to move in response to the flame. Webs hung like lace shawls from outcrops, catching in their hair and across their faces.

'Look for a gap in the rock,' said Bree. 'Like a tunnel or a vent or something.'

'Do you think there will be one?' asked Honey.

Bree said, 'There's water coming in from somewhere.'

Sandy took the torch from Bree and screwed up his face in thought. 'And, if there's enough air for this to burn there must a channel nearby.' As he stepped past them he tripped and stumbled to the floor. Holding up the torch he yelped at two blank eye sockets staring back at him. He jumped and pulled back. The torch gleamed off the yellowed teeth of a dusty skull.

'Bones,' breathed Bree, stepping over carefully. 'They're all over the floor.'

Sandy got to his feet and held up the torch. A skeleton was huddled in the shadows and around it ribs and arms and thigh bones stuck out of the dirt at angles.

'I guess we're not the first ones down here,' said Honey.

The skeleton was covered with cobwebs. All that was left of its clothes hung in tatters. In the torchlight the skull seemed to grin, like a Halloween pumpkin.

'It's hard to imagine this was someone like us at one time,' said Bree.

'It's got its hand on something,' said Honey, nodding down at a dark shape under the finger bones. Bree knelt down and blew away the dust.

'It's a leather bag,' she said, picking it up. When she lifted the flap a huge spider jumped out and scuttled over her hand. She squealed and made Sandy and Honey jump.

'Is there anything inside?' asked Sandy.

The first thing Bree saw was a dusty rope, wound into a tight coil. 'This might come in handy,' she said. She removed it and tied it around her waist. In a side panel there was a small roll of paper, so brown with age that it looked like it had been soaked in tea. It crackled as Bree unrolled it, to reveal three shapes cut in the centre with an arrow drawn between two of them, pointing off the page.

'A square and two halves of a heart,' said Bree, holding it up so the light from the torch projected through the shapes and onto the wall. At that, something dropped out of the scroll and landed with a clink on the ground. Bree picked it up and held it up to the light.

'What is it?' asked Honey.

It was a small flat tool, rusty and rough, like an ancient spoon. At the centre were three holes, the same shapes as those cut into the scroll.

'Looks like Old Bones here came down equipped for something,' said Honey.

'Yes, but it's a shame he can't tell us what,' said Bree. She sighed, rolled up the scroll and put it and the spoon into her pocket. They turned to see Sandy peering at the wall. 'Come and look at this,' he said. They crept over the carpet of bones and stopped beside him. 'Looks like scratches,' he went on.

'By an animal?' asked Bree.

'No, they're too regular. Like letters.'

'What? You mean graffiti?' said Honey. 'Down here with all these bones?'

'Someone has tried to scratch a message into the stone,' said Sandy. 'Bree, bring the torch closer.'

'Maybe it'll be directions out of here,' Bree said as she shone the torch on the wall. In the flickering light two words jumped out at them:

DEATH AWAITS!

Honey gasped.

'Or, then again, maybe not,' said Sandy.

The flame dipped and with it Bree's hope faded. 'There must be some way out,' she muttered, and walked off into the shadows. After a moment she screamed and dropped the torch.

'What's up?' called Sandy.

Honey, ran over. 'Are you ok?'

'There's someone else here. Look.' The word stuck in Bree's throat as she pointed to a pair of dirty feet poking out of the shadows. Sandy picked up the torch and tilted it to bring the flame back to life. Slowly, it illuminated a little hooded figure crouched like a wild animal ready to pounce. 'Stay back!' Sandy warned, lunging with the torch.

The figure shrank against the wall and shielded its face. It looked smaller than Bree, Honey and Sandy, perhaps even smaller than Mimi.

'It's a little kid,' Bree said, pulling Sandy back. 'Don't be scared. We don't want to hurt you.'

The cloak shivered in the corner.

'And we need your help,' said Honey.

Slowly the cloaked figure stood up as though in a trance, but did not step out of the shadows.

'My name is Bree. What's your name…?'

Slowly the cloaked figure moved away from the wall and out into the circle of torchlight. Two white hands appeared out of the sleeves and lowered the hood. It was a little boy with matted white hair and scarlet, staring eyes. He was covered in dust and twigs and his cloak was stained. His eyes looked old and his expression was tired, making Bree wonder what terrors he had seen. 'He's too afraid of us to talk,' she told the others.

'Offer him some chocolate,' said Sandy.

Honey rummaged inside her satchel until she found the bar of chocolate. She snapped off a corner and thrust it out at the child. He cowered, fear flashing in his red eyes.

'It's nice,' smiled Honey. 'Look, I'll eat a piece too.'

The boy looked at them distrustfully but gingerly stepped forward and snatched it out of her hands.

Honey said, 'We'll deal with the table manners

another time.' Bree shot her a warning glance. 'Can you help us to find a way out?' she asked the boy. He shook his head firmly.

'Please?'

He shook his head again.

'I think we'll have to speak his language,' said Honey holding up a stick of bubble gum. 'Look what I've got for you.'

The boy's eyes gleamed. He reached out to take it but Honey pulled it away at the last minute. 'Naughty, naughty. First, you have to help us.'

The boy greedily licked his lips. Then to Bree's surprise he nodded. He stepped aside and before they could say anything he put a dirty finger to his lips and pointed to the floor. Sandy lifted the torch to reveal a trapdoor with an iron ring.

'The way out,' he said. 'He was sitting on it all along!'

Bree dropped to her knees and heaved the ring but the door would not budge. 'It must be locked,' she sighed. The boy put his hand into a pocket in the front of his robe and pulled out a large key. She reached out to take it but the boy pulled it away. He held out his other hand to Honey.

'You pick things up fast,' Honey laughed and gave him the stick of gum. He smelled it suspiciously before nibbling the corner. When he was satisfied, he put the rest into his pocket and handed her the key. She immediately dropped down beside Bree, pushed the key into a hole and turned it. A grinding click echoed around the cave. She tugged on the ring and the door opened onto a set of steps leading into darkness. The air rising up from the depths smelled earthy and damp.

'Come on, let's get out of here,' said Honey, but the boy blocked her way. He held out a grubby hand. Honey looked puzzled. 'What now? You got your gum.'

'We don't have anything else,' said Bree.

'Maybe he wants this torch back,' suggested Sandy.

'We'll need it,' said Bree, her voice sharp with desperation.

'I guess he does too,' sighed Sandy as he reluctantly handed it over. The boy stepped aside and Bree stared down into the unyielding darkness. Who knew what was waiting for them at the bottom of those steps. 'I don't suppose you've got night vision goggles in there?' she said, eyeing Honey's bag.

'Everything but,' replied Honey as she made for the first step. The boy pulled her back. 'What now?' she said impatiently. He leaned close and kissed her on the cheek. It took them all by surprise, not least Honey. She turned pink and touched her cheek tenderly as the boy pulled up his hood. 'You're welcome…' she whispered.

The faint glow from his torch gave them just

enough light to see the uneven steps. When Bree reached the bottom she stepped off and peered ahead. An earth-floored passage stretched into the distance. Above them the trapdoor slammed shut. The absolute darkness drowned them out.

9.

THREE BECOME TWO

Bree blinked and waited for her eyes to adjust to the darkness. Suddenly a magnesium flare of white dazzled her. She spun around to see Honey holding up a tiny bright light.

'It's the flash on my phone's camera,' she smiled. 'I can keep it on, but it'll only last until my battery runs out.'

Its bluish light cast an agitated dance of shadows all around them as they hurried down. The deeper they went the lower the roof became until they had to stoop to avoid bumping their heads. Soon, they had to drop onto their stomachs and wriggle over the ground. Bree fought waves of panic as the tunnel became as narrow as a chimney, and their wriggling brought down showers of stones and dirt. She felt the roof might collapse at any moment and had the terrible urge to back up, when Honey, in front of her, panted, 'Guys, I can see light up ahead.'

They reached a small opening and Honey popped her head through. She pulled herself back and turned her head to Bree and Sandy, the ghostly brilliance of her phone painting her features in a chalk white aura. 'There's a corridor out there,' she explained, with a glint in her eye. 'I'm going to see where it leads.' She pulled her bag over her head and pushed it towards Bree. 'Watch my bag while I'm gone.'

'Be careful, Honey,' urged Bree but she was already halfway out the hole. From her squashed position all Bree could see beyond it was a floor that looked slimy. Honey stood up and walked out of view.

After a few moments Bree said, 'She's gone very quiet.'

'What's going on out there?' Sandy whispered.

Bree wriggled forwards, pushing aside Honey's bag, and poked her head out. Honey was tiptoeing along a torch-lit passage.

'Hey – do you see anything?' Bree hissed.

Honey turned around. 'Nah. Bad news. It's just a dead end.' She started to walk back when something startled her. The thunder of footsteps, heavy and rough, crashed from the darker end of the corridor. Not one set of feet but an army of them, all marching with angry purpose.

'Find them!' barked an approaching voice. 'Alive or dead! Preferably dead.'

Honey stopped in her tracks, trembling, her eyes darting wildly to the approaching shadows and then back to Bree. 'Hide!'

Bree ducked inside the tunnel. 'What about you?' she cried.

'They'll see me if I make a dive for it, then they'll catch all of us.'

From inside the tunnel Bree and Sandy heard the angry roar and marching steps as a clot of shadow spread along the wall until it fell across Honey. Her lips were moving but above the noise her voice could not be heard. The ragged hems of a dozen red cloaks hustled past the opening as the boots crowded towards Honey.

'Take her,' the voice bellowed. 'And bring her to me!'

For a second, between the boots, Bree caught a glimpse of Honey's striped leggings as she was marched away.

•••

Once the pounding in her chest subsided, Bree lay with her cheek pressed against the dirt, her breath tight in her throat. There was only silence now, which made everything worse.

'What do we do now?' sniffed Sandy, sticking a finger behind his glasses to rub a bloodshot eye.

Bree could not think straight. She blinked away hot tears and took a deep breath. 'The only thing we *can* do. We get her back.' She picked up Honey's satchel and crawled out of the tunnel. In the passageway she put the satchel over her shoulder and walked cautiously towards where she had last seen Honey. Behind her, Sandy slid out of the opening.

'Do you think they'll come back?' she whispered, casting a glance at the end of the corridor.

'It depends. They might make Honey tell them we're here too.'

Bree opened her mouth to reply but the sound of rumbling stopped her. Fear pinned her to the spot.

'The tunnel!' hissed Sandy as he spun round, his face blotchy in the flickering light. A gust of dirt and dust blew out of the hole as for a moment the corridor shuddered. 'It's collapsed.' The hole filled with rocks and soil that tumbled out onto the floor. Just then there came the terrible echo of footsteps from the dark end of the corridor.

'Here they come,' said Sandy.

Bree bit her lip as dread washed over her. 'They know we're here.'

'We must be able to run somewhere,' said Sandy pleadingly as he and Bree backed away. 'There must be another way…'

As he said this Bree felt something throb inside her pocket. 'Wait a minute. The book…' she yelped. The glow from the locket lit up the walls in red pulsing waves. She threw open the cover and turned the pages, aware that the footsteps were closing in. 'Wish four!'

'Hurry!'

As soon as the mist cleared on the transparent page she whispered the words to Sandy:

'A RING OF GOLD, SO BRIGHT AND CLEAR,
GO THROUGH THE HOOP AND DISAPPEAR.
NO-ONE WILL SEE OR HEAR YOU THEN,
INVISIBLE TO FOE AND FRIEND.
BUT EVEN WHEN YOU'RE OUT OF SIGHT,
YOU'LL STILL HAVE TOOLS TO WIN THE FIGHT.

BEWARE! JUST AFTER VICTORY,
THIS WISH WILL END AND ALL WILL SEE.'

As she said the last word, something swelled under the word 'Hoop'. It rose up like a bubble until a gold ring broke through the page. Bree and Sandy watched as it drifted off the page and floated a few inches above the book where it rippled like a smoke ring.

'Is it my imagination, or is it getting bigger?' said Sandy.

The ring *was* growing. Larger and wider, until it was the size of a dinner plate. Soon it was bigger than a hula hoop, a molten ring of light. It turned on its side and hovered at waist level in front of them. Bree closed the book but the locket continued to throb in heavy, rhythmic waves.

'Quick! We have to go through it,' she urged Sandy as the voices and footsteps grew closer. Without hesitating she stepped through but neither looked nor felt different once she had. She could still see her body and she could still feel the stickiness of the floor. As soon as Sandy ducked through the gold ring it disappeared. With the locket still glowing in the gloomy corridor, Bree thrust the book into Honey's bag. 'Can you still see me?' she said.

'Of course. Not very invisible, are we?'

The wall torches guttered and flared, lengthening the shadows. Two large hands seemed to reach out for them.

'It's too late. They're going to see us,' said Bree. She turned as a cloaked figure appeared at the end of the corridor. His features were shadowed by a hood so all she could see was the glint of his sword. He seemed to stare straight through them.

'There is nothing up here,' he shouted, then turned and ran back, his shadow shrinking down the walls.

'It did work,' laughed Bree, holding up her hands and waving her fingers around, 'We're actually invisible!'

'Just not to each other…' smiled Sandy. 'Let's follow the cloak. He might lead us to Honey.'

They hurried after him but when they turned the corner, there was no-one in sight.

'How could he have got away so quickly?' hissed Sandy.

'He can't have gone far,' replied Bree. 'I can still hear his footsteps. In fact, they're getting louder.'

She turned to see an army of figures in red hooded cloaks surging towards them.

'Quick! This way,' shouted Sandy, pulling Bree's arm.

'Hang on. They can't see or hear us. They don't know we're here…'

At that, the cloaked figures were upon them, elbowing one another out of the way, their blood-coloured cloaks brushing the stone walls. Before they could step aside Bree and Sandy found themselves being carried along by the sea of bodies.

'This is probably not the best time to point this out,' began Sandy, his face pressed up against the back of one of the figures so that his glasses sat squint. 'But if we become visible soon we're in big trouble.'

Bree dipped her hand into Honey's bag and was reassured when she felt the steady pulse of the locket. They would remain invisible for now.

The stampede rushed them towards an open doorway flanked by guards with ferocious-looking Cleptathorns that snarled and pulled at their chains.

'I hope we're invisible to all things furry too,' said Sandy. Bree gritted her teeth as they passed but the Cleptathorns' amber eyes looked straight through them.

It led into a large arena lit by a forest of torches and surrounded by tiers of seats. When the crowd that had carried them in surged towards the audience Bree pulled Sandy aside and they looked around, still unseen. 'It's an amphitheatre,' said Sandy. The audience was assembling on seats around the curved walls. Bree swept the sea of bodies with anxious eyes. All their faces were covered by hoods. The hot air was filled with whispers and a sense of anticipation. A rope bridge stretched across a pit to the centre of the arena, where there was a circular stage on a raised platform. On it stood a wooden box roped to a hoop high above.

'Do you think Honey is inside that box?' Sandy asked.

'I hope not,' Bree replied.

A few of the figures started to point to the door and Bree turned to see the crowd jump apart to let another hooded figure through. He strode to the bridge, his black cloak drifting out behind him like smoke. He faced the audience and raised his hands until a hush fell over them. With a dramatic gesture he threw back his hood. There was a collective gasp from the audience. Bree felt a sudden, stabbing terror.

'It's Tanas Theramonde!' she blurted, her words strangled by fear.

He stood head and shoulders above all others, eyes shining like black marbles in a face twisted into a sneer by the long diagonal scar on his cheek. The belt around his waist looked like a serpent swallowing its tail. Around his neck was hung a large silver letter 'Z'. Bree felt the hairs on her neck prickle as she recalled the last time she had seen it.

The crowd began to chant their approval as two helmeted figures stepped through the crowd and tossed what looked like a rag doll down onto the ground before him.

Sandy gasped, 'Honey!'

Bree opened her mouth to scream but choked. Honey tried to scramble to her feet but her hands were tied behind her back. Breaking away from Sandy, Bree ran over. Up close she could see

Honey's face was blotchy and tear-stained.

Theramonde dragged her up by her ponytail until she stood on her tip-toes, her chin jutting out stubbornly. Bree knew Honey could not see or hear her but it felt right to whisper in her ear, 'We've found you, Honey. And we'll get you out of here.' But Honey stared ahead obliviously. Sandy put his hand on Bree's shoulder as she fought back tears. Theramonde shoved Honey onto the bridge. Bree and Sandy hurried after them. In the torchlight the black marble stage gleamed like a lake at night.

When he reached the centre Theramonde yanked Honey's hair to stop her. She let out a little yelp but quickly recovered, throwing her shoulders back defiantly. Theramonde grinned and bent down until his mouth was level with her ear. Bree raced over and crouched beside them to hear:

'One down, two to go,' he hissed. The growl of his dreadful voice sent Bree's heart into her mouth.

'You wish. You caught me because I gave myself away,' Honey shot back, her eyes flashing. Bree could feel the panic underneath her rage. Theramonde turned aside and spat on the floor. He sucked in his breath and looked up. 'The other two are here,' he sneered. Bree and Sandy looked at each other. Theramonde leaned in closer. 'And I will sniff them out personally. Now that they're in the Castle, they're as dead as you.'

The buzz of anticipation erupted into an explosion of shouts and cries. The audience started chanting and clapping rhythmically.

'Not even! You don't scare me,' Honey shouted over the noise, although the quiver in her voice betrayed the truth. Theramonde stopped in his tracks and began to laugh. He pulled out a dagger from his belt. Bree and Sandy saw a white gemstone blaze as brightly as a tiny moon.

'What kind of stone is that, can you see?' Bree whispered.

'An opal. It's the Opal Dagger Nevidas told us about. It unlocks the Flame of Irenus.'

A fist of ice clutched at Bree's chest as she watched Theramonde turn and walk back towards Honey, a grin of delicious satisfaction on his face. The crowd were on their feet. Honey took a couple of stumbling steps backwards until she realised she was too close to the edge. She cowered in Theramonde's shadow as he lifted the glinting steel to her face. Little flecks of light reflected off the opal onto her cheek, like fractured glass.

Theramonde lowered the dagger, spun Honey around and sliced the blade through the rope that tied her hands together. She rubbed furiously at the red indents it left and watched as Theramonde slid the dagger back into its hilt.

'You didn't think I was going to kill you straight away, did you?' said Theramonde. 'Where would be the fun in that?'

Honey sprinted past him, sending the crowd wild. Theramonde bolted to the bridge before her and blocked her way.

'The feisty animals are always the most fun to catch,' he smiled as he ran a finger down her cheek. 'You will never cross this bridge again. Unless you win the contest. But I don't think that's likely, do you?'

He dragged her by the arm and threw her down at the centre of the stage. The crowd roared and Theramonde indulged them with a deep bow. Honey looked pitifully frightened.

'Leave her alone!' shouted Bree to no effect. Sandy ran to the edge of the stage and looked over. Bree stayed with Honey, too terrified to leave her for a second. When Sandy ran back Bree knew from the look in his eyes that he did not have good news. 'It's…there's…I…' he spluttered, pointing to the edge of the stage.

'Spit it out, Sandy!' yelled Bree impatiently.

He took a deep breath. 'Over the edge,' he finally managed, 'there's a massive drop around the stage and at the bottom there's wooden spikes. And they're covered in skeletons. They throw people over.'

Fear fluttered in Bree's chest like a bird caught in a net. If the fall did not kill Honey then the lethal spears would. Bree hardly dared process the thought. Turning back she saw Honey eyeing the wooden box nervously. She was trembling as though standing in icy water. Bree felt blanketed in a wave of despair. This felt like a dream that she would wake from at any moment.

The excited murmur from the crowd was gathering in intensity. All at once, every figure lowered its hood. Underneath, they were identical: all were bald with black lips and chalk-white skin that made their red eyelids burn every time they blinked in unison.

'They're like clones,' breathed Sandy in disbelief. Bree grabbed his arm. 'And look who has pride of place.' She pointed to a solitary child sitting at the front, apart from the others. Unlike the adults he had hair. A shock of white hair. 'It's that boy from the cave.'

'Do you think he told them he'd seen us?'

The boy stood up proudly and waved to the audience, his lips forming a dead smile. Bree caught an approving look in his eyes, no more than a fleck of fire, but it made her certain he had betrayed them.

There was a chill of menace in the air, a darkness that seemed to sweat from the walls. A thousand voices chanted the same thing, like an incantation, 'Set It Free! Set It Free! Set It Free!'

Their hideous faces flickered and leapt to the whim of the flames. 'Just to show that I am a fair man I will allow you something to defend yourself with,' Theramonde told Honey, his voice like sandpaper. He picked up a stick from behind the box and handed it to her. Honey took it from him without hesitating, her fear growing by the second.

'Defend herself? What from?' asked Sandy. Bree was too terrified to speak.

'SET IT FREE!'

They watched Theramonde walk across the stage and wave at the white haired boy to come over the bridge. By now the noise from the mob was so intense Bree could not hear herself think. When the boy stepped off the rope bridge, Theramonde reached for his sword and gestured for him to step forward.

'He's going to kill him,' cried Sandy, throwing his hands over his eyes.

Theramonde whipped his sword out of its scabbard with a ringing noise and the crowd roared their approval. The polished blade shone mirror-bright in the torchlight. He handed the sword to the boy, who took it, his knees buckling slightly under the weight.

'He hasn't killed him. You can look,' Bree whispered. Sandy opened his fingers and peered through the gaps. 'Is he going to attack Honey?' he asked.

All kinds of thoughts were racing through Bree's mind. Honey would not stand a chance against anyone wielding a sword. The chanting continued like a string of echoes.

'What is he doing?' Sandy hissed.

Suddenly the noise from the crowd settled to a hush. Theramonde waited for complete silence before lifting his arm above his head. His mouth was quite expressionless, curving neither up nor down. This seemed to be only another contest for him, another killing. Following him, the boy lifted the sword with both hands. Firelight glanced off the metal and reflected in his ruby eyes. When Theramonde dropped his arm the boy brought it down on the rope, slicing through the silence like a whip crack. The rope fell to the ground, throwing open the front of the box with a smash.

'Let the battle commence!' yelled Theramonde lifting the boy's hand in triumph and sending the audience into a frenzy of baying and stamping. Deranged shouts rose into the air, hands clapped and fists pounded.

As she watched, Bree became aware of a presence stirring at the back of the box. She was sure Honey felt it too. A dark and terrible shape was crouching in the shadows. The thing waited.

'What is in there?' whispered Sandy, barely able to look.

It crept out. The roar from the spectators nearly knocked Honey off her feet. The thing made a horrible hissing sound, like a slow wicked whisper. Bree's throat tightened as cheering washed over her like a wave.

'It's a g-giant s-scorpion,' she stammered, her face turning the colour of chalk.

Sandy said, 'It's a duel. And they want Honey to fight it.'

All around, dark shapes squirmed in anticipation of what was to come. Hundreds of them. Bree studied the sea of gawping white faces as they roared their appreciation.

'This is entertainment to them!' she cried disbelievingly. A thousand eyelids flickered eagerly, the crowd's anticipation raw and palpable. No-one in this place expected Honey to walk away from this. They were here for the thrill of the kill, to witness the destruction of an innocent girl. Honey tightened her grip around the stick.

The scorpion scuttled forwards, dwarfing Honey in its impenetrable shadow. She stumbled back, her sapphire eyes darting frantically around the arena. Bree gasped, when for a moment they settled on her. But Honey looked through Bree and glanced away, searching for something.

'She's looking for us,' said Sandy. 'She thinks we've left her.'

'We're right here,' Bree whispered sadly. 'You're not alone.'

The words were meant to be reassuring. Instead, Bree felt she was saying goodbye.

10.

TIPPING THE BALANCE

The scorpion loomed over them, its shell gleaming like armour. Its pincers snapped the air as the coiled, segmented tail arched over its body, the bulbous stinger aimed towards Honey. Panic had drained her face of colour as she shook from head to foot at the edge of the stage. Resolutely, she tightened her grip on the stick, as if to reassure herself that she was not completely powerless.

'How is she seriously supposed to fight that?' said Sandy.

'She's not,' cried Bree, wiping away angry tears. 'That's the whole point.' Bree was vaguely aware of a pulsing sensation at her hip and her blood rushing in her ears, but the spectators' chants and taunts drowned everything else out. Her heart was pounding and her skin prickled with tension.

At the bridge Theramonde grinned and crossed his arms. His mouth curved in a smirk of anticipation.

Honey edged to the side, never taking her eyes off the shiny black scorpion. The crowd roared as it lunged at her, its pincers like open jaws. Quickly, Honey swung the stick like a bat, smashing them away. She ducked, rolled under its belly and jumped to her feet behind it. The crowd gasped as the scorpion fell sideways onto the box smashing it like a house of cards.

Bree jumped and punched the air. 'Atta girl!'

Splinters of wood flew across the stage. Hoots and jeers flowed from the audience. Turning, the scorpion rose on its eight legs and began advancing again from the shadows. Honey had barely time to react when it slammed against her, knocking her backwards and crushing the air from her lungs. She hit the ground with a bone-jarring crash, sending the stick spinning from her hands. It rolled to the edge of the stage, where it see-sawed for a moment, before it tipped over into the darkness. The cries of the audience rose to a deafening crescendo.

'Oh no…' breathed Sandy as Honey struggled onto her elbows.

'Get up!' screamed Bree although she knew Honey could not hear her.

Theramonde's mouth twisted into a wicked grin as he watched Honey stagger to her feet, defenceless and terrified.

'We have to help her. Bree, what can we do?' said Sandy. Bree could not think straight. Paralysed with fear, she watched as the scorpion stood over Honey, its spiked tail curled like a giant whip. The stage seemed to shake with the sounds of raucous shouts and the stamping of feet.

Bree said. 'Didn't the wish say, "You'll still have tools"?'

'Which tools? There's nothing here to give her.'

A thought suddenly struck Bree. She zipped open Honey's bag and dug around for something.

'Hurry up,' cried Sandy. 'It's trying to sting her.'

Honey was on her back, swerving the deadly barb as it stabbed at the floor. Bree's fingers curled around something cold and glassy at the bottom of the bag. She pulled out a bottle of perfume and ran over to Honey. The scorpion drew back its tail aiming to strike again.

Bree aimed the perfume nozzle at the scorpion's head and pressed down until a stream of fruity liquid shot into one of its eyes. With a piercing scream the creature reared up on its hind legs. It staggered before it slammed back down, missing Honey by a fraction of an inch. Bree jumped close and pressed the nozzle again above its other black beady eye, keeping her finger on it until the bottle was empty. For a moment Honey looked puzzled and then, realising her opportunity, jumped to her feet. Theramonde muttered a curse between his teeth as the angry jeers from the crowd grew louder. The scorpion rolled onto its back, eight legs churning in the air. Honey ran for the bridge while she had the chance.

'Come on!' yelled Bree, dropping the empty bottle and grabbing Sandy.

Theramonde blocked Honey's way, arms folded across his chest. Bree felt anger burn like acid in her veins. 'But she won the contest!' she screamed in his face. Theramonde pulled Honey up by the scruff of her t-shirt like a helpless kitten and stared her right in the face.

'There's only one way to leave the arena. Fight to the death,' he hissed, furious spittle sizzling in the corners of his mouth. He tossed Honey back onto the stage like a bone for a dog. A sudden roar from the spectators made her spin round: the scorpion had righted itself and thrashed its lethal tail angrily at Honey. Black fear tugged at Bree's heart.

'She'll never beat it on her own,' muttered Sandy, holding his head in his hands. Honey tried to get away but she slipped on the polished floor. That gave Bree an idea. Peering into the satchel she found the very thing: the tube of sun cream Honey had taken from the rooftop garden.

Sandy watched her point the nozzle at the scorpion's hind legs. 'What are you doing?'

'Tipping the balance in Honey's favour,' replied Bree and she squeezed the tube. A jet of cream spurted out and splattered on the floor between Honey and the scorpion, which immediately started to slip and slide while Honey got back to her feet and circled it warily. The scorpion skidded for a moment before its legs finally slid out from under it.

'Good thinking!' said Sandy.

'It's not over yet,' she replied as the scorpion rose to its feet again.

Honey ran to the edge of the podium and

glanced at the spikes in the pit. For a horrifying moment Bree thought she was going to jump but Honey turned and started yelling at the scorpion. 'Over here! Come and get me!'

Sandy buried his face in his hands. 'What's she doing? Has she lost her mind?'

The scorpion took a few steps forward and scrabbled for traction in the spreading pool of sun lotion.

'You remember how she beat the spider last time,' smiled Bree, 'Miss Pizazz always has a plan.'

Honey stared ahead watching the scorpion. It moved clear of the puddle and, with the crowd chanting and clapping, it stalked towards her, curling and uncurling its tail. Honey stepped back until her heels were over the edge of the stage.

'You have one shot at me spiky,' she smirked. 'Make it count.'

It ran. Bree thumped the tube of sun cream. The scorpion did not have time to stop. It skidded through the greasy puddle, flew past Honey, Bree and Sandy, and off the edge of the podium. The crowd gasped and went quiet. Bree looked over the edge of the stage to see the plummeting scorpion land on the spikes with a terrible crunch. It echoed around the arena in the eerie silence.

Honey dropped to her knees and sobbed with relief.

'You did it, Honey,' smiled Bree.

'We all did it,' said Sandy, patting her on the back.

As Honey wiped the tears away with the back of her hand, she accidentally smeared some sun cream across her cheek. She furrowed her brow and smelled her fingers. Looking up with tear-filled eyes her mouth fell open. 'Are you guys real?' she said, staring at Bree in disbelief.

'Of course we are,' replied Bree.

'B-but how did you get here without me seeing you?'

'You mean you can see us now?' said Sandy stepping forwards.

Honey threw her head back and laughed. 'What? Oh wait. Are you saying you were *invisible?* No way!' she shrieked with envy and awe.

Bree nodded and helped her up. 'We've been here all along. Right beside you.'

'You know, I thought I got a blast of my perfume, Raspberry Rebel…'

'That was me!'

'Oh, I can't believe I missed out on that wish,' pouted Honey as she hugged Bree.

Sandy shook his head, 'Trust me. It's a lot less fun than it sounds. The minute we saw Theramonde we…'

Tanas Theramonde stared at them in astonishment. Bree caught his eye and for a second a flicker of recognition passed between them. A single voice rose from the crowd and echoed off the walls. 'Cheat!' They looked around to see the entire arena rise to its feet.

'I think it's time we got out of here,' gulped Sandy.

Bree remembered the words from the wish: '*Beware! Just after victory, this wish will end and all will see.*' She realised the throb from inside the satchel had stopped. 'Run for the bridge!' she shouted, pulling Honey and Sandy with her.

As they ran, Bree saw guards unchaining the Cleptathorns. They let out vicious snarls that revealed liver coloured gums.

'They'll never let us past,' panted Sandy.

'It's our only hope!' said Bree.

The theatre boomed with shouts from the spectators as they began stampeding to the stage. 'Tear them limb from limb!' they screamed. Some were trying to jump across the gap and falling down onto the spikes. 'Kill the cheat!'

Theramonde strode across and grabbed one of the Cleptathorns.

When they reached the bridge Honey turned to Bree with pleading eyes, 'What do we do now?'

Bree did not know what to say. Dread weighed heavy in her chest. There was no way forward or back.

'You may cross the bridge now,' instructed Theramonde.

'For you to kill us?' said Honey.

'I am a man of my word. I said you could leave if you survived the contest.'

'Don't trust him,' spat Sandy, clenching his fists.

Theramonde threw back his head and laughed. 'You have no choice!' He gestured to the spectators who had managed to pull themselves up onto the podium. Their eyes were wild and they looked hungry for revenge. Honey took a hesitant step onto the bridge. Theramonde grinned. 'That's it, just a few more steps...' The spectators started running towards them, their arms outstretched.

'Come on!' Sandy cried, shoving Bree. 'Before they throw us down to the scorpion for round two!'

As soon as Bree stepped onto the bridge she caught Theramonde's dark look. His eyes were burning. She wanted to turn back.

'Stop where you are, there's something I should have told you,' Theramonde announced as they reached the middle of the bridge. He lifted his sword above his head and brought it down hard on one of its supporting ropes. It sliced in two, tipping the bridge to one side. Bree, Honey and Sandy fell sideways, clinging on to each other as the bridge toppled.

'The contest is not over yet,' said Theramonde, lifting the sword again. 'But you're about to lose.'

As the floor tilted out from under her feet Bree remembered the rope around her waist. She tightened it and managed to hoop the other end around the handrail. 'Give me your hands!' she told Honey and Sandy. They threw themselves at her as Theramonde's sword whistled through the air and chopped the other support. Immediately the end of the bridge snapped away from the ledge and swung down into the chasm. It slammed against the stone wall at the other side, jarring Bree, Honey and Sandy to their marrow. Bree could see it was very dark below and was not sure how far they had to fall.

'At least there are no spikes on this side,' she said to them. 'Try and climb down the bridge like it's a ladder.' Sandy and Honey gripped the spars of wood and started to clamber down. Above them the air was torn with shouts and angry demands. When she looked up Bree saw Theramonde toss his sword across the chasm. It was caught by one of the crowd who grinned at Bree and started sawing through the last supporting ropes.

'Get to the ground, quick!' she called down into the darkness that Honey and Sandy were disappearing into.

'We're almost there,' came back Sandy's voice. 'What's keeping you?'

Her fingers trembled as she tried to pull apart the knot around her waist. It had tightened.

Snap!

Bree heard Honey scream from down below as the bridge collapsed and dangled from a single rope. She clawed at the knot until it came apart and raced to the bottom.

'Don't let them escape! Kill them!' shouted Theramonde as Bree jumped the last few feet to the ground. It was cold and damp and there was a smell of things rotting. She tried not to think about what was causing it.

'Are you ok?' asked Sandy.

'Only if you two are okay.' She nodded and hugged him and Honey tightly. She looked up to see the edge of the stage a long way away. Theramonde screamed a chilling order, the words leaving his lips in cold and measured syllables. 'That book must be mine. Bring it to me—even if her hands are still attached to it!'

A bright blue light caught Bree's eye. Honey had turned on her phone camera's flash, lighting up the darkness to reveal the mouth of a tunnel.

'Come on,' said Bree. 'Let's see where it takes us, while we've still got a chance.'

Suddenly Honey yelped and covered her mouth in disgust. Bree and Sandy crowded round her.

'What is it?' asked Sandy.

'Are these what I think they are?'

She held the light close to the ground and lifted it up around the cave mouth. The entrance was built of yellowish-white bones stacked one on top of the other.

'T-they could be animal bones,' he tried.

'Then what about those?' said Bree.

Beyond the archway piles of open-mouthed skulls grinned in the faint light from candle stubs. The groans of wretched souls seemed to echo around them as they crept under the archway and into the tunnel. It ended at a wooden door. Sandy pushed on it but it didn't move. 'It's locked.'

Bree pulled something from her pocket. 'Just as well I still have this then, isn't it?'

'Don's magic key,' smiled Honey.

Bree pushed the key into the lock and the door sprang open to reveal a small candlelit room with a cobbled floor. At one end was a heavy iron gate but it was too dark to see what lay behind it. As soon as they stepped inside, the door slammed behind them. There was no keyhole on this side of the door.

'Only one way out then,' said Bree, pushing the key back into her pocket and walking over to the gate. She peered through the bars but could only see darkness. An icy blast rippled her T-shirt and made her shiver.

'I just remembered,' she said, lifting the strap of Honey's satchel over her head. 'You might want this back.'

'It feels much lighter,' Honey said, patting it affectionately.

'You get it back minus a bottle of perfume and a tube of sun cream,' said Sandy, cocking an eyebrow.

Honey pushed her hand inside. 'That's okay. There's only one thing in here I don't want to lose.' She pulled out the photograph of Mimi and held the picture up for them to see. There was nothing left of Mimi below the neck. 'She's getting further away,' she said sadly.

'Look at it this way, we're under the same roof as Mimi,' said Bree. 'She's here somewhere and we'll find her. We just have to get out of here first…'

'What do you reckon these are?' said Sandy, indicating two small doors halfway up the wall. Above them were three raised shapes: two jagged halves of a heart and a square, and above each was a button.

'Maybe they've got something to do with this stuff?' said Honey, nodding towards a set of silver scales and a bowl of marbles in the far corner. Sandy walked over to them and knelt down beside the bowl. 'They're all different sizes, and they've got numbers on them.' He picked a marble from the bowl and squinted at it. 'Kelly's Eye, number one,' he said, and placed it down on the floor. He picked up another and held it to the flickering light. 'Key of the door, number eighteen.' Bree could see that it was bigger than the last one. 'Burlington Bertie, number thirty.' He stopped when he realised Bree and Honey were staring at him. 'What? My Gran likes Bingo. She's too deaf to go on her own. I know them all off by heart now…'

'Well, I'm guessing no one's playing it down here,' said Bree. 'What do you think these are for?'

'They must have something to do with the scales,' said Honey. She took a step back and looked up at the hatch.

'Lay the marbles out in the right order, Sandy.'

There were thirty marbles in total, each slightly bigger than the last. Honey scratched her chin as she studied the row of shapes above the doors. 'Gimme that scroll we found on the skeleton,' she said to Bree. Bree pulled it from her pocket and handed it to her. Honey carefully unravelled it. A square and two jagged halves of a heart. 'The cut out shapes on this match the shapes up there,' she said, holding it up to the candlelight.

'So they do,' gasped Bree, taking it from her. She held it up against the wall and unrolled it over the shapes, finding they fitted perfectly through the holes in the paper. The arrow on the parchment pointed to the button above the square.

'Press it,' Honey squealed.

'What if something awful happens?' said Bree.

'And it's likely to happen,' said Sandy. 'Statistically, I mean. Just look at all these bones. People didn't leave their skulls here of their own accord…'

'Oh for goodness sake,' muttered Honey and without another word hit the button.

Bree ducked just in time as the wooden doors sprung open and crashed against the walls, sending the scroll to the ground like an autumn leaf. Bree looked in to see what had been hidden behind the doors. Nothing but curtains of dusty webs. She pulled them aside then wiped her hand down her leg. 'Euch!'

'What's that on the wall at the back?' said Honey, squinting at some loopy writing painted onto the stone. Blowing away the last stubborn skeins of web, she stepped back and read it out to Bree and Sandy:

'On the road to Upper Knox,
I passed a lady with a box,
Inside the box were fourteen cats,
a snake, a bird and seven rats.
I said 'Good Day' and let her pass,
this lady and her laden ass.
I noticed on the creature's back was
strapped a brown and tattered sack,
I peered inside and saw a fox.
How many went to Upper Knox?
Think about your answer clearly,
One wrong choice will cost you dearly.'

'It's a riddle,' said Sandy scratching his head. 'A riddle that will give us a number.'

Bree said, 'And the number should point us to the correct marble.'

'At least there's only thirty to choose from,' shrugged Honey, picking up the scroll. 'Eeeny meanie…'

'No, we have to get it right,' warned Bree.

'Actually, it should be quite easy,' said Sandy, pushing his glasses up his nose. 'It's a straightforward case of addition.'

Honey laughed. 'On you go then, master of all things mathematical.'

Sandy studied the riddle with narrowed eyes. 'Let's see. First of all we count the man who wrote this. Add the woman he meets, plus her fourteen cats, one snake, one bird, seven rats and a fox. Not forgetting the ass she was riding on...' He looked lost in concentration. Bree and Honey exchanged looks. After careful deliberation he arrived at an answer. 'Gateway to Heaven.'

'Enough of the bingo lingo,' said Honey. 'Give it to us in English.'

He ran his finger along the row of marbles until he stopped at the third from last. 'All together it comes to twenty seven.' He held up one of the largest balls and smiled proudly.

'Are you quite sure?' asked Honey.

'Absolutely positive,' replied Sandy as he held the marble over the scales.

Suddenly Bree spun around in a panic. 'Wait!'

Sandy jumped and dropped the marble, which rolled across the ground. 'Now look what you made me do.'

'It's not twenty seven,' said Bree, kneeling down beside him. She pointed up at the riddle. 'Everything there might add up to twenty seven but that's not what it asks. Only *one* of them was going to Upper Knox.'

Honey looked doubtful. 'And how did you arrive at that?'

Bree reached over for the first and smallest marble. 'Look at what it says. On the road to Upper Knox I passed a lady with a box.'

'So the answer is two? The guy who wrote this and the woman.'

'No, because it doesn't say they were going in the same direction,' explained Bree, picking up the marble marked with a one.

'Ah! Smart.'

'You might be right,' Sandy admitted.

'Don't worry, Sandy,' Bree smiled, holding the number one marble up to the light. 'Some things are different when you look past the obvious.'

'Yes,' he said thoughtfully, 'I know exactly what you mean…'

Bree dropped the marble into the scale with a clink. They fell silent as they waited to see what would happen next.

'Nothing,' said Sandy, his eyes darting around the room. Just then the scale tipped until the bottom touched the floor. The doors in the wall instantly slammed shut and the portcullis rolled up with a sudden rusty squeal.

'Yes!' Honey shrieked, clapping her hands together. 'You were right!'

Bree bolted under it into the other chamber. A slap of cold air made her suck in her breath. She rubbed away a spattering of goose bumps that had sprung up on her arms.

'What can you see?' asked Sandy.

'Darkness,' replied Bree, 'and it feels like a freezer.'

When she stepped forward a square tile lit up under her foot, washing the room in a digital blue light. It illuminated Bree's face and formed thick shadows all around her. She could see a few more tiles in front of her but not where the chamber ended. The cold coiled around her ankles like skeletal hands. She took another step. This time the tile under her foot lit up red. The portcullis slammed down behind her with a crash. Honey ran over and tried to lift it but it was stuck firm. 'Let us out!' she shrieked.

A great rumble and a crash was followed by a tremor that almost knocked Bree off her feet. When it stopped she turned around to see Honey and Sandy clinging to the other side of the portcullis, covered in dust and rubble. Sandy had turned a nasty shade of green.

'What did I do?' croaked Bree.

Sandy glanced over his shoulder. 'Whatever it was don't take another step.'

'Seriously,' said Honey, her tone making Bree's blood turn cold. 'Do not move an inch.'

'W-why?'

'Because you made half of the floor collapse through here,' said Sandy.

11.

A Rock and a Riddle

Bree fought back her tears and struggled to balance on the two illuminated squares. 'What should I do?' she wailed, terrified to move. She looked down at her feet; one on a blue tile, the other on a red tile.

'The floor must have fallen in when you stood on the wrong one,' replied Sandy.

'Blue is good,' said Honey. 'Red is very bad. Don't step on any more red ones.'

Bree's teeth started to chatter uncontrollably. 'But I don't know what colour they'll light up as until I step on them. How do I know which ones are red and which ones are blue?' As she blinked away tears she noticed that underneath her right foot, the blue tile was changing. 'Something else is happening,' she said over her shoulder to Sandy and Honey.

'It's not turning red is it?' groaned Sandy, tightening his grip on the gate.

'No, it's staying the same colour. But some words are appearing on it.'

She carefully slipped her foot aside and squinted down at the tile. The words were as wobbly and faint as wreaths of smoke, but soon she was able to read them out. 'It says *Blind Mice*.'

'What the heck does that mean?' said Sandy.

Bree looked back as the words shifted under the tile like fish under ice. 'There were three blind mice.' Suddenly an answer sprung to her mind. 'Three...' She took three steps forward. Honey gripped the portcullis and screamed, 'What are you doing?'

'Don't panic, I've got it. I know what I'm supposed to do. ' She stopped on a tile that turned blue. Honey and Sandy whooped with relief and Bree let out a satisfied sigh, her breath billowing out in front of her. 'The tiles are like glass,' she called, 'with clues underneath.'

'What can you see?' shouted Sandy. Bree spread her feet apart as the words came into focus. 'It says *King Cole's Fiddlers*.' She heard him recite the nursery rhyme under his breath.

'He called for his pipe and he called for his bowl. And he...and he...Oh, how does it go?' Sandy snapped his fingers trying to remember the rest.

'And he called for his fiddlers three!' Honey piped up with delight.

'That's it!' laughed Bree. 'The answer is three again.' Counting her steps out loud she moved forward another three tiles. With every step the room got colder. Bree was shivering wildly now but she managed to plant both feet firmly on the tile and keep them there until it turned blue. She could hear Sandy and Honey celebrating but their voices sounded distant. She looked ahead at the floor which now glistened with ice. The tile beneath her feet started to swirl and she could see some new words emerging.

'Is there another clue?' Sandy shouted.

Bree tried to control her chattering teeth. She could barely feel her fingers anymore. 'Yes. It says *Hickety Pickety's Eggs*.'

There was a silence during which Bree could hear only the hammering of her heart. Her mind had gone blank, numbed by the cold. Eventually Honey shouted something. 'Hickety Pickety, my black hen.'

A memory seeped through into Bree's mind. 'She lays eggs for gentlemen!'

'How many eggs?' cried Sandy, his voice one step away from hysteria.

Bree's voice dropped to a whisper that only she could hear. 'Sometimes nine and sometimes ten…'

'Bree, how many eggs were there?' echoed Honey.

'I don't know. The nursery rhyme says sometimes nine and sometimes ten.'

'But h-how do we know which one it is?' stammered Sandy. He wasn't looking at Bree. His gaze seemed to be fixed on the tile beneath her feet. She shook her head, her lips too numb to answer.

'Nine or ten, how are you going to pick?' cried Honey.

Bree said, 'Sometimes you never know…' She would have to risk it. She stepped forwards, her heart pounding and her mouth dry. After nine steps she stopped but made a split second decision to move forward another one.

'It has gone red!' she heard herself gasp.

'NO!' screamed Honey and Sandy, but their cries were drowned out by the crash of stone, as the floor – and their luck – crumbled beneath their feet.

•••

In the cold stillness that followed, Bree could only hear the sound of her own breathing. It seemed magnified by the plumes of white mist that billowed from her mouth. She gulped and looked over her shoulder. Sandy and Honey were clinging to the bars, perched on a narrow strip of what was left of the floor. Behind them dust clouds rose out of a yawning hole. Honey's eyes were wild with panic and Sandy's mouth hung open, but they were alive. Bree drew in a shaky breath. 'Are you all right?' she asked, the first hint of tears breaking her voice.

'Why did you do that?' screamed Honey, her face flushed with outrage.

'I didn't mean to,' sobbed Bree. 'Everyone makes mistakes.'

'Just don't make any more!' hollered Sandy, his eyes enormous in his face.

'I have to keep moving,' Bree said through chattering teeth. 'I can see something up ahead that looks like it has controls.'

By the light of the tiles she could see a pillar with a dome-shaped button on the top. It was perhaps ten tiles away. All she wanted was to get Sandy and Honey into her side of the chamber. She tried to concentrate before the next clue appeared. But nothing came. The whirling mist got colder, and to Bree's surprise, snow started to fall.

'As if it's not cold enough in here already,' she cried, wrapping her arms around her body. Soon pea-sized balls of ice were raining down from the darkness overhead.

'Hailstones?' ranted Honey. 'But we're indoors! What next?'

As soon as the hail speckled the tiles, Bree kicked it aside so it would not hide anything that might appear. As she did, the ice pellets sprouted legs and scuttled towards her. She screamed. 'Next we have ice that turns into spiders!' She stamped on them as hard as she could, crushing them like ice cubes. But there were too many of them and they kept coming. She felt them climb up her legs, so cold they burned her skin. Terror seized her, squeezing so hard that for a moment she couldn't breathe. She started to dance around, shaking her leg.

'Help!' screamed Bree, her voice echoing a hundred times around the chamber.

'Bree, stop moving,' pleaded Honey.

'I can't. They're crawling all over me!'

Sandy cried, 'You're going to set off another red one!'

Bree wanted to fight but she was so cold and scared that she clawed the ice spiders off her face and broke into a run. As she did, every tile she stepped on lit up red. Honey screamed, but in Bree's head it sounded distant. Knowing that at any second that tiny ledge would collapse beneath Honey and Sandy, Bree lunged at the stone column and slammed her hand down on the button.

The chamber was flooded with a blaze of light and the portcullis thundered up. Honey and Sandy dived off the ledge just as it crumbled into the chasm. As they staggered to their feet the gate slammed down again.

Exhausted, Bree collapsed. Immediately, a line of ice spiders raced over to her. They climbed onto her hands and up her forearms. She didn't have the strength to brush them off as more poured over her feet and up her legs. They started to cluster together and froze. Their cold seeped into her bones, chilling her to the core. Soon she was buried up to her neck under a pile of ice. Frost crusted her eyelashes and made her lids heavy. Entombed in whiteness, she felt herself slipping further away until the sound of hurried footsteps and someone shouting her name pulled her back. She prised open her eyes and saw the shifting fog. There it was again, the echo of her name.

'Bree! Bree! Where are you?'

She was too exhausted to move or to answer.

She tried to speak but her throat closed over and all that escaped between her lips was a puff of air. Honey cut through the mist holding a tiny light out in front of her.

'Here she is,' she shouted. She threw herself down beside Bree and clawed the ice spiders off Bree's body. 'Hold on, we're going to dig you out of there.'

'H-help me,' murmured Bree.

Sandy stared down at them, his face as pale as curdled milk.

'Don't just stand there,' cried Honey, throwing fistfuls of ice at his feet, 'help me!'

He got down on his knees and wiped the frost off Bree's face. 'Her lips are blue.'

'Then kiss her! Do anything to get her warm.'

Honey did not notice the tear that ran down his cheek and onto Bree's face. He took her in his arms and laid his cheek against hers. 'Please,' he whispered into Bree's ear. 'Please. You can't leave me on my own.'

Once Honey had shucked the snow from Bree's arms and legs she started rubbing her limbs between her hands to create some heat. 'Get up McCready!' she shouted. Bree didn't move. 'I mean it! Seriously, Adam Eastbough is on the phone for you right now.'

Bree's eyes snapped open and she gasped.

Honey smiled. 'Well, that did the trick. My my.'

Bree was shivering and soaking wet. 'I'm…am I…?' she stammered as the colour returned to her lips. Honey and Sandy huddled close together and soon Bree was able to sit up by herself. 'Where am I?'

'Your guess is as good as mine,' said Honey. She shone the light on her phone around them. Marble walls glistened in the light, stretching up to a ceiling lost in darkness. 'It looks like we're inside an igloo.' Everything about this place was bright and sharp.

'It's certainly cold enough,' groaned Sandy, rubbing his forehead. 'This place is giving me the worst brain freeze ever.' Droplets of ice had started to form in their hair and on their eyelashes.

'Let's get up off the ice,' said Bree. They helped each other to stand, and while Honey and Sandy got their balance Bree steadied herself against a strange column that stood alone in the middle of the floor. 'What do you reckon this is for?' she said. Sandy and Honey clung to each another as they slipped across the floor, the ice groaning with their every step. Sandy craned his neck. 'It must be to support the ceiling. And yet it slants further up, and I can't see the top.'

Bree circled it, tracing its powdery surface. Halfway round, her fingers met something round and sharp that stuck out. She brushed away some ice crystals to reveal four cogs. One of the larger ones was embossed with three shapes at the centre: two half-hearts and a square. 'Hey, come and look at this,' she said.

Honey and Sandy looked at the jagged wheels.

'It looks like the shapes in that spoon thing we found in the skeleton's bag,' said Honey. Bree fumbled in her pocket and held up the rusty device. Their eyes flitted between the cogs and the metal tool.

'Let me see it for a second,' said Sandy. 'It looks like it's a sort of spanner for – '

Before he could finish they heard a crack. They spun round to see a long, silvery splinter spread across the floor like a fracture in glass. Bree placed the device over the cogs and tried to turn it. The cogs were stiff.

'Hurry up,' hissed Honey, as another crack edged towards their feet.

'I'm doing my best!' Bree pushed her weight against it and after the first few turns the cogs loosened and spun freely.

'Look. Something is happening to the pillar,' gasped Sandy. As the cogs turned, metal rods spaced a few inches apart gradually emerged all over the pillar. Sandy reached out and gripped one as the floor shook beneath them.

'That's as far as it'll turn,' said Bree.

'The rungs look wide enough to stand on,' he said.

Honey saw the enormous crack was sending smaller fractures spider-webbing in every direction. 'We can use these like a ladder. Let's climb up.'

'You guys go first,' said Sandy, helping Bree and Honey up. Once they had started to climb he planted his foot on the first rung. A deafening crash shattered the floor into a thousand pieces. From halfway up Bree saw it fragment and tumble away into nothingness.

'Hold on everybody,' she called, 'We're nearly there.'

Once they had climbed the straight section of the column they found it sloped up at an angle. Bree heaved herself out of the opening onto the flat top and kneeled to offer a hand to Honey, then Sandy.

'It's not holding up anything,' said Honey once she stood up. 'It just feels like we're standing at the top of a very tall building.'

'Yes, and it's too dark to see where we go from here,' said Bree.

'Unless we follow the directions…' said Sandy.

'What do you mean?'

'Look what's under our feet.'

An arrow had been scratched into the stone. It pointed to the rim of a wide hole. Bree looked over the edge to see there was a hollow tube inside the column. 'It almost looks like some kind of chute,' she said. She stared into the blackness and wondered what might be at the bottom. Before Sandy could tell her not to, Bree lowered herself into the pipe and let go. Her stomach shot up to her mouth as she dropped into complete darkness. The rushing air plucked the breath from her mouth and she fell for what seemed like an eternity before the pipe levelled out and she bulleted along on her back. Just as she was getting used to the sensation she was spat out the end, and to her surprise landed, standing up. She was in a small wood-panelled room. She was relieved at how warm it was but she didn't have a chance to think anything else before Honey came shooting out of the pipe like a slippery fish, closely followed by Sandy.

'That was wicked,' laughed Honey. Sandy did not look so sure. He steadied himself and straightened his glasses before taking in their new surroundings. The room was silent except for the cackle and hiss of flames in an enormous stone fireplace that took up an entire wall. Bree wandered over to it, the heat bringing prickles to her cold numbed hands and feet. She had wondered if she would ever feel warm again but now she could feel her body thawing from the inside out.

Honey tossed her satchel down beside her and sat on it. She rubbed her hands together and held them up to the fire. 'That's more like it,' she grinned.

'What a strange place,' Bree mused as she watched Sandy running his hand over the wooden panels. The room was empty apart from a small statue, partly concealed in the shadows in the corner. Bree walked over for a closer look. Its stone fingers gripped a stack of irregularly shaped slate tiles. The one at the top had the word 'Grand' carved into it. She prized them out and turned them over. 'They've got hooks on the back,' she observed and knelt down to spread them over the floor. There were eight in total, each etched with a single word: Grand, Small, Orange, Green, Star, Ten, Red, Three.

'Very odd,' said Sandy with a puzzled frown.

'Could it be another riddle?' said Honey.

'I didn't mean those,' he said. 'I was talking about that huge shadow on the floor.'

They looked up to see a massive rock hanging above them. It was roped to a hook in the rafters with the other end of the rope anchored to the floor by a rusty bolt. Bree swallowed nervously. 'That doesn't look very promising.'

'If that falls we're meat paste,' Sandy gulped.

'Then the sooner we get out of here the better,' said Honey, shifting around on her satchel.

Sandy pushed his glasses up his nose. 'There's no door. I already looked. However, there is this…' He put his ear against the wall and tapped a panel with his knuckles. 'This one sounds different to the others. Hollow. I think it's fake.'

They nodded in agreement as he knocked again to demonstrate. 'And it's covered in nails.'

'Aha!' said Bree. 'How many?'

'Eight.'

Sure enough, in a straight, vertical line were eight rusty nails driven into the wood.

'So, eight nails for eight slates. We have to hang those up,' smiled Sandy, as if it were the simplest idea in the world.

'You're right,' sighed Bree, 'but I don't think

we're here to decorate the place. There must be a specific order.'

Sandy considered this for a moment. The smile slipped off his face as he stared down dejectedly at the slates.

Oh, help us out,' begged Bree, looking up at the statue. 'Please?'

Unseeing eyes stared blindly ahead. In the flickering light from the fire its face seemed to twitch. Suddenly Honey jumped to her feet as if something had bitten her.

'It's vibrating! In my bag!' she shrieked, pointing at her satchel as if it were an unexploded bomb.

'The book?' gasped Bree, running over. 'I forgot I put it in there earlier.' She pulled it out and stared at the throbbing locket. 'Yep. Here we go. Wish five,' she said, turning the brittle paper until she arrived at the fourth page. She flattened it with her hand and waited for the page to turn transparent. Once the swirling mist had cleared, more words than usual came into focus:

ANOTHER GAME YOU MUST PARTAKE,
BE CAREFUL OF A SMALL MISTAKE.
A MINOR ERROR SEES YOU DOOMED,
FOREVER IN THIS ROOM ENTOMBED.
THIS HELPFUL RIDDLE HOLDS THE KEY,
THE PROPER ORDER SETS YOU FREE.

CHOOSE THE DISMAL LOT WHO ARE DEAD FIRST.
ARE THEY HONEST ENTITIES,

MEAGRE ENTITIES, OR ANGELS
WITH REEDY VOICES AND LONG, RANDOM HAIR.

Bree read it out three times, slower and slower in the hope it would make sense.

Sandy scratched his head and narrowed his eyes.

'Could be something to do with the Shrillflitters,' suggested Honey, putting the satchel strap over her head. 'Remember how the old woman in the alley called them dangerous angels.'

Sandy looked uneasy. 'They'd better not be coming back,' he blurted.

Honey knelt down beside the tiles and ran her fingers over them. 'How about arranging them into colours first? So, red, orange, green...'

'Then the numbers in order?' said Bree. 'Followed by small then grand?'

Sandy looked unconvinced. 'Too obvious,' he said, taking a step back to study the slates. 'And we can't make a mistake.'

Bree looked up at the rock as it swung on the creaking rope. Sandy was right. She knelt beside Honey, laying the open book next to them so they could refer to the wish. It was supposed to be helping but Bree had never felt more confused. She stared at the tiles hoping that somehow the answer would spring out at her but after a few minutes the words started to swim in front of her eyes.

'My brain hurts.'

Honey was undeterred. 'Meagre means small, and small and grand are opposites aren't they?'

'But how does that relate to 'Green', 'Star' and 'Three'?' said Sandy.

They did this for a while but nothing made sense. Then Sandy noticed something. 'Look at the words 'dismal' and 'lot'.' he said, tilting his head and screwing up his eyes to read the fading riddle.

'I'm looking, but I'm not getting,' shrugged Honey. Sandy pointed to the words which were faint but still legible. 'Pushed together they spell out the word 'small'.'

'Oh yes,' gasped Bree. 'The last four letters of 'dismal' and the first letter of 'lot.'

'I see it now,' smiled Honey her arms folded across her chest. 'Well whad'ya know.'

'So, the others might be hidden in here too if we squash words together.'

Once the code had been broken the rest of the riddle was easy to solve. ''Are' and 'dead' together make 'red'!' Honey clapped excitedly. 'And 'first' and 'are' spell out 'star'!' added Bree, shuffling the slates around so they were laid out across the floor in order. The glow from the locket was starting to dim and the words on the page had all but faded. The paper glass had changed back to plain, brittle parchment but it didn't matter. Now all they had to do was hang the tiles up on the nails.

'Are we ready?' asked Sandy, picking up the tile marked 'small'.

'Yes' replied Bree confidently. She closed the book and put it into her pocket.

'It's now or never,' smiled Honey. One by one, Bree handed Sandy the tiles and he hung them in order.

small
red
star
ten
green
orange
three

And the last tile to go up was the one that had been at the front of the pile. Sandy carefully hung the word 'grand' onto the bottom nail and took a step back. The statue's jaw lowered with a heavy grinding noise. Bree peered inside its mouth.

'Can you see anything?' asked Honey.

'There's a lever down there,' she said, reaching into its throat until the statue had swallowed her all the way up to her elbow. She flicked the lever and the hollow wood panel slid aside to reveal a torch lit corridor.

'We did it again,' whooped Honey. Bree smiled and pulled her arm out. She was about to remove her hand when the mouth snapped shut, clamping around her wrist. 'Ouch!' she yelped as she tried to yank her hand free.

'Pull it out,' said Sandy, trying to prise the

mouth open.

'I can't, I'm stuck!' yelped Bree.

Just then a small hatch sprung open under the rope tied to the floor. A candle popped up like a Jack-in-a-box. The rope started to smoulder and a few of the strands snapped and frayed.

'Blow it out!' she screamed as she tugged on her wrist with all her might. Sandy threw himself down on the floor and blew hard. The flame vanished, then sprung back and continued to burn. Honey threw her arms around Bree's waist and tried to pull her out but it was no use. Above their head, the rope creaked. Honey screamed and threw her free arm up to protect herself when the rock dropped a little.

Sandy ran over to Bree and Honey. 'The rope keeps burning. There's no way to blow it out and there's only seconds before it snaps.'

'Get out of here quickly, leave me,' cried Bree, her body melting with despair.

'We can't leave you,' sobbed Honey.

'You have to. If you don't, there will be no one left to rescue Mimi. All four of us will be dead.'

Honey looked shocked with the realisation. The rock dropped again as the flames burned through the rope's last remaining cords. Sandy kicked the statue with frustration. 'We're not leaving without you.'

'Then you will never leave.'

12.

REFLECTIONS

'We-are-not-leaving-without-you,' Honey resolved through gritted teeth. She tightened her grip around Bree's waist and tugged as hard as she could.

The strands of the rope smouldered and snapped.

'It's almost burned through,' cried Sandy.

Bree yelled. 'Get out of here!'

Sandy's eyes darted to the corridor and back to Bree. Honey turned her satchel upside down and emptied the contents over the floor. As soon as her strawberry lip-gloss rolled out she grabbed it. 'This is what I was looking for,' she said.

'Have you gone mad?' shrieked Sandy.

'It's like grease,' she answered, yanking the lid off with her teeth.

'And?'

'And that's exactly what we need to pull Bree out.'

Bree was too terrified to speak as Honey squeezed the sticky pink gloss all over her wrist. 'Now PULL!' she screamed, looking at the one remaining strand of rope smouldering above the flames. Bree pulled as hard as she could. Her hand popped out of the statue's mouth like a cork from a bottle. Breathlessly Honey swept everything back into her satchel. Sandy grabbed her and Bree and pushed her out into the corridor just before the huge rock crashed to the floor. A wave of dust and debris blew over them and they collapsed on the other side of the door.

'Talk about a close shave,' said Honey, applying the lip-gloss round her mouth. Bree stood up and looked back inside. The rock filled the entire room, with the bottom embedded in the floor. The statue's head stuck out from underneath with the same empty expression as before, only now its mouth hung open as though in a scream.

'That could have been me,' she muttered, wiping away tears with the back of her hand.

'We would never have let that happen,' said Sandy.

Honey handed her a tissue so she could wipe away the gloss from her wrist. Damp air whispered down the corridor and sent shivers up their spines.

'The draft is coming from that way,' said Sandy, pointing towards a door cut into the wall at the end of the corridor.

'Please let it be the way out!' said Honey. Just then the walls shook around them. They exchanged troubled glances. With a flush of icy horror Bree saw a thick stone partition lowering between them and the door. 'Quick!' she yelped, sprinting ahead. 'Or we'll be trapped!'

They bolted up the corridor, but the wall was coming down so quickly Bree knew there would only be the smallest gap at the bottom to get through.

'Dive, dive, dive!' squealed Honey, skidding onto her back and rolling under it. Bree and Sandy did the same and stopped on the other side of the wall just as it ground into the floor. The only sound to be heard was their relieved breaths. Bree lay on the cold stone floor and stared up at the cobwebbed ceiling.

'We are in serious need of a break,' said Sandy, sitting up. Honey stood up and brushed herself down. 'Talk about a roller-coaster ride,' she sighed, staring at the giant slab of stone behind them.

'Let's open this door before anything else happens,' Bree said. She pulled Don Daines's magic key from her pocket and got up. Sandy stared at the door knob as Bree curled her fingers around it.

'As long as there are no snakes, hanging rocks, furry creatures, big insects, skeletons or killer plants I'm ready,' he said.

'Oh, but where would be the fun in that?' Honey grinned. The door sprung open into another wood-panelled room. At first it looked like the last one, only twice as large, until they realised that one wall was a floor to ceiling mirror. It reflected the burning torches on the opposite wall, and a wooden door next to an hourglass on a high shelf.

Honey gasped. Terrified, Bree looked up at the ceiling for any falling rocks and Sandy at the floor for any cracks.

'My hair is a total mess,' Honey chuckled at her

reflection. 'Just look at it.'

Bree sighed. 'As if. Your hair is never a mess.' She combed her fingers through her own unruly tangle. Sandy closed the door behind them and something dropped to the floor with a clink.

'It's a key,' said Bree, bending to pick it up. It was heavy and rusty with a heart shaped hole at one end. At the other end some blunt curves and lines made up the teeth.

'Maybe it's the key to that other door,' said Sandy, nodding towards the far end of the room.

'Have you ever known things to be that simple?' Honey smiled at him in the mirror.

'Let me see it.'

Bree gave him the key. He turned it over in his hand and ran his finger over the teeth at the end. He pushed it into the keyhole and found that it turned. A lock clicked into place. 'Well, it locks this door,' he said, holding it out in the palm of his hand. 'And apart from the doors there's nothing else here that the key would fit.'

Honey stopped tidying her hair and stared at him. 'Sandy, do that again.'

'What? This?' The key glinted in his hand.

'Bring it closer to the mirror.'

He came up beside her and pressed the key against the glass.

'Look at the teeth,' Honey said with awe.

Reflected in the mirror, the metal teeth looked like two words.

'It says CHECK BOOK,' said Sandy.

'Chequebook?' asked Bree.

Honey's eyebrows lifted as she pressed her glossy lips together. 'No. *Check* book. As in check it out.'

Bree pulled the book out of her pocket and stared at the little screen in the centre of the front cover.

'Something is happening,' she said.

'Is it another wish?' asked Honey.

'I don't think so. The locket isn't glowing.'

Some words emerged but Bree could not read them.

'What kind of language is that?' snorted Honey, tilting her head.

'Gobbledegook,' sighed Sandy. 'There's something wrong with it.'

'Maybe not,' said Bree, holding the book up to the mirror.

In the reflection the words jumped out at them.

SOMEWHERE FAR AWAY IN ANOTHER TIME AND PLACE,
THROUGH THE LOOKING GLASS IS WHERE YOU'LL
FIND A FRIENDLY FACE.
A CHANCE FOR ONLY ONE OF YOU TO
SPEND SOME TIME AWAY,
TO PROVE THAT FRIENDSHIP MATTERS AND
YOU NEVER WOULD BETRAY.
THE OTHER TWO WILL WATCH THE SCENE
BUT WILL NOT HEAR A SOUND,
MAKE SURE YOU'RE BACK TOGETHER
WHEN THE HOURGLASS TURNS AROUND.

Once the words had disappeared from the screen Bree put the book back in her pocket. Honey looked puzzled. 'What do you think it means?'

'Well, last Christmas when we were here I went through a mirror,' said Bree. 'Maybe I have to do it again?'

Honey nodded. As they looked at themselves, their reflections began to fade. In their place a wobbly, indistinct picture started to form. It eventually filled the entire mirror and at first they could not make out what they were looking at, but slowly the image came into focus.

'It's three people,' said Bree, 'sitting around a dining table.'

They watched as the blurry edges became crisp. It felt a bit like being at the cinema, watching a movie without sound.

Sandy gasped. 'Look who it is…'

'I don't believe it,' Honey smirked. 'Ruthless Renshaw!'

Bree groaned. Alice was not who she wanted to see at this precise moment. It felt like looking through one of the two-way mirrors on TV, where the detectives could see the criminal but the criminal couldn't see the detectives. Everything in the room was full size and felt close enough to touch, as though they were actually standing in the Renshaw's dining room. Bree knew they could not see her but nevertheless she felt uncomfortable.

'Well, it's good to finally get a look round the palace of Miss Prissy Pants,' Honey grinned.

'And it'll be the last time,' muttered Sandy.

Alice looked as grim as a maths lesson on a rainy afternoon. She sat rigidly at a chair in the middle of the table, between a man and woman sitting at either end. Alice was fiddling with a lettuce leaf at the end of her fork.

'I'm guessing that's her dad,' said Honey, pointing to the plump bald man in the dark suit and horn-rimmed glasses, 'and her mum.' She nodded towards a disappointed-looking woman with fuchsia lips and a sharp blonde bob.

'Yup,' sighed Bree forlornly. 'That's Alice's parents.'

'You've met them?' said Honey.

'Not really. I saw them once before...'

Mr Renshaw studied a newspaper as he stabbed a slice of quiche. He kept looking at his watch impatiently.

'I wish this thing had sound! I *need* to know what Alice talks about at home,' Honey laughed.

Mr Renshaw's rubbery lips moved but his fishy eyes did not leave the newspaper. Mrs Renshaw raised her eyes and laid down her cutlery. Her lips narrowed to a tight slit as she slid the salt cellar over to her husband. Alice said something to her mother, causing her to glare back as though she had caught the smell of something nasty. Alice dropped her eyes and began to twist her hair between her fingers. Bree searched Mrs Renshaw's face for a sign of affection or interest but there was none and he continued to read his newspaper in silence.

'Alice looks different from how she is at school,' said Sandy. 'Kind of quiet and lonely.'

'Get real. She gets everything a girl could ever want,' scoffed Honey. 'How could she be lonely?'

Bree said, 'Sometimes you can be lonely in a room full of people.' As she spoke the image faded and was replaced by another. Sunlight was streaming through open windows onto a group of adults talking animatedly to each other.

'That's my living room!' Bree said. 'And there's my mum…'

'And my Gran,' said Sandy.

'And there's my parents too,' added Honey. 'Everyone is round at yours.'

Mrs Pizazz was staring gloomily into a mug of tea.

'Mum!' sighed Honey, her hands pressed against the glass. Her father was pacing up and down speaking into a phone. Although they couldn't hear what he was saying they could tell from his expression that he was feeling desperate. Annie Hooten was lying back on a chair in a shaft of sunlight, stroking Bustopher, Bree's beloved cat, on her lap. Bree's mother was moving between them all, passing out cups of tea and slices of cake on saucers. Bree felt a pang of sadness as she watched her trying to hold everything together. 'Typical Mum. Always thinks a cup of tea will solve everything.'

'I've never seen my folks like this,' said Honey,

choking back tears. 'They look so lost.'

The image disappeared and they were left staring at their own reflections.

'Come back!' cried Honey.

'Listen, we're going to find Mimi,' Bree told her firmly, 'and everything is going to be fine.'

As she spoke the mirror started to vibrate. Honey jumped back. 'What was that?'

'It's time for one of us to go through,' said Bree, noticing a small fracture appear in the mirror. It grew until it was a black seam running down the centre of the glass, splitting it into two halves. They moved slowly and silently apart until there was a space between big enough to walk through. Honey turned to Bree, her teary eyes shimmering in the torchlight. 'What are you waiting for?' she asked.

'I think you should go this time,' Bree replied.

'Why me?' asked Honey, staring uncertainly at the dark gap in the glass.

'Your mum and dad could do with a cuddle. Go to them.'

'What about Sandy?' she asked.

'No!' he spluttered. 'I would only say the wrong thing and end up getting us into trouble.'

'All right then,' said Honey, wiping her eyes. 'I'll do it.'

The hourglass turned on the high shelf, and the first grains of sand started to trickle through.

'Don't stay too long,' said Bree as Honey stepped into the mirror. 'You don't have much time.'

'But bring back some food!' shouted Sandy.

Bree looked at him reproachfully. When she turned back the gap in the mirror was gone – and so was Honey. The surface of the mirror rippled as another blurry scene started to appear.

'Wait a minute. That's not my house any more,' said Bree with a note of concern in her voice.

Sandy looked at her. 'Where's Honey gone to then?'

'Something is taking shape. It looks familiar…'

The picture sharpened to show an old war memorial clock, under a bright blue sky.

'It's Rockwell!' said Sandy.

'I don't believe it. It's only 12 o'clock back home,' said Bree. 'But it feels like we've been gone for days.'

'Any sign of Honey?' asked Sandy, watching the steady trickle of sand inside the hourglass.

'Not yet. But I can see someone.'

On the bench beneath the clock was a figure with a mop of dark hair. As the picture came into focus Bree saw it was a handsome boy in a white T-shirt and baggy khakis. He had a book balanced on his knee. Her heart fluttered wildly in her chest.

'It's Adam…' she breathed, trying to control her voice.

'Where? Let me see,' gasped Sandy, pushing her out of the way.

'Careful.'

'Sorry. I just wanted to make sure Alice wasn't there with him.'

'Well, she's not. He's by himself.'

Adam looked up from his book and waved at someone out of sight.

'I bet that's her now,' said Sandy with a glower. 'She always has to butt in.'

But it wasn't Alice who stepped forward. It was Honey. Adam laid his book on the bench and stood up. He flashed a dazzling smile and ran his fingers through his floppy fringe in a way that made Bree's skin tingle.

Sandy grinned. 'He's going over to speak to her!'

Bree felt strange watching her on the other side of the mirror; it was like seeing one of your best friends on television. Her mouth was so dry she couldn't speak. She could tell by the sparkle in Adam's eyes that he was glad to see Honey. That made her stomach lurch. Anyone who spent time with Honey fell in love with her and her mischievous energy. Bree felt a flicker of envy in the pit of her stomach.

'What is she telling him?' fretted Sandy, his fists clenched in frustration.

'He's holding out his crisps,' said Bree, analysing every movement, 'and she's giving him something in return. Looks like a bit of paper,' Bree took a quick glance at the hourglass. The top half was nearly empty. She turned back to the mirror to see Honey pressing buttons on her mobile. Her face lit up just before she disappeared out of view.

'She'd better hurry,' said Sandy, chewing his lip.

Bree watched Adam going back to the bench to sit down. He was smiling at whatever Honey had put in his hand. Her stomach felt strangely light and fluttery, like she was on a swing. Adam took a swig of water from a plastic bottle and returned to his book.

'Sorry, Sandy. What did you say?'

Sandy put his hand on her shoulder. 'You like him, don't you?'

Bree felt her whole body stiffen. 'Pfft. I don't even know him that well,' she tried.

'You don't have to. If you like someone you want to be close to them, don't you?'

'I'm not going to get close to him.'

'But you'd like to,' he said softly.

Bree could hear the sadness and defeat in his voice and it scared her. She turned to look at him. He was staring at Adam with an expression that she could not read.

'You don't have to worry. Whatever happens, you'll always be my favourite guy. You know that, don't you?' said Bree, searching his face. Sandy looked surprised. He held her gaze for a moment then lowered his eyes and looked away. 'I guess so,' he said quietly. For a brief moment neither of them knew what to say. Bree searched his face again but he was giving nothing away.

The mirror had started to quiver. The image of Adam and the blue sky over Rockwell faded and a crack tore down the middle. Honey stepped through just as the last few grains of sand filtered into the bottom of the hourglass. The two halves of the mirror moved back together and the crack vanished. In an instant, the mirror turned to plain glass, becoming a window through which they could see another corridor.

'Perfect timing!' smiled Bree. Honey hugged her. She smelled of fresh air and cheese and onion crisps. When she pulled away Bree could see that her face was glowing and she felt another unwanted twinge of jealousy.

'What are you so happy about?' she asked with a forced smile.

'I phoned my mum while I had a signal,' smiled Honey, looking at her mobile. 'I told her we were busy but we'd be back soon.'

'Did she ask where we were?' Sandy gasped.

Honey shook her head. 'She just said everyone was round at Bree's having lunch and waiting for news about Mimi. I so wanted to say we'd seen them and we know where Mimi is. But they'd think I needed a lie-down if I told them the truth.'

'You did well not to say anything,' said Bree.

'Were you not tempted to stay in Rockwell?' asked Sandy.

'What? And split up the three musketeers? No chance.'

'One for all!' Bree giggled.

Sandy looked down at his trainers. 'We saw

you with that guy…Thingmebob.'

'You mean Adam, don't you?' smiled Honey, with a knowing glint in her eye.

'What were you talking about?'

'Nothing much. He was just hanging around waiting for Alice to finish her lunch.'

'See I told you. Alice has her claws into him already!'

'Calm down,' said Honey, putting her phone away. 'I get the feeling he's not interested in her.'

'Why, what did he say?' asked Bree, her heart hammering wildly.

'Well,' smiled Honey, enjoying keeping them both in suspense, 'he asked where you were. Of course, I couldn't tell him. So, he's intrigued.'

A shot of something warm and wonderful spread through Bree's veins and she shyly covered her mouth to hide her smile. Sandy's shoulders slumped.

'And Sandy, he said he thought you were cool,' continued Honey.

'Me? Really?'

'What did you give him?' Bree asked.

Honey tapped the side of her nose. 'That's for me to know and you to find out.' She turned round to check her hair in the mirror. 'Hey, it's gone.'

Sandy pressed his nose up against the glass and peered into the corridor behind. The wall torches flickered as a shadow appeared. He jumped back. 'There's someone out there,' he whispered.

Cold terror struck Bree when she saw a figure striding down the corridor, tall and fluid, his cloak flying out behind him like a shadow.

'It's Tanas Theramonde,' she gasped.

'He can't see us through this—can he?' said Honey.

'I don't think so, but he's coming this way.' She ran to the door at the far end of the room. 'Give me the key.'

Sandy threw it to her with fumbling fingers. 'Quickly!' he hissed. 'The doorknob is turning!'

'Thank goodness you locked it,' whispered Bree, turning the key in the other door. It creaked open into a tunnel, letting in a gust of cold air. Honey grabbed a torch off the wall and hurried after Bree and Sandy. Bree closed the door behind her and locked it, leaving the key in the hole.

The torch cast an uncertain light on the greasy floor and threw their shadows up onto the walls. They faced the tunnel's dark beginnings, corrupt with damp air.

'Follow me,' whispered Honey, thrusting the torch out in front of her.

Their feet made muffled splashes in pools of slime and a bitter draft elbowed its way down the tunnel. With it came a strange, unidentifiable sound, a steady drone that was getting louder with every step. Bree could feel the hairs on her neck start to rise. She jerked her head, feeling they were being watched. But the shadows swallowed up everything behind them. Turning a corner they heard a distant rumble. Bree turned to Sandy. 'I hope that was your stomach.' He shook his head and jabbed a finger at an opening a few feet ahead. They tiptoed through the slime until they arrived at an archway. Inside was a small cave, saved from total darkness by two guttering torches. A door the shape of a tombstone was flanked by two stone heads on pillars in the far wall. Beside it, in the shadows, was an enormous dark shape.

Bree's breath caught in her throat. She pulled back, her eyes darting between Honey and Sandy.

'What's wrong?' hissed Sandy, his terrified eyes mirroring Bree's.

'That's a Magnentity, I'm sure of it,' she breathed. 'It was mentioned in Don's letter. It said *the Magnentity guards the final door.*'

Sandy put his hand over his mouth to catch his gasp. He glanced around the corner and gulped. 'It's even bigger than I imagined.'

'Don't make any sudden moves,' urged Bree, her breath quickening.

'We must be close to the Flame then,' he said.

'And Mimi,' added Honey. She laid her torch on the ground where it sputtered in the slime. Bree stole another glance at the creature. It had its back to them. It sounded as though it was eating something.

'Let's try and get past it while it's distracted,' she said. They edged under the arch, hardly daring to breathe. Keeping their backs to the wall, they took careful steps towards the stone door. Bree's stomach roiled when she caught sight of an army of bluebottles guzzling a heap of rotting meat. Sandy retched. The creature froze. Slowly its massive horned head turned.

'Don't move,' Bree whispered out of the corner of her mouth.

The Magnentity was a creature Bree could not have imagined in her wildest nightmares. Flies clouded its head and crawled over its bubbled, leathery hide. Two bulging reptilian eyes rolled above a long purple tongue that licked strings of bloodied meat from the side of its mouth. It snorted and swiped at the flies with hands like pincers, grasping fingers that ended in long gnarled claws.

In an instant its eyes fixed on Bree, Honey and Sandy. It licked its lips and prowled towards them.

13.
ELEPHANT SHOE

The Magnentity roared. Inside its massive mouth were rows of razor-sharp teeth. Without warning, Honey dashed for the door. In one swift spasm the creature pounced at her, its jaws wide. She dived, sending it ploughing into the wall head first. Stunned, it got up and shook its head. One of its horns had snapped and stuck out at an angle. Honey threw herself into the shadows but the Magnentity saw her and snapped its pincers.

'Quick!' yelled Bree. 'Use a Slumber Bud!'

Honey rummaged inside her satchel as the creature's shadow fell across her. A great rumbling erupted from its chest making the torchlight flicker.

'Hurry!' cried Sandy.

'They've fallen out of the tissue,' said Honey, her hands shaking. As she spoke she found it. She held up the little clear ball. Inside, it swirled with blue mist.

'Throw it to the ground. It'll explode!' shrieked Bree, covering her face in anticipation. Honey threw the Slumber Bud at the Magnentity. It snapped the air and caught it between its teeth.

'You missed,' wailed Sandy, throwing his hands up in the air.

'There's a couple of others somewhere,' said

Honey, searching the bottom of her bag. Just then there was a muffled crunch as the Magnentity bit into the Slumber Bud.

'Cover your mouths!' yelled Bree, pulling her T-shirt over her nose.

Blue smoke curled out between the Magnentity's teeth. At first it looked confused but then its eyes rolled back in its head and it staggered.

'I think it's working,' smiled Honey. Bree and Sandy peeled themselves away from the wall and ran over to her. The Magnentity caught sight of them and jumped, gnashing its teeth. Sandy dragged the girls out of the way. 'Look out!' he yelled. The floor shook as it crashed against the wall, bringing dust and grit down from the ceiling. The Magnentity's head flopped to the side. For a moment nobody dared move.

'Is it d-dead?' asked Honey.

Sandy prodded it with his toe but jumped back when it twitched. Bree circled the huge body warily. In the torchlight its sides rose and fell in slow and steady breaths.

'No, it's sleeping,' she whispered.

'Then let's get out of here before it wakes up,' said Honey, going to the other door. On either side of it was a carved stone head on a column. One was of a woman with her hair piled high, and the other was a man with wavy hair and a beard that curled out from his chin like a shoehorn. They looked too beautiful to be in this dank cave.

Sandy felt round the outline of the door. 'There's no way to open it. How are we supposed to get out?'

Bree looked over his shoulder. 'If there's a lock we could use Don's key.'

'No, there's nothing. It's just a solid stone panel,' cried Sandy, his breathing fast and shallow.

The Magnentity started to stir and claw the ground.

'The Slumber Bud is wearing off,' hissed Honey.

'We can't risk waking it, let's get out of here,' said Bree.

Sandy's eyes darted around the room. 'There's no way out, except the way we came in.'

He accidentally elbowed the statue of the man and for a moment thought he had broken off its beard. It flicked under the chin with a grind of shifting stone. Sandy jumped aside while the panel lowered like a drawbridge.

'Well done Sandy, you found a secret lever,' laughed Honey.

But her relief was short-lived. Behind them, the Magnentity rose to its feet and bounded towards them. Dizzy with horror, Bree snatched a wall torch and swung it in front of the beast's face. The Magnentity flinched, reared back and bellowed.

'Go!' Bree urged, shoving Sandy and Honey through the doorway. She tossed the torch at the Magnentity, where it struck it between the eyes in an explosion of crimson sparks. She flipped the statue's beard and jumped in after the others. The stone panel started to lift immediately so she vaulted over, just in time for Sandy and Honey to grab her and pull her to safety. It had almost closed when a scaly head burst through the gap, gnashing its razor sharp teeth and sweeping its staring eyes across them like searchlights. Froth and blood sprayed over their heads and trickled down the wall. They dived for cover, not daring to look up in case the beast had crashed through. The thick stone door started to crush the great snout and with a strangled cry the Magnentity had no choice but to pull its head out.

After what seemed like a long time Honey made a move. 'I think it's safe to get up now,' she said.

The panel had slid back into place, leaving them in silence. Bree straightened her clothes and studied the corridor which curved away into darkness. Sandy looked from one end to the other apprehensively. 'Look, up there,' he gasped, his voice ricocheting off the damp stone.

At the end, a blade of yellow light sliced out from underneath a door. Bree stood up on wobbly legs and stared at it in awe.

'We're here. It's the final door.' she breathed.

• • •

It was a large door, glinting with iron studs. Nothing about it gave an indication of what lay beyond. On the wall were two illegible words made up of broken sticks:

'It makes no sense. Could it be a different language?' wondered Bree.

Sandy narrowed his eyes and studied the letters closely. 'Looks like an anagram. Maybe it's 'A house'?'

'Whose house?' asked Honey as she tried to shove the door open. It was stuck fast. 'Mimi is in there. I just know it,' she said dejectedly.

'I think you're right,' agreed Bree, 'we need to find a way in.'

Sandy took a step away from the door and threw back his shoulders. 'How about brute force?'

'No offence, Sandy,' smiled Bree. 'But I think it will take more than your shoulder to break through this door.'

'You don't have to bother. It doesn't matter any more,' said Honey. They turned to see her eyes were filled with tears. She held up her picture of Mimi. 'We're too late. Mimi is gone. Look.' Her sister had almost completely disappeared from the photo, leaving only the smallest tuft of hair. Honey started to sob and fell into Sandy's arms.

Bree slumped against the wall. She thought sadly about everyone in Rockwell waiting for news about Mimi. How could she tell them when they got home that Mimi was not coming back? *If* they ever got home again. How would Honey cope with losing her little sister? Bree thought about the people she herself had already lost—her father, Agora Burton, Don Daines—and wondered how some people could be in your life forever and never make a jot of difference, when others who changed it forever were gone in a moment. Her Dad had taught her about love and letting go, Agora had shown her how to keep a secret, and Don had helped her find the strength to stand up to Alice Renshaw. He told her the door to her heart could be opened from the inside. 'Remember my name when the door won't open...'

Don's voice swooped into Bree's thoughts like a flock of darting birds. She shot up from the floor, making Honey and Sandy jump.

'What is it?' said Sandy.

Bree stared at the broken sticks, her heart hammering with excitement. 'I think I know how to open the door.' She moved the stick that formed the bar across the middle of the first letter. Now it looked like the letter D. The next letter was rearranged to form an 'O'. Bree's fingers were shaking now in anticipation. She slid the stick at the bottom of the letter 'U' upwards and it stopped at the top to form the letter 'N'. Sandy tilted his head and peered at the new word. 'It says...Don,' he said. Bree smiled as she moved the other sticks up and down until the name sprung out at them.

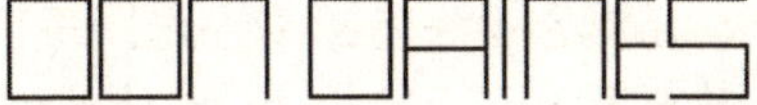

Honey's eyebrows went up sharply. 'Well I never!'

Bree stepped back and folded her arms. 'He left a clue in the letter he wrote me.'

'It's still shut though,' shrugged Sandy.

Bree gave the door a push. With a click it sprung open a fraction of an inch. 'Now let's go and get Mimi.'

•••

They found themselves in a large empty room divided by a long velvet curtain. A black and white tiled floor stretched to an enormous fireplace that yawned like a lipless mouth. Above their heads hung an iron chandelier that looked like a wheel of candles that crisscrossed in shadowy lines. The air was thick with the smell of burning wax.

'No sign of Mimi,' whispered Honey, her voice conspicuous in the silence.

'And no sign of the Flame either,' added Sandy.

'Maybe this is the wrong room,' Honey sighed, her body sagging with disappointment.

Bree shook her head decisively. 'It can't be. That was definitely the final door.' A flash of something bright caught her eye, rippling dread over her skin like icy water. Hanging above the fireplace was a long chain pulled taught by the weight of a silver letter Z.

'We're still not out of danger,' Bree said, tiptoeing towards it. 'So let's be careful…' She was stopped by the sound of a click. She froze. One of the floor tiles had sunk under her foot. 'Uh oh. It might be an alarm or a trap or something!'

'Move!' cried Honey.

'Don't move!' shouted Sandy at the same time.

Bree cautiously lifted her foot and let the tile rise up again. As it did, the velvet curtain drew aside with a mechanical hum. Sandy groaned with relief. 'It's just a remote control for the curtain.'

It slowly pulled back to reveal a glass dome on top of a stone pillar. Underneath the dome was a flame. It pierced the darkness like a fiery planet.

'It's the Flame of Irenus…' breathed Sandy.

In the top of the glass dome was a small slit. 'That must be for the opal dagger,' said Bree. Inside, the Flame of Irenus floated in a shallow pool of oil that kept changing colour: green, blue, gold, red. It was quite hypnotic but something else nearby had caught Bree's attention, something which made her heart feel like a tight knot in her chest.

Mimi's face gleamed ghost-pale in the gloom, her enormous eyes two dark pits framed with smudges of grey. In the candlelight it looked like she was glowing from the inside out.

'Mimi?' Honey gasped, and pressed her hand over her mouth. Her mood ring shone in the candlelight like a black marble. 'Meems, it's me,' she said gently, tears of regret scalding her eyes. 'It's your big sis.'

Mimi's face was contorted with grief, her eyes red and swollen from crying. They were filled with fear and mistrust.

'What have they done to her that would make her wary of her own sister?' cried Honey.

Bree was not prepared for the torrent of emotions that racked her body. And yet her horror was nothing compared to Honey's. Shock was making her shudder as if something had been released within her and was now erupting to the surface. When their eyes met Mimi smiled feebly. Honey bolted for her but an explosion of sparks sent her flying backwards. Bree let out a scream and Sandy helped Honey up from the ground. Honey looked at Bree with desperate eyes. 'I can't get near her!'

'There must be some kind of force field protecting her,' said Sandy.

Bree stood up and reached out to Mimi but her hands met a flat invisible surface. She felt an odd fizzing sensation as though her fingers were magnets being repelled. Mimi pressed her fingers to the force field and the tips turned white before Bree's eyes. Her breath misted in front of her as though she was breathing in a glass booth.

'I just want to hug her,' sobbed Honey.

'Talk to her,' said Sandy softly. 'I'm sure she can hear you.'

With tears rolling down her cheeks Honey looked at her sister. 'I'm sorry I was mean to you. I'll never take you for granted again.'

The sisters had been cut from similar cloth; different, yet the same. Their pasts and futures were twisted together but now it seemed the slender threads connecting them were unravelling. Seeing them divided by the invisible barrier, Bree realised the curtain between hope and despair was very flimsy. It only took a second to tear it down.

Suddenly Honey's expression changed. It became firm, resolute. 'We're not leaving without you.'

The wind howled down the chimney and with it came the sound of footsteps outside the door.

'Somebody's coming,' hissed Sandy but it was too late to react. The door sprang open and a shadow spread out over the floor. Mimi looked terrified. When Bree heard her shallow, ailing breath her heart almost stopped beating.

The figure heaved itself over the thresh-hold and into the murky candlelight. Bree could tell it was a man but his face was formless. As he moved closer he emerged out of the gloom like a ghost, slowly taking shape. He was not much taller than Mimi and very plump. He had dough-like skin and his head was completely bald. A tattoo of a flame was branded on his forehead. Bree knew she had seen that tattoo before. She gulped and tried to conceal the fear that threatened to overwhelm her.

'So you made it past the Magnentity?' the man grinned, revealing liquorice coloured gums. 'I am impressed.' His mouth twitched to a grimace before settling into a cruel, thin line. He had no eyebrows, which exaggerated his large bald head. As he shuffled closer Bree noticed his eyes were two different colours, one iris was black and the other the colour of an egg yolk, with a small black pupil. She remembered staring into those eyes the last time they had escaped from Castle Zarcalat and for a second she was transported back to the final moments with her dad.

'Nobody has ever managed to get this far before,' he continued, jerking Bree back to the present moment. She glanced at the doorway and considered making a dash past him. But what about Mimi? He advanced on Bree, his decay-stained teeth glinting. She took a couple of stumbling steps backwards.

'So, you have seen the Flame of Irenus?' he said, pointing to it. A diamond ring flashed on his meaty index finger.

'We're not here to see that!' blurted Honey.

'We don't care about the Flame,' said Bree. 'We only want the girl.'

'And I,' the man began, 'only want the book.' His mismatched eyes gave Bree the unsettling feeling that two people were watching her. She hardly trusted herself to speak.

Honey stepped forward. 'We'll hand over the book if you let me near her.'

Shocked, Bree stared at Honey disapprovingly. The small, rotund man seemed surprised, then puzzled. Finally he looked suspicious. He rubbed his hands together and licked his lips, making Bree shudder with a chill of revulsion. 'How can I be sure this is not a trick?' he frowned.

'Can't you see I only want to hold my sister?' cried Honey.

'Then you will give up the book?' he queried suspiciously. 'You will give it away?'

Bree nodded sombrely and pulled out the book. The man gasped as his eyes fastened on the half-heart locket. 'I suppose the time has come to let it go,' she said.

The man cursed to himself and shuffled across the floor with snuffling breaths. He stared at Mimi, his buttery eye twitching. 'Aufero Obexis!' he bellowed and pointed the finger with the diamond ring at her. Mimi cowered and shielded her face.

For a moment Honey was frozen with fear, but nothing happened. Bree noticed the man's tattoo burned red. He withdrew his finger with a flourish and took a steadying breath. The tattoo cooled back to black. Mimi slowly unfurled from her frightened ball, her face splashed with coloured light from the Flame. She looked around as if the air had changed suddenly. Her face broke into a smile that showed off the gap in her front teeth.

'What are you waiting for?' the man hissed venomously.

With a cry, Mimi jumped to her feet and ran towards Honey, tears of joy running down her cheeks. She threw herself into her sister's arms and sobbed. Honey held Mimi as if she was the most precious, wonderful being ever to have walked the earth.

'Enough! We had a deal,' spat the man.

'And I'll do exactly what I said I would,' Bree replied calmly.

'Bree! What are you doing?' said Sandy, putting his hand out to stop her.

'Take it,' she said, and handed the book to Mimi. Mimi looked at the book then to Honey with a puzzled frown. The man's face fell.

'I said I'd give it away,' said Bree, her eyes darting to the open door and back to the man, 'and I have. Now, I would love to stay and chat but we really ought to be going…'

Molten anger seemed to bubble up from inside him and ooze from every pore on his face. Without warning Bree grabbed Mimi and pushed her towards the open door. 'Everyone run!' she screamed. Bree, Mimi, Honey and Sandy sprinted for the doorway.

'Solvo Volatilis!' bellowed the man. Before they could reach the door, a whining wind and a thunderous rumble came from the fireplace. A deluge of rubble fell into the grate and a swarm of bats poured from the chimney. There were hundreds of them, a tornado of flapping wings with a deafening high pitched shriek. Mimi covered her ears and screamed as they circled her head. The man laughed as he watched them cower.

'Get off!' shouted Sandy as he fended them off. His glasses were knocked to the ground and as the bats slashed the air above his head he fumbled blindly for them.

'Evolvo Volatilis!' the man barked with a sharp clap. Some of the bats changed direction and flew out through the open door. The others quickly followed in a steady stream, brushing Bree's face with their leathery wings. As soon as they were gone the door slammed shut leaving a deathly silence. The man shuffled across the floor with heavy grunts and Mimi started to cry. 'That will teach you to play tricks with me,' he said.

Honey stood in front of Mimi protectively, as the man loomed over them. 'She's only a kid. Leave her alone,' she spat.

'I'm afraid that is not possible,' the man replied, looking down at the book in Mimi's hands before he turned away. While his back was turned Bree nudged Sandy. 'Are you all right?' He nodded dazedly and put his glasses back on. 'For the moment,' he whispered. 'What's he saying now?'

The man was muttering under his breath and fiddling with his diamond ring. He bowed his head in concentration and started to pace the room. Ten podgy fingers wriggled like fat worms and as his words left his thick lips in dark whispers the tattoo on his forehead once again turned a vicious red. 'Sororo Duplicatas...'

Honey shook her head then started to twitch and moan. Mimi ran to Sandy crying, 'What's happening?'

The man's voice was louder now, his words rhythmic and sinister, a chant that sent an icy chill through to Bree's soul. 'It's some kind of spell,' she said.

The man pointed his fat finger at Honey's head, the diamond glinting in the firelight. 'Planto duos of lemma videor!'

Honey started to convulse wildly. As they watched, something slowly emerged from her body. At first it came out stretchy and wobbly, like a lump of modelling clay, but soon it materialised into the solid figure of a blonde-haired girl.

'It's a-another Honey,' stammered Sandy. Honey stood side by side with her double, who stared back at her sceptically. They walked around each other, looking each other up and down. They were identical in every way, right down to the chipped nail polish on the middle fingernail, and the frayed strap on her satchel. Mimi backed away from them with an open mouth and disbelieving eyes. The Honeys stared at one other then together turned to Mimi. 'Give me the book,' they said.

Mimi was confused and frightened. She looked from one Honey to the other.

'I'm the real Honey,' said one of them. 'I'll take it.'

'No! Whatever you do, do not give it to her,' shrieked the other.

'Don't listen to her, Mimi, I'm your sister. That's just a copy.'

'Mimi, she's trying to trick you.'

Mimi clutched the book to her chest. 'I don't know who to believe…'

'That one is not real,' said one Honey. 'Now, come here, Mimi.'

'Help me,' pleaded Mimi, her large eyes spilling over with tears. Bree's eyes darted between the two Honeys. She thought she knew which was which but now she was not sure.

'I can't tell them apart,' she whispered to Sandy.

'Me neither,' he admitted.

One Honey held out her hand. 'Mimi, you must do as I say. We're all in trouble if you don't.'

Mimi's eyes flitted between the two Honeys, terrified and uncertain.

'Ignore her,' insisted the other Honey. 'She doesn't care about you, Mimi. I love you.'

Mimi bit down on her lip and held the book out to her.

'Stop,' yelled Bree. 'That's not Honey. Honey doesn't say I love you. She says…'

'Elephant shoe,' the other Honey smiled as a tear rolled down her cheek. Mimi pulled the book back just before the imposter could grab it and yelled at her. 'You're not real!'

The clone clenched her fists and screamed then disappeared in a flash. Mimi dropped the book and threw her arms around her sister. Bree ran over and scooped it up, pressing it to her chest.

Cursing, the man's lower lip twitched like a fat slug. He stamped his foot and grabbed Mimi by the arm. She cried out and Honey pulled her back. With one violent tug the man pulled Mimi away, kicking and crying. His laugh quickly turned into a deep rasping cough that made the veins in his neck bulge. Once he had composed himself and adjusted his cloak his expression became cruel again. 'You really thought you could trick me, didn't you?' He drew a small knife from his boot.

Bree's heart wrenched as he spun Mimi around and jabbed the blade against her throat.

14.
Playing with Fire

The blade glinted in the candlelight as the man tightened his grip on Mimi. She started to cry. Her tears landed on the man's hand but he did not seem to care. 'Help me,' she whispered.

Bree glanced at the book in her hands and then at Mimi. A violent draught sent the candles into a flare, making the shadows sharpen then blur again, as at that moment a tremendous force ripped the door from its hinges. They all turned to see the doorway filled by the same clot of shadow they'd seen before Honey was captured in the tunnel earlier. Tanas Theramonde grinned devilishly at the scene before him. A wild, mindless terror rushed over Bree and she shoved the book into her pocket.

Theramonde locked eyes with Bree and strode towards her, the heels of his boots clicking on the tiles. He stopped directly in front of her and leaned close.

'We meet at last,' he exclaimed. 'You were all in such a hurry to leave the last time. And now, not only have you outwitted my prize scorpion, you also escaped a rather hungry audience.'

Up close his skin was worse than Bree had remembered, pitted like a barren moon, with a vivid pink scar that ran down the length of his cheek.

'Your talents never cease to amaze me.'

The wink of a white stone caught Bree's eye. The opal dagger was nestled inside a leather pouch attached to his belt. It took her all her effort not to make a lunge for it and run.

'And I see you've already met my second in command, Hallux Valgus.' The name filled the air like a bad smell. Theramonde's face changed when he saw him pressing the dagger into Mimi's neck. 'Put that away, man!' he spat angrily. 'If there's any killing to do, I'll be the one doing it.'

With a sneer Valgus pulled the knife away from Mimi's throat and threw her onto the floor. She scrabbled on her hands and knees and crawled out of sight behind the curtain. Honey started to run towards her but Valgus blocked her way. She stared at the blade and took a couple of steps back. Tanas Theramonde turned back to Bree. She held his gaze for one fearless moment and his mouth curled into a sly, tight-lipped grin.

'Why, up close you're even more like your father,' he said.

Bree flinched.

'It's the eyes,' Theramonde sneered. 'They're the windows to the soul.' He turned his back on her and started to walk away.

'And yours are dead,' she spat.

Theramonde stopped in his tracks. His shoulders shook as he chuckled, a horrible menacing laugh. It stopped as suddenly as it had started and he whipped around to face her.

'So are your father's,' he said flatly, and walked back towards her. 'And speaking of dead things, I have your friend Mister Daines to thank for missing you the last time.'

Bree squirmed under his intense glare. He started to circle her like a vulture. Fear glued her to the spot as his eyes snaked over her skin. It felt as though the book was burning a hole in her pocket.

'Don had nothing to do with it!' she blurted.

'Surely you realise there is nothing you can do to protect Mister Daines now?' he spat, the name twisting his ferret-like features.

'Of course I do,' said Bree. She hoped he would spare her the details. 'So why have you brought him up?'

'Your loyalty impresses me. To him, and to that child...'

'Let us take her home. You don't need her.'

'I will trade her for the book.'

It should have been a simple negotiation but Bree could feel her tongue turn to sandpaper. She felt crushed under the weight of responsibility. Honey tugged at Bree's sleeve and pulled her out of Theramonde's earshot. 'Just give him the book. Please, for Mimi.'

'It's not that straightforward,' said Bree.

'How can you say that? We're talking about trading my only sister for a mouldy old book.'

'But don't you realise? As soon as he gets his hands on the book he'll still kill us all.'

Bree felt her chest tighten and her eyes sting with tears. Theramonde watched the two girls with malicious satisfaction.

'I hope your little friends are listening,' he shouted. He then addressed Honey and Sandy. 'She's showing her true colours now. When it comes to saving a friend's life, she chooses not to do it. She may keep her book. But the little girl is coming with me. We have a pit full of very hungry Cleptathorns looking for some dinner.'

Mimi gasped from behind the curtain.

'Bree, please don't let this happen,' said Honey. 'If *I'd* had to choose between saving the book and saving, I dunno, let's say *your dad,* I wouldn't have had to think twice. *I* would have saved your dad.'

Bree looked at Honey as though she had been slapped by her.

'Trust your instincts, Bree. You always have. I'm sorry Honey, but I'm with her. Don't do it,' Sandy said with a sudden flare of dark energy. Theramonde's eyes narrowed and he turned sharply. Although Sandy was terrified he clenched his jaw and stuck out his chest. Bree felt for the outline of the book in her pocket.

'What did you say?' Theramonde hissed through gritted teeth. Before Sandy had a chance to speak Theramonde lunged at his throat, his black eyes burning. Sandy choked and turned the colour of dough, too shocked even to struggle. Pure, blank terror seized at Bree's heart. 'Let him go!' she heard herself scream.

Theramonde laughed. 'Not until I have the book.'

Bree could feel the tears well in her eyes again but she refused to buckle. 'It has to be given willingly. And if you hurt him, I'll make sure you never get it.'

'And I'll make sure you leave here without the only friends you have. Will you miss them as much as you've missed your daddy?'

'I said let him go.'

Theramonde stared directly into Sandy's eyes, enjoying his squirming and gasping for air. After what seemed like an eternity he made a sneering, dismissive sound and released his grip on Sandy's neck, dropping him like a puppet with its strings cut. Theramonde cracked his knuckles, making a sickening sound like dry wood snapping. His face darkened as he looked at Sandy. 'I could kill you all right now if I wanted to. Bring me the youngest one first!'

Bree's stomach roiled. She knew she would have to act now.

'Is this what you want?' She kept her voice firm even though her heart was thumping hard enough to press against her ribs. Theramonde spun round. His angry eyes flashed like onyx and his mouth twisted as if he wanted to spit. 'What?'

Bree pulled the book from her pocket and waved it in the air. She noted a faint flicker of surprise on Theramonde's face. He licked his lips and lifted his hand dubiously. Bree snatched it back. 'Over my dead body.'

Theramonde's face twisted into an expression of wild fury. 'As you wish, child,' he said. 'You will not be the first to fall by my hand.'

He started towards the curtain. Bree could see Mimi's feet poking out from underneath and her heart did a somersault.

'Did you kill my father?' she blurted, her voice little more than a strangled croak. Theramonde stopped suddenly and turned. 'I need to know the truth,' she said softly.

'Why does the truth matter to you now? This is the end for you too.' His tone, low and menacing, made Bree's stomach clench. Mimi peeked out from behind the curtain, her eyes filled with terror. Bree nodded at her to get back.

'Are you going to tell me the truth about my father's death?' said Bree, trying to buy time.

Theramonde spun on his heels, his face red with fury. 'Are you going to give me my book?' he growled from between his teeth.

'If you won't tell me about my dad, then no, I won't give you it.' Bree slipped the book back into her pocket and shook her head defiantly. The muscles in Theramonde's face tightened. He stared her directly in the eyes.

'You can ask your father when you see him in the afterlife. You'll be joining him shortly.'

He turned back to face the curtain. Bree thought her heart might burst through her chest at any moment. He marched over to where Mimi was hiding, his huge boots thudding on the stone. 'But the little one must die first.'

Honey screamed in protest but Valgus grabbed her and pressed his hand over her mouth. Out of the shadows Sandy appeared like an apparition. He stuck out his chest and jumped in front of Theramonde, his jaw clenched. At first Theramonde did not react, then moved to flick him aside like a mere insect but before anyone saw it coming Sandy swung a fist and punched him in the face. Theramonde staggered and fell head first, the air escaping from his chest in a guttural humph. As he landed, the dagger shot out of its pouch and skidded across the floor, coming to a halt at Bree's feet. She grabbed it and ran over to the Flame of Irenus.

'NO!' shrieked Valgus, releasing Honey. 'M-master,' he stuttered, 'the Flame must not be extinguished.'

Theramonde rose up from the ground, his expression a mixture of disbelief and rage as he realised what had just happened. He glowered at Sandy, spite twisting his mouth. He felt for the missing dagger at his hip. He looked up to see Bree holding the dagger above the glass dome.

'Give that to me,' he bellowed, sending a shower of spit into the air.

Bree gulped and thrust the tip of the dagger into the slot. Valgus whimpered like a wounded dog. Theramonde threw him a silencing glare before turning back to Bree. He held his hands up in a gesture of surrender and took a couple of measured steps forward.

'Stop right there or I'll push it in,' warned Bree, her voice quivering.

He stopped immediately. 'What do you want from me?' he asked. The hideous scar on his face moved like a worm as his hand felt for the bejewelled handle of his sword.

'Tell me who killed my father.' Bree tightened her grip on the dagger.

Theramonde blinked and ground his teeth as he considered his answer. His tongue poked out and moistened his lips. 'I cannot tell you...'

'You liar.' Bree pushed the dagger in a fraction more. The opal shone in the candlelight.

'Stop,' cried Theramonde throwing his hands up in the air and taking a step backwards.

'Who killed my father?'

Theramonde's scarred cheek twitched. 'It was an accident,' he hissed, his eyes never leaving the dagger.

Bree felt the slow burn of grief build inside. She hoped the truth would make it stop. 'Tell me!' she screamed.

Theramonde flinched. 'I needed to find the book,' he began, 'and he would only tell me if I promised not to hurt the old woman or your mother.'

Bree thought she could feel her heart breaking all over again. There was a bitterness in her mouth she thought she might taste for the rest of her life. She felt her grip loosen on the opal dagger. Through her wall of hot tears Bree could see Theramonde and Valgus edging forwards but she felt helpless to stop them.

'And you killed him anyway?' she whispered.

'Only after he did this,' spat Theramonde, tapping his scar with a finger.

Suddenly the grief slipped away from Bree, leaving behind an anger that burned like acid in her veins. 'I HATE you!' she screamed and rammed the dagger all the way down into the hole without a second thought. The opal in the dagger turned black and the glass case sprung open, letting the Flame dance erratically in the pool of coloured oil. Valgus let out an anguished moan and steadied himself against the wall.

'Quickly! Blow it out,' shouted Honey.

Bree inhaled deeply, and prepared to extinguish the Flame of Irenus. But she wasn't quick enough. Theramonde launched himself at her in a blur of black, and landed just in front of the case. He tripped and pushed the pillar over. The dome crashed to the ground sending the dish with the Flame, still alight, spinning through the air. Bree jumped back as it landed on the flagstones, showering them with burning oil and shards of glass. The opal dagger shot across the floor and hit the wall.

A fierce orange flame sprung up and tore along the trail of oil towards the velvet curtain. It caught instantly, exploding in a terrifying wall of heat and light. Honey screamed. Theramonde sprung to his feet and stamped on the falling embers. Valgus removed his cloak and whipped them but this only fanned the fire. Sensing a chance to escape, Bree grabbed Sandy and Honey. 'Come on,' she cried, making for the door. 'We have to get out of here!'

'We can't leave,' cried Honey. 'Mimi is trapped behind the curtain.'

Bree searched the room for something to quench the fire but there was nothing. And now the curtain was a great sheet of fire. The flames darted and licked and smoke swirled up in thick banners.

'How are we going to get her?' she screamed over the harsh roar of the flames. Honey looked desperate. She tried to get close to the curtain but the heat was too intense and she was forced to step back. The stone walls had taken on a glaze of yellow as burning embers drifted up in spirals. The rafters cracked and smoked above their heads and with a crash of sparks one of the rafters fell between them and Theramonde and Valgus, bursting into flames immediately. With that, the last remnants of curtain disintegrated and were consumed, and there in the corner, curled up like a ball was Mimi.

'There she is!' cried Honey.

The fire snaked in rippling bands, twisting and turning in malevolent flames. Candles melted in their holders and ran like milk down the walls. The flames raced and met each other, trapping Valgus inside a circle of fire. His face bore a half mad expression of fear mixed with hate. His mismatched eyes were wide and he was breathing in rapid, snatching gulps. Behind a wall of flames Theramonde's mouth was gaping. An inhuman scream erupted from within his chest, sending a mist of spittle up into the air. 'I will NOT let you get away this time!'

He searched blindly around the floor, all the time shielding his face from the raging inferno. Spotting the dagger he bent to pick it up and cursed as it hissed on his skin, branding the centre of his palm. He held it up and Bree could see the taut, crimson tissue had been singed into the shape of a triangle.

There was a deafening crack as the beams fractured in the heat. Timber crashed to the floor in an eruption of crimson sparks, trapping Theramonde and Valgus.

'Come to us, Meems!' called Honey. Mimi tried to crawl over the tiles but great tongues of fire leapt and writhed around her, making it impossible. Bree could feel her hair sizzle like dried heather. Her throat blazed with each lungful of breath she took. 'I need to help her,' cried Honey, removing her satchel.

'How?' choked Sandy.

Squinting against the heat, Honey climbed up onto some fallen debris. 'Be careful!' cried Bree.

Honey threw the strap of her satchel up to the iron chandelier. It looped over one of the candle holders and after quickly testing to see if it would hold her weight she pulled back.

'Grab my feet,' she instructed. She swung out through the red embers and over the tongues of fire. Mimi leaped into the air, grabbed her shoes and was whipped up from the ground.

'Look out,' cried Sandy, seeing Theramonde aiming his sword at them. He threw it, and it spun over their heads, flames glinting off the mirror-bright steel. The blade sliced through the rope that held the chandelier. Just as Mimi swung over Sandy she let go and dropped into his arms. But Honey was swung back through the smoke on the lopsided chandelier, the rope fraying and snapping.

Sandy was coughing violently, his breaths coming in thin whistles. Reeking palls of smoke stung Bree's eyes and caught in her throat, making her choke for air. She pushed Mimi to the floor where the air was clear and told her to crawl towards the door. As the heat pressed down she felt dizzy and disoriented. A crash knocked her off her feet and in the smoke and burning dust she realised Honey had landed on her. As she did, a shower of crimson sparks fell from the ceiling scorching the bare flesh on Bree's arm. She heard herself yelp. They would not leave this room, she thought.

'The door is this way!' choked Mimi, tugging Honey's arm. Down low, their cheeks pressed to the cold stone floor, there was just enough clean air for a lungful. They crawled over the tiles until they reached the doorway. Bree stood to see Theramonde shielding himself from a wall of fire.

'They're getting away,' screamed Valgus, dodging a hot cascade of sparks.

'Do something then, you stupid man,' barked Theramonde. Through the rippling heat he stared straight at Bree, livid.

Hallux Valgus was robed in thick smoke, his head haloed in tongues of fire. The room was suddenly filled with the sickening smell of singeing skin. He grabbed at his forehead and writhed under the weight of his blistering skin. It bubbled and fizzed before Bree's eyes, causing a horrible sore to burgeon on the side of his face and up over his forehead. He choked and convulsed and cried out, an unnerving mixture of agony and rage. His inhuman eyes lifted to Bree's in a blaze of anger. He pointed his finger at her and the flames reflected off the huge diamond ring, turning it to amber. He spat some words, barely audible over the hungry cackle of fire. He said them over and over again, all the time getting louder until his scream reached a flaring crescendo.

'Floodus Spectacularis!'

He threw up his arms and laughed until his eyes disappeared into the fleshy folds in his face. Bree and Sandy stumbled into the corridor with Honey and Mimi and pulled the door shut. The candles flickered wildly in their holders and thick smoke swirled along the length of the corridor like fog.

'Is everyone okay?' Bree coughed.

'Just about,' wheezed Sandy. 'Are you?'

Bree nodded and put her arm around his shoulder.

'And I'm okay now we've got what we came for,' smiled Honey, ruffling Mimi's smoky hair.

'We should get moving before the fire spreads,' said Sandy.

Mimi grinned and pointed to the floor. 'It's all right. Someone is putting out the fire.'

Bree said, 'What?'

Mimi pointed to the floor, where large pools of water were collecting near their feet. It was pouring from under the door, spreading a dark river over the stone. Bree thought the water smelled strange; metallic and sharp, like rain on a hot pavement.

'Where's that coming from?' said Honey.

'Valgus and Theramonde have done this. It's a spell to stop us.'

'Come on, move!' shouted Sandy, heading off. They sprinted after him with wave after wave rising over their trainers. Panic bloomed in Bree's chest. 'Quickly,' she yelled, her voice merging with their splashing footfalls, 'there's no knowing how high this will get!'

Water gushed under the door and sprang from cracks in the walls as though they were on a sinking ship. The candles sputtered into tiny points of light in the thick smoke. Mimi stopped running and stood, paralysed with terror.

'We have to hurry,' Bree said urgently, 'what's the matter?'

Mimi wailed as the water rose up over her knees. 'I can't swim…'

15.

A Sight for Sore Eyes

Bree searched the corridor with anxious eyes. If they stayed where they were the water would swallow them. It gurgled around their knees, rising like their terror.

'Mimi never learned to swim,' explained Honey. 'She was always too frightened.'

'Then I can carry her. Lift her up onto my back,' said Sandy. Honey grabbed Mimi around the waist and heaved her up. Mimi threw her arms around Sandy's neck and squeezed her eyes tight.

'Let's try and get back down that way.' Bree pointed down the corridor to the tombstone door and started to wade through the water, dodging fallen shards of wood. A swell curled at their waists and pulled them away from the Magnentity's den. It poured through cavities in the walls and cascaded from cracks in the ceiling extinguishing the wall candles. Darkness closed around them like a cloak.

Each rolling wave lifted them off their feet and it took all their efforts to keep their heads above the surface. Every time Sandy stumbled, Mimi let out a scream and grabbed him tighter. 'Where's it taking us?' he cried. But water flooded Bree's mouth and stole her words. She choked and struggled to catch her breath before the current sucked her under and sent her tumbling. In the watery darkness she could just see Honey's arms and legs flailing but she lost sight of Sandy and Mimi. As soon as she felt her feet touch the floor, Bree sprung up, cutting through the water and breaking the surface. Shaking her wet hair away from her face she realised the water felt warmer, the air close and hot.

'Woah! Fire up ahead!' yelled Sandy. Bree spun round to see Sandy gasping for air. A few metres ahead of them a blistering waterfall of fire poured sparks into the water, sending up clouds of sizzling steam. Just then, Honey and Mimi bobbed to the surface. Mimi let out a high-pitched scream, her pale face reflecting the dripping flames.

'How are we going to get past that?' Honey gulped.

'There's only one way,' said Bree. 'We're going to have to go under it.'

'No! Please!' Mimi begged hysterically. 'I'll drown. And then get burned to a frazzle.'

'We've no choice,' Honey said gently. She grabbed a length of driftwood and tucked it under Mimi's arms. 'This will keep you afloat. You have to trust me.' Mimi stopped struggling and bobbed silently in the shimmering water. Honey reached under the surface and removed Mimi's belt.

'Now, take a long, deep breath,' she instructed, 'and hold it until we come up on the other side.

Got that?'

Mimi's bottom lip trembled and her eyes filled with panic but she nodded. A hard knot of dread tightened in Bree's chest as she watched her prepare to go under the water again. Bree was a good swimmer—a great swimmer in fact—but even she was terrified at the prospect of swimming under the fire-fall. Sandy swam over and put a hand on Mimi's shoulder.

'It'll only take a few seconds,' he tried with a smile, 'and I'll be right behind you.'

Bree noticed Sandy looked troubled and a shiver of fear ran up her spine. He swam back to her as Honey fastened the belt around Mimi's wrist.

'What is it?' Bree whispered.

'B-back there, the way we came,' Sandy said. 'I think I saw something.'

Bree tried to peer through the darkness but all she could see was the water reflecting the flames and smoke curling down the corridor. 'I don't see anything,' she said, pushing her wet hair back from her face.

'It's gone now. Or maybe it was my imagination...'

'Guys are you ready?' said Honey before she turned back to Mimi. 'You'll be fine as long as you keep this belt on.' Mimi nodded and clung desperately to her piece of wood.

Out of the corner of her eye Bree saw something which made her stomach lurch. Something was under the surface of the water, swimming towards them through the flickering shadows and quills of smoke. When it lifted its head above the surface she grabbed Sandy. 'The Magnentity!' she hissed. Sandy started shaking violently. 'I knew I'd seen something.'

The creature swam like a giant crocodile, using its tail to propel itself. Water churned behind it. Bree could hear its sharp, snorting breaths as it got closer.

'Mimi, we have to hurry,' urged Bree, trying to keep the panic from her voice. Mimi started to whine but Honey knew there was not a second to spare. She turned Mimi's head away and spoke firmly. 'After three, take a deep breath.'

'Oh no. The Magnentity has gone again. Where did it go?' said Sandy, his eyes darting furiously. Bree wiggled her toes fearfully, expecting it to brush against them.

'One…' yelled Honey. Bree saw the water erupting as the giant body and tail broke the surface. The Magnentity threw back its head and opened its jaws.

'Two…'

Sandy threw the driftwood as hard as he could but the giant jaws bit down, ripping right through it.

'Three!' Honey and Mimi both gulped a lungful of air and disappeared under the water. Wasting no time, Bree and Sandy dived after them, kicking their legs furiously. Bree felt her skin poach as the currents turned to liquid gold under the boiling orange fire-fall. Glancing back, she was sure she would see the gaping jaws of the Magnentity, there was nothing but swirling amber water.

Just when her lungs started to burn for oxygen she felt the water around her start to cool. Above her head there was a shift from gold to grey and she knew with a flush of relief this meant she had made it past the fire-fall. She kicked her legs and rocketed through the surface at such speed that she hit her head on something. For a moment she saw stars, but they cleared to reveal that she was floating near the ceiling of a dimly-lit tunnel. Her heart hammered wildly in the silence. There was no sign of the three others, and for a moment she had to consider that they might not have made it. Then, to Bree's wild relief, Sandy's head broke the surface. 'I c-can't see them,' he panted.

Bree's eyes swept the water like a searchlight. 'They've been down there too long. Maybe Mimi started to panic. Oh, Sandy what if…'

Before she could go on Honey erupted from the water a few feet away. She looked distraught. She held up the empty belt. 'I lost her. Help her, please…' she begged, her tears mingling with the icy water.

Without hesitation, Bree flipped down into the murky depths. She flailed blindly, feeling for a limb, a piece of clothing, a fistful of hair. But her hands met only empty water. Down she went, tumbling and swirling. She spun round in a cauldron of darkness, trapped in a chaos of tangled clothing and spiralling bubbles. She soared back up to the surface, where she gasped and swallowed air, before dropping down again. Everywhere there were bubbles. She had no idea which way was up. And still she could not see Mimi. She was ready to give up when she felt something cold and hard under her fingers. She grabbed it and, kicking a swarm of bubbles, dragged it to the surface. When she broke through she gulped a lungful of air and peered through bleary eyes to see she had caught Mimi's string of beads. Mimi was limp and deathly pale.

'She's not breathing,' cried Honey, supporting her sister's head.

'Mimi?' shouted Sandy, staring down at her helplessly.

'Help her!'

Bree pushed Honey out of the way and clamped her mouth over Mimi's. She blew a long single breath and Mimi's chest lifted in response. Her eyes remained closed, her lips a mottled blue. Bree tried again, this time listening closely for signs of life, but all she could hear were Honey's sobs echoing around the tunnel. Mimi's ghostlike face was framed by her hair, which floated on the surface like seaweed. Droplets of water glistened on her unmoving eyelashes.

'Don't you dare do this to us Mimi Pizazz!' Bree screamed and thumped the water with an angry fist. For the third time she covered Mimi's mouth with her own and breathed life into her. This time water gurgled in Mimi's throat like a drain. Suddenly, wonderfully, Mimi coughed up a mixture of snot and water. Her eyes shot open and she gasped for air.

'Mimi!' Honey yelped and pulled her close. Bree jumped back and started shivering wildly, her breath wheezing in her raw throat.

Mimi was deeply shocked and crying but she was alive. Her face slowly returned to its usual shade of pink, a constellation of freckles decorating the bridge of her nose.

'Flipper saves the day,' laughed Sandy as he smacked an open palm on the water.

'Thank you,' breathed Honey as she wiped Mimi's tears away, 'I don't know what to say.'

Bree was exhausted and trembling. 'Let's celebrate once we get out of here,' she said. 'Before that thing comes after us.'

'What *thing?*' cried Mimi.

'It's nothing for you to worry about,' said Honey briskly.

'Not yet anyway…' muttered Sandy adjusting his glasses, provoking a stern look from Bree.

'There's a hint of light up ahead,' she said. 'Let's head for that.'

Honey offered Mimi one end of her satchel strap. 'Grab hold of this.'

'And don't let go this time,' Sandy added.

After a while the floor climbed and the water level dropped until it was no higher than their ankles.

'I'm c-cold. And soaking!' whimpered Mimi.

'We all are,' replied Honey, 'but we'll get out of here soon, I promise.'

'That light up ahead…' said Bree trying to lift everyone's spirits. 'It's getting closer. And I think it's the way out.'

'Quiet!' hissed Honey and everyone fell silent. She threw up a finger and turned to look back into the darkness.

'What is it?' asked Sandy.

'There's something there. Can't you hear it…?'

Bree could hear the hammering of her heart but then another sound emerged. The low echoes of distant splashes, of footsteps racing towards them.

'Something is coming after us!' Mimi cried, grabbing her sister.

'It sounds like more than one something,' said Bree, breaking into a jog. 'Come on, run!'

As they raced through shallow pools of water, the sounds of stamping feet and wild cries grew louder and more violent. The bloodthirsty howl of a Cleptathorn tore through the air and made them jump.

'There's the light,' said Bree.

'That's not a torch flame,' said Sandy. 'I think its daylight!'

'Come on! We're nearly ther—'

The word caught in her throat as something hot and acidic choked her. She coughed and spat. Then all four of them were coughing. Bree's stinging eyes ran with tears and her nose dripped.

'It's some...kind of...poisonous...gas,' wheezed Sandy, his knees loosening beneath him. Bree pulled her shirt over her nose and hauled him up from the floor. 'Get up Greenfield!' she screamed. 'If you sit down now you're done for!'

They stumbled towards the shaft of daylight, the thick gas burning their throats. Honey picked Mimi up and ran with her. All the time the thunder of voices and barking intensified. All but blinded by the noxious fumes they found themselves staggering up a slope towards the shifting light, smelling fresh air. As they reached the top Bree caught a smell of burning but it was nothing compared to the gas. When her vision cleared she noticed a heavy iron grille blocking their path.

'There's the courtyard,' said Sandy. It was still raining outside but the wet cobbles glowed as though they were baking. Everything was enveloped in a furious haze of orange and red, sparks showering down through swirling smoke.

'What's happening? Is the whole castle on fire?' panted Honey, throwing a glance at the lengthening shadows coming up behind them. Mimi sped past her and threw herself at the grille, gulping greedily for air.

'I can see the bridge from here,' Bree said, rubbing her sore and bloodshot eyes.

'They're coming! Let us out!' sobbed Mimi, rattling the metal grid.

'It's no use, Mimi,' cried Honey, 'it's locked.'

'There's only one thing for it,' coughed Sandy, leaning forwards, his hands on knees. 'Don's magic key.'

Bree made the mistake of glancing back. An army of cloaks was approaching the bottom of the slope. 'Mimi, give me your necklace,' she ordered. Mimi looked puzzled but lifted the beads over her head and handed them to her. 'Sorry about this,' said Bree, 'I'll replace it as soon as I can.' She snapped the elastic and scattered the rainbow beads down the slope towards the army. There were shrieks and angry yells as the guards slipped and crashed, tripping the others coming up behind.

Bree pulled out the key and rammed it into the lock. As soon as the grille swung open on its rusty hinges they ran through, then together pushed it back until it clanged back into place.

'Come on, run!' cried Honey, grabbing Mimi and making a bolt for the courtyard. Bree started after them, but doubled back when she had an idea. 'I should lock it again…'

'Hurry up!' yelled Sandy. Bree fumbled with the key with trembling fingers and tried to block out the shouts and bloodcurdling barks as she groped for the keyhole. The guards were on their feet and pounding towards them. Bounding ahead were the Cleptathorns, their great jaws wide in anticipation. Just as the lock clicked one launched itself at the bars. Sandy yanked Bree back as its massive jaws snapped shut where her head had been. Staggering back, Bree slipped the key into her pocket.

'The guards might have a key too,' hissed Sandy.

'Then we have to get to the bridge.'

They ran across the courtyard without looking back.

Once outside they saw the castle was ablaze. Shoots of fire were sprouting out of collapsed sections in the roof, showering flakes of ash like a blizzard of red-hot snow. Acrid smoke billowed out of every crack and fissure.

'Honey and Mimi are already there,' yelled Sandy over the crackling roar. They dodged a flurry of embers and raced towards them over the shuddering wooden bridge. At the other end Honey was staring at her photograph of Mimi and the others. It was soggy and dog-eared but she was smiling. 'We made it!' she laughed and held it up to them. Smiling out from the middle of everyone, whole again, was her sister. She grabbed Bree and Sandy and gave them a tight hug but Bree flinched and pulled back. Her forearm was raw and glowing red.

'That's a nasty burn,' Honey frowned, digging in her satchel. 'These will take away the sting and stop it blistering.' She plucked a few lavender buds from the sprig she had taken from Dunubas's garden and rubbed them over the burn. Bree grimaced and bit down on her lip. 'Sorry, but you have to trust me on this one.'

• • •

The rain had eased but it still fell in glittering ribbons, cooling them and washing away the black streaks of soot on their clothes and skin.

'Let's go and get Dunubas,' said Sandy running towards the fringe of trees.

'Yeah, he'll be waiting for us,' said Honey.

'Who will?' asked Mimi starting to chase Sandy.

'A good friend,' replied Honey absently. She let them run ahead and turned to see Bree staring back at the castle. Fire clawed through the windows, sweeping up in wraiths of smoke towards the cloud of burning sparks. Through the belching smoke the castle looked like a skull screaming in fury.

'Come on, Bree,' said Honey, 'it's over now. We can go home.'

For a few moments neither girl said anything. But they jumped when Sandy burst back through the trees. Bree could tell from his expression that he did not have good news. 'Dunubas isn't there,' he said. 'He's gone.'

They searched the bushes but there was no sign of Dunubas anywhere. Bree shouted his name but only her own voice answered with an echo.

'I don't understand,' she said, turning to Honey.

'He'll be here somewhere,' she replied. 'I mean, you don't think he'd go without us. Do you?'

'Well, where is he? I can't believe he's left us,' Bree breathed. 'I thought we could count on him.

I guess I was wrong.'

'Maybe something happened,' shrugged Sandy. 'Maybe he had to get back to his sister.'

'We could try their cottage,' suggested Honey as she squeezed the water from her hair.

Bree shook her head angrily and fought back tears. 'He should be here. A promise is a promise.'

They walked together in silence, with the only sounds coming from their squelching shoes. Bree did not feel like talking. How could Dunubas have abandoned them when he knew how much they would need him?

An eerie muted light came from the smoke-choked sun, as motes of black ash swirled between the trees like moths. Crows stared down at them with yellow eyes from high up in the dripping branches, cackling like witches as they rattled their glossy feathers. Their presence made Bree feel uneasy.

'Can you remember which way to go?' asked Honey, holding Mimi's hand.

'Let's go back another way,' said Bree, 'so we don't run into the Crimboids again.'

Sandy shuddered at the mention of their name.

They walked for a long time, pushing through the undergrowth and tackling steep hillocks. Even this far into the forest the air was still heavy with the pungent smell of smoke. The rain fell steadily but there was a little shelter under the branches. Bree heard a twig snap and she stopped in her tracks. An icy shiver trickled up her spine.

'What was that?' she whispered, feeling for the book.

There it was again.

She whipped around, terror seizing her. It took a moment for her frightened mind to register what she was seeing. There, standing in a clearing was Dunubas, his drenched hair hanging like rats' tails over his face. Bree broke into a run and crashed into him.

'Are you a sight for sore eyes!' she laughed.

Pain and disbelief sparked in his steely eyes. 'When I saw the flames I thought the worst…'

'Flames, floods, gas. They tried everything,' said Sandy.

'But it takes more than that to get rid of us,' said Honey mischievously.

When Winrad bounded through the undergrowth Mimi let out a strangled yelp. Terrified, she jumped at Honey then heard Bree laugh as Winrad jumped up on her and licked her face.

'This is the friend we were telling you about Mimi,' said Honey, gently pushing her forward as a way of introduction. Dunubas smiled at Mimi and bowed down. She giggled behind her hand. 'I have heard so much about you,' he said. 'You are a lucky girl to have people care about you enough to risk their lives.'

Mimi blushed and looked shyly at her shoes.

'Anyway, we're cold and wet and hungry. Can you help us?' said Bree.

Dunubas nodded. 'I know a way out of here.

It'll take a bit longer but it's a safer route.'

They had only walked a short distance before Bree realised they were heading to Strangledoor. Far in the distance the dark clouds petered out letting sunshine thread its way through the forest. The heavy silence on this side of the border made Bree uncomfortable, but she shook it off and followed the curving path through the trees.

Behind them, dark shadows detached themselves from the tree trunks and moved swiftly towards the path.

16.

Every Path Has Its Puddle

'The rain's stopped. We must be getting closer to the border,' said Bree, glancing up through the branches.

'What difference does it make?' replied Sandy. 'It's not like we're going to be drying out any time soon.'

A murder of crows scattered into the air in a sudden eruption of flapping wings. Mimi jumped like a frightened rabbit and threw herself at Honey.

'Something has spooked them,' muttered Honey, wrapping a protective arm around her.

Something at the edge of Bree's vision distracted her. Shadows were shifting between the trees.

'Over there,' she stammered, pointing a shaky finger.

A clutch of shadows were emerging, and they were taking on a roughly human form. It was as if they had come into existence between one blink of her eyes and the next.

Sandy and Honey whipped around, wearing identical expressions of shock. The figures crept into view, still nothing more than a featureless cluster of dark shapes.

'A-are they ghosts?' asked Mimi.

'They don't look dead enough,' said Sandy.

As they stepped into a shaft of light it became clear that they looked like people but the deadness behind their eyes told them that whatever had made them human had long gone. Their faces were pale and gaunt, their cheekbones poking through their skin. They looked like evil scarecrows, cut down and set free. As they lumbered towards them Mimi screamed. The noise still hung in the air as Dunubas grabbed her and started to run.

'It's the Fearless!' he yelled. 'Come on!'

They plunged through the tangled thickets until their breaths seared in their lungs, drawing on reserves of energy they didn't know they had. Branches whipped Bree's face and caught in her hair and all the time she could not get Dunubas's words out of her head. *The Fearless, the Fearless…*

'They're following us!' shouted Sandy, stumbling and tripping in his panic to get away.

Bree glanced back to see the figures blundering through the undergrowth, tearing at their hair and faces with anguished moans.

'We can outrun them!' panted Bree, ducking to avoid a low branch.

They broke through a line of trees without realising that the ground fell away suddenly down a steep slope. They skidded down the bank, tearing through bushes, flipping and rolling. They landed in a heap at the bottom, in a marshy area full of rotten tree stumps and boggy pools. Bree was aware of a jumble of sounds; Winrad's agitated bark, Mimi whimpering, crows squawking. She staggered to her feet, her senses on high alert.

'Are are we all in one piece?' asked Dunubas, paying particular attention to Mimi, who was sitting up and rubbing her ankle. Her face was tearstained and smudged with dirt. She nodded, her bottom lip quivering.

'Where have they gone?' asked Sandy breathlessly, his glasses dangling from one ear.

'They were right behind us a minute ago,' replied Bree.

'Let's not hang around to let them catch up,' said Honey.

Bree started to walk over the spongy leaf mould but after only three steps it turned to marsh. The mud was so thick and deep it tried to suck the shoe right off her foot. She pulled her foot out before it could sink any further. Her footprint immediately filled with stagnant water and disappeared.

'Oh no,' she breathed, backing away.

Sandy got to his feet. 'What is it now?'

'We're surrounded by quicksand,' she said. Shifting ooze stretched out before them in a vast brown puddle.

Mimi struggled to her feet and hobbled over to join them at the edge of the marsh. Dunubas held Winrad back from the bubbling mud by the scruff of his neck, although it looked clear to Bree that the dog was wise enough not to venture any further.

'Quicksand?' wailed Mimi. 'We'll never get out

of here!'

'This part of the forest is well known for it,' said Dunubas grimly.

'I thought you said this was the safe route?' cried Sandy.

'I said *safer*.'

There was a faint bubbling noise coming from the patch of thick, soup-like mud. It drifted up in watery pops. Mimi looked up at Bree. 'Do you think those people followed us?' she whispered. Bree's senses had pricked again but she thought better of telling Mimi that. 'I think we've outrun them, we'll be home soon,' she said.

At first all was silent except for the quiet popping of the bog. Then the sound of a snapping twig sent a crow into the air and shot through Bree like a jolt of electricity. Then another branch cracked loudly behind them and Bree whipped around. Winrad growled and the fur around his neck stood on end.

'What is it boy?' whispered Dunubas. 'What do you see?'

All around her Bree could sense movement, yet could see nothing. And then they appeared. Emerging into the light from the shadows of the trees were dark shapes. Not just one or two, but dozens of them. For a moment the Fearless were silhouetted against the sky as they crested the ridge of the hill, but soon they were descending the steep bank with lumbering steps. Bree's eyes flicked between them and the thick mud.

'We're trapped!' Honey wailed.

Winrad was barking and lunging forwards but it was no deterrent for the Fearless. They kept coming, staggering woozily towards them. Mimi clung to Honey, howling with terror.

'Stay behind me!' ordered Dunubas. He drew his dagger and prepared himself to fight. Honey stared desperately at the flimsy weapon and then back at the descending mob. 'It's no use,' she cried, 'there are too many of them!'

The Fearless stalked them, gaining in substance as they moved closer. They moved in an odd, jerky way, as though their legs would not bend at the knees. They reached out hungrily, their eyes empty and haunted, staring without seeing. Their low moan made Bree's head swim. 'What are we going to do?' she sobbed, glancing back at the quicksand.

'We could take our chances with the mud,' said Sandy, but Bree shook her head firmly.

'It'll swallow us alive.'

'By the look of things, so will they!'

Bree felt a vibration against her hip and nearly jumped out of her skin. Quickly realising that the book had sprung to life she pulled it out of her pocket.

'Wish six!' cried Bree, turning the brittle pages. Mimi stared in awe at the throbbing locket.

'What does it say?' yelled Dunubas, his voice lost amongst the anguished moans. The change from paper to glass happened in a flash as though the book sensed the urgency. Bree tried to swallow her fear as she waited for the words to emerge. When they did, she shouted them out over the rising cries of the Fearless.

THE FEARLESS ONES HAVE BEEN RELEASED,
ON HUMAN FLESH THEY LIKE TO FEAST.
NOW FROM YOUR MOUTH WILL BLOW A BREEZE,
A BREATH THAT MAKES THE QUICKSAND FREEZE.
WANT THEM GONE? HERE'S SOME ADVICE,
CLOSE THE BOOK TO THAW THE ICE.

'Do as it says!' screamed Dunubas as the army of figures reached the bottom of the hill. Mimi was rigid, locked in a world of nightmares. Her lips mumbled two words over and over again in horror, 'Human flesh, human flesh…'

Bree turned to the bog, took a deep breath and slowly blew it out. As she did, a white plume curled from her mouth and travelled across the mud turning it, inch by inch, to ice. Mimi stared in astonishment. Her lips were still moving but no words were coming out.

'Hurry!' urged Bree, pushing her onto the ice. One by one they stepped onto the frozen quicksand and walked as fast as their sliding feet would allow. Bree held the open book out in front of her, terrified that if she slipped the cover might close and the ice would return to the hungry, sucking mud. When they reached the other side, Bree turned back to see Dunubas fighting off three of the Fearless at the same time. Winrad was snapping at their arms and legs, tearing at their clothing but they did not seem to feel his teeth pierce their skin. Their expression did not change, even when Dunubas thrust his dagger into them.

'They're not even blinking,' said Sandy. 'It's like they're already dead.'

Bree stared down at the fading words on the page. 'There are too many of them for him to fight alone.'

'They're going to make it onto the ice,' hissed Honey, 'You have to close the book!'

Bree stared at her disbelievingly and then her eyes dropped to Mimi, who was looking up at her with pleading eyes. 'Not without Dunubas' she said firmly.

Dunubas plunged his dagger into one of the Fearless and pushed another to the ground. They both got straight back to their feet, unfazed and unwounded.

'Come on!' Bree yelled, her desperate voice echoing around the trees. Dunubas kicked one of them away and grabbed Winrad by the scruff of his neck, dragging him onto the ice. Three of the Fearless had already made it to the middle of the ice as Dunubas and Winrad reached the other side.

'Shut the book!' he ordered and Bree slammed it closed with an echoing thud. The locket stopped glowing and with it the ice cracked and thawed, replaced in an instant by the thick, slimy quicksand. One by one the Fearless stepped onto the mud and one by one they were swallowed like pebbles in a puddle.

'They can see what's happening,' said Honey, shielding Mimi's eyes, 'and yet they're still following each other.'

As they were pulled under, the Fearless let out bloodthirsty cries that seemed to carry indescribable torment. Bree could not pull her gaze away. She watched in horror as they yawned their silent shrieks, before they were pulled down into the shimmering ooze. Their eyes remained blank even when the mud rose up over their mouths and sucked them into the airless depths. Soon they were all gone. The mud settled, the bubbles stopped rising and the silence settled like dust.

'It's over,' whispered Honey as she rocked Mimi gently. Bree was not so sure. Her fear was still keeping her on edge. 'I want out of here,' she said, pushing the book back in her pocket.

'I'll second that,' muttered Sandy, eyeing the brow of the hill. He turned to Dunubas, who was inspecting the blade of his dagger. 'Any more nasty surprises we should know about?' he asked sarcastically.

Dunubas slid his dagger back into its sheath and swept the trees with his steely eyes. 'We should always be ready for the unexpected,' he replied coolly.

'I feel so much better now,' said Sandy with mock delight. 'Thanks…'

• • •

After walking for a while, they stopped to rest in a glade ringed with trees that cast skeletal shadows on the grass. Mist rose up in feathery wisps around their ankles. Although the sun was hidden behind a damp grey bank of cloud, it had stopped raining long enough for them to dry out a little.

'I feel much warmer than I did back there,' Bree said, smoothing out her damp tangled hair.

'That's because we are near Strangledoor,' smiled Dunubas. 'You can see the sky above it from here.'

Not too far in the distance they could see the distinctive change in weather. The sky was a watercolour painting of peacock blue where the steely grey stopped. It warmed Bree's soul to think how near they were to safety.

'I'm thirsty,' groaned Mimi. She got up and wandered over to the trees.

Dunubas tapped his empty hip flask. 'We all are, little one,' he said apologetically, 'but I know a place where we can drink just across the border.'

'Your house?' smiled Honey, relishing the prospect of Nevidas's cooking and the sanctuary of their quaint little cottage.

Dunubas shook his head and looked to the east. 'I'm afraid not. We are still some way from there.'

Mimi raced up the brow of a hillock to look towards the border.

'Don't stray too far, Mimi,' Honey warned. 'Stay where I can see you!'

Mimi looked petulant then disappeared out of view. Honey shook her head at Bree and Sandy. 'Honestly,' she said, keeping her voice low. 'I sometimes think I'm the mother.'

'I know what you mean,' said Sandy. 'You're the one who's always got to pick things up.'

'Exactly! It's like my mum expects *me* to be the one who's in charge.'

'It's the same with my Gran. It's not that I mind, but sometimes it's a bit much...'

Bree was not listening. A bud of apprehension had begun to bloom inside her chest. The mist was slinking through the trees now, slipping in and out of the trunks like a cautious animal. She got up and strolled over to the hillock. From the top she saw Mimi bending to pick a handful of blue flowers. The twists of pearly mist had somehow worked their way up Bree's legs and she could feel a damp chill seeping through to her bones. 'This mist is getting thicker,' she muttered to herself, staring down at her feet, which were now completely concealed in the swirling fog.

Mimi turned and grinned, but something just beyond Bree's shoulder caught her eye. She dropped the bunch of flowers as the smile melted from her lips. Her whole body stiffened. Bree felt something hovering near the bare skin on her arms, nothing more than a breath, but enough to turn her blood to ice.

'What is it, Mimi?' she whispered, even though she knew without looking that something was behind her.

Mimi pointed a trembling finger and Bree turned slowly. A tall figure in a white sheet had appeared at her shoulder, floating above the ground. She took a step back and saw it carried a heavy sword.

Dunubas came running towards her, waving his arms and brandishing his dagger. 'Get out of the way! Run!' he was yelling.

Bree came to her senses with a sickening jolt as Mimi darted up and threw herself at her. The cloaked figure loomed over them, faceless and silent. Silver light glinted off the length of the sword as fleshless fingers curled around the handle. In its other hand was a coiled whip. The sleeves of its cloak looked like they had been dipped in blood and the hem was trimmed with bright red feathers.

As Sandy and Honey ran towards her, Bree could see the mist shifting and fading in their wake. It curled up from the ground in revolving columns like rain off a hot pavement. Honey, Sandy and Dunubas stopped at the foot of the hillock, their breaths rasping in their chests. Behind them more solid forms started to materialise until there was a barricade of cloaked guards standing shoulder to shoulder with one another. A faceless army armed with bows, whips, swords and shields.

'It's the Phasmitis!' yelled Sandy.

Mimi winced and let out a strangled yelp. Bree remembered the vision of her nightmare in the ball of secrets and pulled her closer.

'Get them away from me!' cried Mimi, in a voice choked with shock.

Below, the Phasmitis were poised and ready, six on either side of them. The first two dropped to their knees and thrust their terrifying swords forwards and up, forming an impassable phalanx. The silver tips of the burnished weapons glinted threateningly. Black and purple shields shone like giant beetles. The next four pulled arrows from their quivers and placed them onto the bows.

'Mimi!' screamed Honey from the foot of the hill.

Crows darted into the sky with a chorus of angry shrieks and this momentarily distracted the figure in front of Bree and Mimi. Sensing a chance, Bree grabbed Mimi's hand and they bolted down the slope.

'Run for the border!' Bree yelled to the others and they all sprinted across the open ground. No sooner had they started running than the sound of vibrating bow strings shuddered through the air. Arrows whistled past them, spearing the dirt and missing them by inches. Winrad led the way, his fur rippling as he ran. He was the first to cross the border, turning and barking his encouragement to the rest of them.

Stumbling over tree roots and clawing their way past dipping branches they could hear the approaching Phasmitis close on their heels. The border into Calvaria was within reach now but Bree's muscles were locking into painful spasms. She could almost feel the angry breath of the Phasmitis on the nape of her neck as she stumbled on, expecting an arrow through her back at any moment. Mimi was pulling her now, not the other way round. She let go of her hand, sure that she was only holding her back.

'Run, Mimi,' she panted, 'as fast as you can!'

Bree felt something wrap around her ankles and jerk her tight. The next thing she knew she was lying face down in a pile of wet leaves. Spitting and gagging she tried to get to her feet. She quickly realised that her ankles were bound by the end of a whip. The more she struggled, the more the leather bit into her skin. A scream bubbled up in her throat as she scrabbled around, her palms digging against the dirt for purchase. The Phasmitis were closing in. As if from a distance she heard herself scream. 'HELP!'

Sandy turned back and dived over. He tried to loosen the leather but it was wrapped too tightly. Suddenly a sword spun through the air, glinting in the sunlight.

'Duck, Sandy!' screamed Honey from the other side of the border. Sandy dodged it just in time, letting the sword slice through the branches and into the ground with a thud. He snatched the handle, and hoisted it up. Dunubas ran to Bree and flicked his dagger underneath the leather, slicing through it with a yank.

'Are you all righ–' he began, but the word was cut short when out of nowhere another whip slashed the air, coming down with an angry slash across his face.

Bree felt his strong hands taking her under the arms and lifting her from the ground. Sandy swung the sword above his head, holding the biggest Phasmitis back. A barrage of arrows flew between the trees, whizzing past his ears.

'Get the girls out of here!' he screamed at Dunubas, not daring to take his eyes away from the huge figure.

Dunubas pulled Bree but she would not budge. She wanted to run but the fear of turning her back on the cloaked warriors was too great. She stood there helpless, rooted to the spot.

'Come on,' commanded Dunubas, pulling on her arm. 'We're nearly there!'

She turned and ran as fast as her legs would allow, towards the shaft of brightness that split the clouds above. She kept running, all the time aware that the gap between her and the Phasmitis was closing. They weaved from side to side as arrows struck tree trunks. As she jumped over Strangledoor into Calvaria the wind died to a gentle breeze, leaving behind only the echo of terror. Birds chirped among the lush green leaves and the sun glittered on the forest floor.

Bree had expected Sandy to be running behind her, so shock stole her breath when she saw him pointing the sword at the cloaked figure. She started to cross back into Swarnbideah when Dunubas pulled her back.

'We have to help him!' she wailed, trying to struggle free.

'I can't let you go back,' hissed Dunubas. 'They'll kill you.'

'They'll kill Sandy!' she screamed, hot tears welling in her eyes.

'He has a weapon. You don't,' replied Dunubas without much conviction. 'He stands a chance. You wouldn't.'

Despairingly, Bree watched the Phasmitis closing around him like a pack of hungry wolves. The tall cloaked figure came at Sandy, slashing the air with its sword as if it was scything wheat. Sandy backed away. With nowhere to run, he swung his sword in great heedless sweeps. Arrows bounced off it as whips cracked the air.

Bree winced as the two swords collided. Sandy stumbled backwards, grimacing. He managed to stay on his feet, ducking under another arcing slice. The swords smashed together again with a terrible clang, flipping Sandy's from his hand. Bree watched in horror as the Phasmitis floated towards him, slicing the air with its sword. Sandy fell backwards to the ground, writhing. The long steel curved through the air towards him.

'Watch out, Sandy!' screamed Bree. Sandy

rolled out of the way just in time, his feet kicking in the dirt. He was struggling to get something out of his pocket with one hand and fighting to keep hold of his glasses with the other.

'What's he doing?' sobbed Bree.

'I can't look any more,' answered Honey softly.

If she had, she would have seen Sandy pull a small blue bottle from his pocket just as the cloaked figure lifted its sword above its head again.

'It's the magnetic powder!' gasped Bree.

Sandy plucked the stopper from the bottle with his teeth and poured the contents into his hand. The light caught the blade of the Phasmitis's sword and momentarily dazzled Bree. When her vision cleared she saw the metallic filings float into the air until they hung like a storm cloud. Sandy cowered under the shadow of the Phasmitis as it brought down its sword. But it didn't even reach halfway. The hovering magnetic blob sucked it out of its hand and in a flash the empty cloak fell to the ground.

'It worked!' squealed Honey, her bangles jangling as she jumped around.

Swords, shields and arrows shot out of the hands of the Phasmitis and stuck to the floating mass. Without their weapons, they collapsed, folding in on themselves like discarded sheets, and dropped lifelessly to the forest floor. Sandy stared up at the clutter of metal and wood that hung above his head then clambered to his feet and ran towards the others. He leapt across the border of tangled roots and landed with a soft thump beside Bree.

'Yippee!' squealed Mimi, clapping her hands excitedly.

'Thank goodness,' cried Bree, hugging him.

'Congratulations, you did it again,' laughed Honey.

Dunubas patted Sandy on the back. 'That was good thinking,' he said. 'You are a very brave young man.'

Sandy threw back his shoulders and straightened his glasses. He looked back at the floating globule as it dissolved to powder, raining the weapons like shrapnel onto the patch of ground below.

He chuckled and turned pink. 'Actually, I've never been so scared in all my life.'

'*Never?*' said Honey. 'What about that time we had to fight that giant spider?'

'You had to fight a giant spider?' cooed Mimi. 'Wait till I tell mum!'

'Don't you dare. What is it?' Mimi tugged on Honey's t-shirt and looked up at her pleadingly. She started dancing on the spot with her legs crossed. Honey smiled tenderly and took her sister by the hand, leading her to a cluster of bushes at the edge of the forest.

'Won't be long guys,' she said over her shoulder. 'Even heroes need to wee.'

Bree looked down at her ankles, braceleted by a thin red line where the whip had curled around them. She looked at Dunubas's cheek and flinched when she saw the long vivid weal.

'You two didn't come off too well,' Sandy said. 'At least I—' Something hit him in the back with a hollow thud. An astonished look creased his face and he fell forward. Bree dropped to her knees and cradled his limp body. Her hands came away sticky with blood.

'What? I don't understand!' she spluttered. 'I thought we were safe?'

'So did I,' cried Dunubas, searching the forest with wild eyes.

Winrad barked at Sandy, his way of telling him to get up. But Sandy did not move. His breathing was short and raspy and his eyes were wide with confusion and terror. Dunubas knelt beside them, saying things to Bree that she could not understand. After a short time Sandy stopped struggling and a tired resignation washed over him. Bree felt dizzy and weak.

'Sandy! Are you all right?' she heard herself say, but in her heart she already knew the answer.

A tear fell from the corner of Sandy's eye and seemed to take a lifetime to travel down his cheek.

Winrad stopped barking and lay down, his head cocked to the side.

'Help us, help us,' Bree begged Dunubas. Dunubas gently lifted the top half of Sandy's body off the ground and let out an anguished moan. Bree threw her hands up to her face and shrieked when she saw the shaft of an arrow poking out of his back, a circle of blood turning his T-shirt dark.

'No!' she screamed.

Dunubas gripped the wooden shaft and carefully pulled the arrow out of Sandy's body. He tossed it aside and shook his head grimly.

'It's too late for him now,' he whispered, his grey eyes glinting with tears.

'Please don't say that! Don't say that!' sobbed Bree, rocking herself backwards and forwards.

Sandy spluttered and reached out for Bree. He was desperately trying to tell her something. His breathing was laboured now and Bree wanted to tell him to stop trying to talk, to rest and everything would be all right but the words could not get past the lump at the back of her throat. Fear had bleached Sandy's face.

Gradually the fight left him. He took a rattling breath. Bree waited for him to breathe out he did not. Sandy's body seemed to lose all its bones, and become loose and fluid.

In the sudden silence even the birds stopped singing.

17.

LIFE AND DEATH

There was nothing dramatic about Sandy's death, just a short gasp between breath and no breath. For Bree, this felt like the end of her life too. Every day after this, for as long as she lived, would be another one without Sandy. Growing up without her dad was bad enough, but she knew this grief would never diminish, her heart had cracked and nothing could heal it.

'I'm so sorry,' breathed Dunubas, brushing his palm over Sandy's eyelids so they would not have to look into his glassy eyes. Winrad padded over and gently licked Sandy's cheek.

'Don't close his eyes yet. It can't be too late,' said Bree firmly. 'The book must be able to help us. It'll bring him back, won't it?' She pulled it from her pocket and stared at the locket, willing it to start throbbing. It lay motionlessly in her palm. 'Do something!' she screamed as she shook it and threw it to the ground. A terrible wave of black horror crashed over her. 'I'll have to tell his Gran he's dead. I'll have to tell her she'll never see him again.'

Dunubas tenderly placed his hand on Bree's shoulder. 'Every warrior has his time.'

Bree pulled away from him. 'How could *this* be his time? He hasn't even had a chance to live yet!'

Dunubas dropped his gaze and pulled Winrad closer, burying his face in his fur.

Bree's chest ached and her throat tightened until she could not swallow or breathe.

'You're supposed to help us!' she screamed at the book, pounding the ground with her fists.

Sandy's milky skin, which never tanned no matter how he tried, was growing more translucent by the second. His lips, frozen into a grimace of pain, had turned a winter blue.

'Sandy?' she whispered as though saying his name would bring him back. 'Sandy, remember that time in the cave, when I was covered in snow? I heard you saying you didn't want me to leave you. That's what made me wake up. Not Honey saying Adam was on the phone. It was you! I fought back because I can't leave you. But I'd rather leave you than have you leave me.'

Trembling, she smoothed down his ruffled hair. The blackest hair imaginable that never lay flat. Tears spilled from her eyes as she rocked his head back and forth, back and forth and she howled into the emptiness.

• • •

Dunubas watched quietly from the dappled shadows under the trees. Bree had laid her head on Sandy's chest and was sobbing. From behind him came the distant sound of Honey and Mimi's laughter. It jerked Bree from her grief as a fresh wave of pain washed over her. Everything seemed muddled, with her mind racing. She was overwhelmed with a sudden urge to shake Sandy's body and yell at him for leaving her like this. But when she looked at him it was clear his essence was gone. Everything that had made Sandy Greenfield special to her had evaporated. She covered her eyes until her palms collected pools of tears. She jumped to her feet. 'Honey! Honey!' she screamed, her voice echoing round the forest. Dunubas walked over and took hold of her shoulders to calm her. 'There's nothing she can do,' he said softly.

Bree struggled free from his grip. 'I've just remembered. Honey still has the Akeso Tears.'

A memory sparked on Dunubas's face. 'Wait here.' He ran into the woods, leaving Bree alone with the dog. She stole a glance at Sandy's body. It looked so small, like a bag of discarded rags. Her eyes flicked back to the trees and to her wild relief she saw Dunubas running back, waving his arms above his head. 'I have them!' he was yelling.

'Hurry up!' she screamed, tears of desperation running down her cheeks, 'we're running out of time.'

Honey came scurrying with him, her breath coming out in panicked sobs. 'What happened?' she shrieked in horror.

'Sandy is…' Bree knew she would have to say it. 'Dead.'

Honey gasped and Mimi screamed.

'He was hit by an arrow.'

Bree threw herself down beside Sandy and cradled his head in her hands. Against the black of his hair his skin seemed bloodless, white as marble. 'Please hold on,' she begged through her tears. 'There might be a way to save you. Come back!'

Dunubas skidded to a halt. He had pulled the stopper out of the horn-shaped bottle before he had even dropped to his knees. Spreading Sandy's lips apart, he tilted the bottle to his mouth. 'There isn't much left,' he said grimly. 'I don't know if it will be enough.'

Mimi stared at Sandy, her face torn into a ragged expression of disbelief. Her eyes darted between Bree and the pool of blood that was spreading from under his back.

'Oh Honey,' Bree sobbed. 'He's gone!' The words made it final and she felt her heart break all over again.

'But he can't be dead, not after all we've been through,' cried Honey, kneeling beside Bree. She fished the photograph from her satchel and flattened it out. Something horrible made her close her eyes and she let it fall to the ground. Mimi picked it up and stared, big tears balancing on her lower lids. 'Where is Sandy?'

'He's not in the picture any more,' said Honey with tears trickling down her cheek. 'Sandy's gone.'

Bree took it from her. She saw her own tangle of mousy hair, Honey making the silly rabbit ears with her fingers, and Mimi's gap-toothed grin. But there was no trace of Sandy. It was like he had never existed.

'That's the last of the Akeso Tears,' said Dunubas solemnly, placing the vial aside. 'I'm afraid we were too late.'

Bree rocked Sandy back and forth. He felt so cold and still. Honey crouched down and put her arms around Bree and the two girls silently wept.

Nobody spoke for a while. It was as if everybody was locked in their own world of grief. Bree's tears dropped onto Sandy's face and mingled with the Akeso Tears on his lips. She started when Mimi shrieked, 'Look!'

Mimi thrust the photograph under Bree's nose. 'Sandy's trainers are in the photo.'

'Show me,' gasped Bree and grabbed it out of Mimi's hand. Her eyes flicked between the photograph and Sandy's trainers.

'What's happening?' asked Dunubas, his steely eyes full of curiosity.

'It's Sandy's shoes,' Bree murmured. 'I'm sure they weren't in this a moment ago.'

'And the blood is drying up,' said Honey, touching the dark earth around Sandy's body. 'What's going on?'

As they watched the pool of blood shrank, disappearing before their eyes. When Bree looked back at the picture, Sandy's bodiless legs had grown out of his trainers. First his legs, then his waist. Bree swallowed and felt dizzy, her chest tight. 'He's coming back to us…' she breathed.

'Let me see,' said Honey, leaning in. They watched Sandy's face slowly form in the image like someone floating up from the depths of the sea; his stilted smile, the reflection on his glasses and his messy mop of hair in front of Honey's rabbit ear fingers. Bree grabbed his hand. 'He's warm!' she squealed. Winrad barked excitedly and Dunubas calmed him with a pat. Just at that, Sandy's lips parted and he suddenly coughed.

'Sandy!' cried Bree, dropping the photograph and throwing her arms around him. His eyelids fluttered and he groggily looked from Bree to Honey, then heaved himself onto his side, wincing.

'It's you!' laughed Honey, clapping her hands together so hard her bracelets jangled.

'Who were you expecting? What happened?' he muttered trying to sit up.

Bree and Honey sprang up from the ground and threw their arms around each other. They danced in circles, laughing and crying. Bree was happier than she had ever imagined possible. Dunubas picked Mimi up and threw her giggling into the air while Winrad barked and leaped after them.

'You're back!' sobbed Bree happily.

'W-here was I?' he asked with a puzzled look. His black hair gleamed in the sunlight and he no longer had hollow smudges under his eyes. Bree was buzzing with joy.

'Are you able to walk?' asked Dunubas, lifting him gently. Sandy straightened his glasses and looked at them all like they had gone bonkers.

'Why wouldn't I be?' he shrugged. 'Look, why are you all acting so weird?'

'It's the effect you have on us, Mr Greenfield,' said Honey and she grabbed him and planted a kiss on his cheek.

'Get off!' he laughed, turning pink.

Bree threw her arms around them both and said, 'Let's just say you never know how much something means to you until you think you'll lose it. I'll explain it all when we get back to mine.'

The sun blazed triumphantly through the trees and enclosed them in a hundred dazzling shades of green.

•••

They followed a winding route through the forest for some time until they caught the glint of water beyond the trees.

'Is it safe to drink?' asked Sandy, licking his lips. Dunubas smiled and nodded. 'You will never taste water as pure as it is in this lake.'

Mimi squealed and ran on ahead, with Honey chasing after her, keen to keep her in her sights at all times. Bree and Sandy followed them down a slope to the shallow beginnings of the lake. Nearby a small wooden raft bobbed at the shoreline.

Mimi and Honey were already on their knees, drinking from cupped hands, and beside them Winrad slurped greedily.

'Do help yourselves,' Dunubas chortled, reaching for his hip flask.

Bree walked to the edge, crunching over the wet shingle. At the water's edge the ground melted beneath her feet. The water was cobalt blue here, not turquoise as it had looked from the hot air balloon. Further out near the middle it sparkled where the current moved swiftly. She bent down and slurped from her hands. It was ice cold despite the boiling sun overhead and so clear that it hardly seemed there at all.

She stood for a moment and studied her wobbling reflection. When she knew no-one was looking she forced herself to smile, to make her dark eyes lose some of their seriousness. What she had always thought of as a plump, round face was actually a pale oval with defined cheekbones and a high forehead. Her hair was still bunched in a halo of frizz, but she noticed that in the sun it was not mousy brown but the colour of chestnuts. She barely recognised herself.

'We'll have to get to the other side,' said Dunubas as he filled his flask beside her.

Bree straightened and stared out across the shimmering water.

'Just tell me we are not crossing on that,' said Sandy, pointing at the flimsy-looking raft.

Dunubas shielded his eyes and nodded. 'It's no

beauty, but it'll do the job.'

'There is a slight problem,' said Honey.

'And that is?'

'There won't be enough room on that raft for five people and a dog.'

Dunubas looked down at Winrad. 'Away! Home, boy!'

Winrad barked once and bolted off towards the trees. Mimi let out a little whimper, prompting Honey to give her a reassuring squeeze.

'Will he find his way home without you?' asked Bree, watching as his furry tail disappeared from view.

'Of course!' said Dunubas, fixing his hip flask onto his belt. 'He knows the forest better than I do.'

Behind them they heard Honey's voice. 'Catch it, catch it!'

Bree turned back to the lake and noticed a shoal of bright fish was weaving close to the surface like shimmering metal filaments. A single silver fish had sprung out of the water and landed flapping at their feet. Mimi was bending to pick it up when Dunubas shouted, 'Don't touch it!'

'It's just a fish,' said Honey, as it flailed around. 'We have them in our world too you know.'

Dunubas poked the fish with a stick. It started to thrash even more violently.

'Please don't hurt it,' begged Bree, 'it's only little.'

At that moment the fish stopped thrashing and

crunched the end of the stick between two rows of razor sharp teeth. 'Whoa!' cried Honey, as everyone jumped back. Its teeth were ragged and within seconds had shredded the tip. 'Just as I thought…' said Dunubas, as the fish wriggled towards his bare toes. He hooked it up and tossed it over their heads back into the water.

'What was that?' asked Sandy, checking that no more had landed on the pebbles.

'A Rubekulah fish,' said Dunubas grimly. 'They hunt in groups but will eat each other if nothing better comes along.'

'Great,' said Honey flatly. 'And do they always jump?'

'No. They're getting hungry.'

• • •

While Dunubas held the raft steady Bree, Sandy, Honey and Mimi climbed aboard. Once he had taken a swig from his flask he wiped his brow and heaved himself onto it.

'Are you all ready?' he asked, lifting the oars.

'Let's just get this over with,' Honey muttered, making herself as small as she could. As soon as Dunubas punted the raft away from the shore he told them, 'Keep your hands by your sides. And don't touch the water.'

Bree's nerves flooded with an icy flush. Beside her, Mimi pressed as close to Honey as she could manage, her hands tucked tightly into her chest. Bree gripped the book in her pocket for reassurance, but felt more when Sandy put his hand on hers. Once they reached the middle of the lake, Dunubas stopped rowing to drink from his flask again. As the raft bobbed Bree tried not to focus on the silver cloud that flitted stealthily through the water and soaked up the warmth of the sun instead. Sandy sat stiffly and looked around them. 'I never thought I'd be homesick for Rockwell. But right now I'd rather be there,' he grumbled.

'We've not far to go,' Dunubas said as he picked up the oars again. The raft started to turn in slow circles. Bree looked at Dunubas as he strained to steer. 'Why are we spinning?' she asked.

'It's the current,' he said with concern. 'It's working against the raft…'

Water lapped over the sides as it started to dip. 'Hold tight!' yelled Honey.

'I can't control this anymore!'

'We're sinking,' exclaimed Sandy, his eyes flitting between Bree and the distant shoal of fish. Mimi started to cry and struggle but Honey held onto her firmly.

'We're too heavy for the raft,' Bree said, scanning the shoreline, which still felt like a long way off. She knew she would be able to swim the distance but the thought of the Rubekulah fish filled her with terror.

The raft started to spin out of control like a toy in a whirlpool of draining bathwater. Its timbers creaked and splintered as water lapped over the sides.

'What should we do?' Honey shrieked, searching Dunubas's face for guidance.

'There's only one thing I can do to help,' he replied resignedly. His expression had become remarkably calm, almost trancelike.

'Then do it! Now! We can't waste time.'

Without a word he handed Bree the oars and stood up. 'What are you doing?' she cried. 'You're going to topple the raft!'

And then it all happened very quickly: Bree locked eyes with Dunubas as a pillar of sunlight shrouded him in gold. He smiled at her once more and before it happened Bree somehow knew he was going to throw himself overboard. She reached out to grab him but before she could cry out he was falling backwards, tipping the raft for an instant one way, then the other, and he was gone.

'No!' Bree screamed. She threw down the oars and peered into the water, her thoughts whirling. There was no sign of him.

'What's he playing at?' cried Honey. 'He's insane if he thinks he can swim the rest from here.'

'He doesn't think that,' Bree murmured blinking down on her tears. 'Every warrior has his time…'

'What do you mean?'

'Bree, the Rubekulah fish are coming this way,' interrupted Sandy. When Bree looked around her heart skipped a beat. The pulsating mass of fish was speeding straight for the raft. They gleamed erratically as though emitting pulses of hungry power. Without Dunubas the raft had stopped taking on water and although they were still lop-sided it was clear they were no longer sinking. Sandy and Honey grabbed the oars and paddled the raft in the direction of the shore.

• • •

As soon as they reached the shallows Bree, Sandy, Honey and Mimi jumped off the raft and splashed towards the bank.

'Grab my hand,' Sandy told Bree when it looked for a moment that she might turn back to go after Dunubas.

'I can't believe he did that!' she cried, slipping up the muddy flats to the shore. 'Dunubas!' she called desperately, the single, wild word bouncing off the waves like a stone. She stared across the lake, looking for any sign of movement on the surface. But a deathly stillness had fallen, and with it a silence so complete that their breathing sounded startlingly loud and intrusive.

'We couldn't make it with him on board. I guess he knew that,' said Sandy.

'How long will it take him to swim over?' asked Mimi.

Sandy and Honey frowned at each other. 'Listen, Meems,' said Honey leaning down to her,

'I'm sorry to have to tell you this. But I don't think Dunubas will be coming back.'

'What? He's just going to stay in the water forever?' Mimi's lip trembled and she started to cry.

'Well, sort of…'

Bree turned on Honey. 'Don't say that! There still might be a chance to save him. Where are the Akeso tears?' She held out her hand impatiently. Honey took it gently and looked at her. 'Bree, we used them all for Sandy,' she whispered. 'There's nothing you can do.'

Bree searched Honey's face for something that would give her hope but all she could see was her resigned despair. Tears burned the back of her eyes and she sank to her knees and cried. She could no longer suppress the fury that welled in her chest.

'*WHY?*' she screamed at the top of her lungs, but nobody could answer her.

'It was his way of saving our lives,' said Sandy, staring gravely at the darkening lake. 'He must have known he was going to die.'

One of the oars was still floating, abandoned in the water. Bree watched it turn aimlessly in the tide. Sandy removed his glasses and rubbed his eyes.

'Guys, we need to get home,' said Honey softly. Bree gave a quick nod and started to follow her and Mimi towards the trees. She stopped and turned, and for a moment was certain she would catch a glimpse of Dunubas scrambling out of the water.

Sandy touched her shoulder. 'He's gone, Bree. We have to go on without him.' His words hung in the air, hard and final.

'That's the story of my life,' she replied.

• • •

Bree spent the next while wrapped in an angry silence. Although the sun beat down from a cloudless sky she was cold and wet and numb, and could not stop reliving the final moments with Dunubas. She accepted that he had made the ultimate sacrifice, and had put their lives before his own, but she wished she could have thanked him for his bravery and selflessness. Her heart ached when she remembered Nevidas waiting at home. Baby Pamela would never know her brave Uncle Dunubas. Bree knew only too well the grief of a bereaved mother and daughter, and hoped that they, like her and her own mother, would eventually find the strength to move on.

She pulled the book from her soggy pocket and examined the locket on the centre of the cover. With a sting of resentment she wondered why it had not come to life when she had needed it the most. What if the locket was dead and that was why it had not saved Dunubas? Could it still protect any of them? Would it still get them home? Her head was a whirlwind of questions.

As if reading her mind, Honey spoke in her ear and slipped a hand through the crook of her arm. 'There's only one wish left. Hopefully it is the one that will take us back to Rockwell.'

A sudden movement on the forest floor brought them to a stop. 'Did you feel that?' asked Bree.

'What was it?' said Honey.

'Another quake like the one when we arrived?' said Sandy, looking down at his feet. The ground had started to tremble as little lumps of earth mushroomed up, then exploded around them. Out of the holes they left poked overgrown insects with gleaming gold heads.

'Cockroaches!' cried Mimi. 'Hundreds of them!'

'And not just any old cockroaches,' gulped Sandy. 'They're huge. And look at their heads.'

Bree yelled at the others to run but as they turned they saw that the entire forest floor for as far as they could see was now teeming with them. The cockroaches scurried in blind circles and more were crawling up through the holes in the ground. Looking around, Bree spotted a fallen tree near the shore and decided to bolt towards it. 'This way. Follow me!' she cried, grabbing Sandy.

Bree, Sandy, Honey and Mimi climbed onto it as the giant insects surrounded them, filling the air with a low scream. Mimi threw her hands over her ears and started humming to block out the terrible sound.

'If we go back down there they'll crush us,' said

Sandy.

'At least they're not trying to climb up the tree,' said Bree. She felt for the outline of the book and willed it to come to life. Just then, the sun slid behind a cloud and the forest darkened. It felt like a warning. Mimi stopped humming and stared up through the trees at a sky that seemed to be on the brink of rain.

Suddenly the sound of thundering hooves rose above the terrible scream of the insects. Bree spun round to see four horses thundering towards the shoreline at the other side of the lake, great divots of earth flying out from their hooves. Their riders were wielding weapons, their cloaks billowing out behind them like rust-coloured sails. The rumbling of hooves came to an abrupt halt. The horses – one black, one red and two pale – shifted from one foot to the other like they were standing on hot coals. The red horse wore a dark blue breastplate with yellow flames in the centre. Its rider appeared to be the leader and was making gestures as he turned his horse to face the other riders.

'Look. The horses have snakes instead of tails,' said Bree incredulously.

'Snakes? Why does that sound familiar to me…?' said Honey.

Sandy said, 'Back in Dunubas's cottage. Don't you remember? He told us about that little girls' vision.'

'*Yes*,' said Bree, hearing Dunubas's voice again.

'Yahala's prophecy…'

'She saw horses with serpents for tails.'

'And infernos and floods and a plague of giant insects!' cried Honey. 'Well, we've done all that.'

'And she also saw many deaths,' said Bree darkly.

The agitated horses scraped the ground with their hooves. Their tails flicked and writhed sinuously, the serpent mouths gaping wide. The black horse edged nearer to the shore, its hooves crunching the shingle. It threw back its head and snorted. Mimi grabbed hold of Honey's hand.

'They're coming to get us and we're trapped,' she whimpered.

'It's okay Mimi,' said Honey soothingly. 'They can't ride their horses across the lake.'

They watched as the black horse turned and cantered around towards the others. The man on the red horse seemed to instructing the other riders. Honey squeezed Mimi tightly and kissed the top of her head.

'See, I told you,' she smiled, 'they're going away.'

The horseman tugged on the reins so the horse turned to face the lake again. Bree frowned. 'What are they doing?' she muttered.

The other three horses parted as the rider dug his heels into the black horse's flanks. Bree, Sandy, Honey and Mimi watched dumbfounded as it galloped full-pelt down the shore and launched itself over the water, the rider's cloak billowing out behind him like a sail.

'It's flying,' said Sandy in disbelief. 'It's going to make it over the lake!'

18.

The Door in the Sky

For a moment both the horse and rider hung suspended over the water before crashing down just short of the bank.

'You said they couldn't get to us,' cried Mimi but Honey was too terrified to respond.

The horse landed awkwardly, its hind legs in the water. It started to kick and panic, black eyes staring and froth flicking from its mouth. It tried to gain a footing but the mud was slippery and it slid backwards. The rider clung to its thick mane, his other hand waving the sword around his head.

'What if they make it up the embankment?' said Honey, her voice spiralling.

'If they do, they'll still have to get through all these bugs,' said Bree.

The horse managed to make it to the top of the slope but to everyone's relief it slid back down again.

'It's getting tired,' said Sandy. With one last burst of effort, it took a run at the slope. The rider fell backwards out of the saddle, catching his foot in the stirrup. He swung there, his long cloak covering his head while the horse skidded down the embankment and landed in the water.

'Look!' said Sandy. 'Over there!'

Bree followed his finger to a spot at the centre of the lake where a blurred shape was twisting rapidly through the water. Her eyes returned to the exhausted horse, flailing around and trying to right itself. Dread and nausea flared in the pit of her stomach as she realised what was about to happen. 'The Rubekulah fish. Hide Mimi's eyes,' she whispered to Honey.

The rider tried to pull himself back up into the saddle but the horse collapsed sideways and landed on top of him, crushing him under the water and pinning him there. Its legs churned in the air, its dark eyes bulging. The serpent tail lay across the water like a piece of old rope.

'He's going to drown,' hissed Honey, pulling Mimi close and covering her face.

The shoal of deadly fish moved like a silvery shadow under the surface of the water, heading straight for the horse. It tried one last time to scramble up the embankment but it seemed too exhausted. Suddenly the fish pounced out of the water like an explosion of silver darts, overpowering the creature and dragging it under.

'It's awful,' said Bree.

'I can't look,' whimpered Honey, turning away.

The horse disappeared in a wild flurry of teeth and scales. A dark red stain spread out through the water and all went quiet. Bree felt the bile rise in her throat and she turned her head to the side.

'Where's the man gone?' said Sandy, his face turning a nasty shade of green. Bree did not want to look but she stole the briefest glance, enough for her to see the rust-coloured cloak floating across the surface of the lake, with nothing filling it. Mimi pulled away from Honey's grip and stared at the red-tinged water that lapped at the shoreline.

'The fish ate them!' she squealed, pressing her hand over her mouth.

'Saddle and everything...' gulped Sandy.

'At least we're safe now,' Bree said.

'No we're not,' said Honey, staring across to the other side of the lake. 'There's still the other three.'

The man on the red horse turned to the other two and shook his head slowly. Despite the fact he was concealed within a hooded cloak, it was clear to see he was huge, twice the size and width of the two men on the paler horses. He seemed to overpower the massive creature beneath him, his feet almost dragging along the ground. It might have looked comical had it not been for that lethal weapon in his hand.

'He doesn't look very happy,' said Bree, her voice breaking. As she spoke, the red horse reared up and the giant man raised his sword high above his head. He roared at the top of his lungs, a sound that seemed to split open the sky. Mimi covered her ears in fright. The bellow stopped abruptly and he cantered away, turning back when he reached the fringe of trees. The horse eyed the water nervously, snorting out through flared nostrils.

'Surely he won't try and do the same thing?' said Honey, trying to hold Mimi still. She struggled away from Honey. 'He's going to come now!'

'There's no way he'll make it over, Mimi,' Bree tried. 'Not unless that horse has wings.'

The rider dug his heels into the horse's ribs and screamed at the top of his lungs.

'Looks like he's going to give it a try anyway,' said Sandy.

'He'll kill us all!' sobbed Mimi, throwing herself into Honey's arms.

'We have to get out of here,' hissed Honey, grabbing onto Bree's sleeve. 'NOW!'

Bree flinched but did not take her eyes off the red horse. The horseman had lifted his sword high, the white sun glancing off the metal like a mirror. He brought it down, smacking the flat part of it against the horse's flank. The creature reared and span around, kicking its hind legs out in protest. Its serpent tail writhed and hissed angrily, bearing two white fangs.

'I know horses,' said Honey. 'You can't make them do something they don't want to do.'

'Even horses with tails like those?' asked Sandy dubiously.

'Apparently so,' shrugged Honey, nodding towards the horse as it bucked and reared, refusing to obey orders. After a few attempts the horseman gave up. He tugged violently on the reins and his horse spun around and bolted off into the trees. The other two men looked at Bree, Honey, Sandy and Mimi, then at each other, before turning and galloping after their leader. When the dust settled Bree allowed herself a small sigh of relief.

'Don't relax just yet,' said Honey. 'We still need the biggest bug spray in the world to get past the million giant cockroaches.'

'I've got an idea,' said Mimi, tugging Honey's sleeve. Honey glanced down at her little sister and smiled tightly. 'Oh Meems, I don't think anything will help at the moment.'

Mimi eyed Honey's satchel. 'Do you still have the lavender you used for Bree's burn?' she asked.

Honey raised her eyebrows as a slow smile spread across her face. 'Of course!' she laughed, her hand already inside her satchel. 'Dad uses it all the time to chase away bugs.'

'Are they giant bugs with gold heads?' gulped Sandy, jabbing his thumb towards the wriggling mass of cockroaches below them. Honey ignored him and carefully plucked the buds from their stem.

'I have a little bit of lavender too,' said Bree, pulling the flowers from her pocket. 'They're a bit crushed but there's a good handful of them.'

'We don't know if it will work yet,' said Honey, taking a tiny pinch and throwing it down among the cockroaches. They immediately panicked and scurried away, creating a clear patch of ground.

'I'd say that's a result!' laughed Sandy, disbelievingly.

'Mimi, you are a star,' whooped Honey, kissing her sister on the cheek. Mimi blushed and smiled coyly.

'If we use the buds sparingly,' said Bree, 'we should be able to clear a path through them.'

'They really hate it,' said Sandy with a satisfied grin. 'Look! Some of them are going back down into their holes!' A few of the giant insects hurried away from the small pile of flowers, scuttling in all directions and burrowing into the soft soil.

'I'm going down,' said Bree, finding a foothold in the moss-covered trunk. She threw another little handful of lavender buds sending more of the cockroaches away, revealing more of the forest floor.

'I can see a footpath,' Honey said, kicking away a stray cockroach. 'We'll be out of here in no time.'

Every few steps, Bree and Honey threw down some more lavender buds to keep the giant insects at bay. By the time they reached the narrow path most of them had disappeared.

The track was overgrown and only wide enough to allow them to walk in single file. Branches and roots jutted out from the dense thicket on either side but soon gave way to an open earth track that wound up the lower slopes of a mountain. The canopy of leaves had gone and now all that hung above them was the wide sky.

After half an hour of steep hiking Bree's legs ached so it was a relief when the slope finally levelled out to a patch of stony ground. On one side was a barren stretch of dusty land and to the other was an almost vertical drop down the side of the mountain.

'Let's stop here for a minute,' panted Bree, seeing the path rise sharply before disappearing around the side of the mountain.

'When are we going home?' groaned Mimi.

'Not long now,' answered Bree, although she had no idea when and how they were going to get back to Rockwell. Shielding their eyes against the glare of the sun they looked down into the deep valley.

'Woah,' said Sandy, noticing the clouds below them. 'We're higher than I thought.'

'We can see the Realm of the Lost from here,' Bree said, pointing at an ocean of green treetops swaying in the breeze.

'I don't suppose you can see Rockwell Tower block too?' asked Honey.

Bree glanced back at her and rolled her eyes wearily. 'If only,' she sighed. 'It's funny. I've spent so much of my life wishing I could get away from Rockwell and now I'd give anything to get back there.'

Far in the distance, through a bank of black clouds above a curtain of rain was Castle Zarcalat, standing stark and grim on top of its jagged rock. Smoke still rose from it in milk-white columns.

Bree dropped her gaze and studied the landscape below. A long path wound its way round the base of the mountain, nothing more than a ribbon of brown interwoven through the carpet of green. It was then that Bree felt a familiar prickling at the nape of her neck, a sense of something approaching rather than a vision. She turned her head to the right and her eyes were drawn towards a swirling cloud of dust, travelling fast along the snaking path. She could not make sense of what it was until she became aware of a sound. Hooves thumping in the dirt. Bree followed the line of the road with her eyes and saw that it led all the way up the side of the mountain. All the way up to where they were standing!

'Okay, before I tell you this, promise me you won't panic,' she said as calmly as she could.

Sandy jumped up from the ground. 'Why?' he yelled.

'I said *don't* panic!' cried Bree, searching their surroundings for somewhere to hide.

'What is it?' said Honey. 'What have you seen?'

Bree turned and looked down. The dust cloud was getting close enough now for the ground to start rumbling under their feet. 'It's the horsemen,' she said, trying to stay calm. 'They've spotted us and are catching up.'

From the cloud of swirling dust appeared three horses, one red and two pale with cloaked figures on their backs. They were already halfway up the mountain.

'I disagree with you, Bree,' said Honey. 'I'd say this is a very good time indeed to panic. Run!' She grabbed Mimi and started to run with her up the steep path.

'Come on!' Sandy shouted at Bree as he made off into a sprint.

'There's no time!' screamed Bree. 'We won't be able to outrun them.'

Honey stopped in her tracks and stared hopelessly at Bree. Mimi's eyes grew as wide as saucers as her eyes fixed on a plume of dust appearing on the brow of the hill.

'She's right. We can't outrun them this time. We're trapped,' said Sandy, his eyes flitting between Bree and Honey. The pounding of hooves seemed to match the speed of Bree's heart as she tried to think what to do.

'Let's hide behind these rocks,' Mimi said, breaking into a run.

'Mimi, are you crazy?' screeched Honey. 'They're sure to find us there!'

'Let's go after her. We've no other option,' said Bree, but her words were drowned out by the thundering crash of hooves. They all ran behind the cluster of broken rocks, keeping low and quiet. Bree sank to the ground and tried to calm her racing pulse. Honey pulled Mimi close and clapped her hand over her sister's mouth. 'Stay very quiet,' she whispered. 'Not a sound.'

Honey started raking around inside her satchel.

'Shh…' hissed Sandy, nudging her in the ribs.

Honey plucked out a hand mirror. 'Now we'll be able to see them without them seeing us,' she whispered, angling it carefully around the rocks.

The hoof beats were deafening now. The horses would be coming over the hill at any moment. Bree pressed her back against the rock and wondered if things could possibly get any worse. She signalled for Honey to give her the mirror, which she tilted until she could see a reflection of the dirt path. The horses stopped right beside the rocks.

'They're here...' she rasped, fighting down the waves of panic.

They were so close that Bree heard the horses' breaths wheezing in their chests. The three men were talking but she could not make out what they were saying. In the mirror she could see the back of the red horse. For a heart-stopping moment she locked eyes with the serpent tail in the reflection. She slid back the mirror and held her breath. Honey nudged her and looked at her questioningly, but Bree shook her head and put her finger to her lips. Honey nodded, her eyes widening. Bree shook her finger at her in fear she was about to say something. Then she realised Honey's expression had changed from confusion to terror. Her eyes had fastened on something over Bree's shoulder. When Bree whipped her head around, she opened her mouth to shriek. Curling around the rock was the serpent head, its tongue flickering over its face. She threw up her hand to catch her horrified gasp before it left her lips. The snake, only inches from her face, stared at her. Bree was not sure whether to run or stay where she was. If she panicked now, the men would find them and it would all be over. She started to shake as she watched the snake open its mouth wide and pull back. It was about to lunge at her when it was suddenly yanked away. In the mirror, Bree saw the horse walk away towards the other two standing at the edge of the mountain. Bree noticed the footprints she and the others had left in the dry earth and she hoped the men did not look down.

The rider on the red horse pushed back his hood to reveal a round ruddy face. Although his head was as bald as an egg he had a bushy ginger beard and shaggy eyebrows to match. He drew his sword from its scabbard and stood up in the stirrups, craning his thick head to look for any sign of Bree and the others. Bree pulled back into the shadows and signalled for everyone to keep quiet.

After a moment she edged the mirror back out around the rock. A jolt of terror pulsed through her body. The bearded man was so close she could almost count the hairs in his enormous nostrils. For a moment his broad frame blotted out the sun. In the small circle of the mirror, Bree got a better look at the other two men. Both were hooded, one holding an axe and the other wielding a long curved scythe. Bree could feel her heart rattling like a drum beneath her ribs.

'They're here somewhere,' growled the giant, his teeth bared in a snarl. 'I can smell 'em. Hunt them out like rats, men.'

At that moment Bree flinched as she felt the vibration of the book against her hip. She elbowed Honey and mouthed the words '*Last wish!*'

A bright light burst above them. Bree looked up through half shut eyes to see a doorway opening in the sky. In the mirror she could see the men shielding their faces and staring up at it. Their horses were whickering and shying away. Thinking quickly, Bree angled the mirror so that it caught the light and bounced a brilliant rectangle on the muzzle of the white horse. She tilted it until the beam moved up into its eyes. The horse whinnied and tried to move away, tossing its head from side to side and backing off the path, towards the edge. The rider yelled and tugged the reins, kicking hard but the white horse edged backwards, and with a sudden cry from all three men, its hind legs slipped over the edge. The rider threw away his scythe and tried to throw himself out of the saddle but it was too late. In the blink of an eye the horse and the man vanished, leaving behind nothing but a puff of dust and the echo of a cry.

'One down, two to go,' Bree whispered as she watched the other two men race over to peer down. Once their backs were turned Bree pulled the book from her pocket and turned to the last page. The paper had already turned to glass as the words stood out clear and bold:

STRIPES AND PATTERNS GRACE THE GROUND,
YOU'LL SEE THEM WHEN YOU TURN AROUND.
A THING OF BEAUTY ON THE FLOOR,
A CARPET THAT YOU'VE SEEN BEFORE.
CLIMB ABOARD AND FLOAT UP HIGH,
A MAGIC JOURNEY TO THE SKY.

'Looks like our ride has shown up,' said Sandy under his breath. Bree turned her head and saw a large carpet hovering close by, a few inches above the ground.

'Where did that come from?' she said.

'It looks like…I think it is…' whispered Honey with a smile. 'It's the rug from the Witch Hammamalis's tent!'

She stared at it disbelievingly. Bree closed the book and pushed it back into her pocket, the locket still throbbing like a heartbeat. She glanced in the mirror to check the two men were still looking over the edge of the drop then turned to the others.

'Right, we have to move. Now!' she whispered. 'We don't have much time.'

'We're not g-getting on th-that are we?' stammered Mimi.

'Trust me,' smiled Honey, 'a flying carpet is nothing compared to some of the things we've travelled on.'

They crawled along the ground, keeping low behind the rocks. Mimi climbed on first, followed by Sandy and then Honey. They spaced themselves evenly so the carpet would be well balanced.

'It's just like being on the raft again,' groaned Mimi as it bobbed in the current of air.

Bree was about to climb on when a bear-like roar stopped her in her tracks. 'There they are!' bellowed the bearded man. She turned just in time to see the smaller man hurl his axe. Its shining blade spun through the air, she ducked and it missed her head by a fraction of an inch, slamming into the dirt beside her.

'Hurry up!' shouted Sandy, holding his hand out for her. As he did, Honey leaned over the side of the carpet, picked up a rock, and hurled it at the horsemen. She missed them but struck the white horse in the rump. It reared and thrashed, throwing its rider out of the saddle.

'Bree!' screamed Sandy, jerking her from her terror, 'come on!'

She reached out to take his hand when the carpet suddenly rose up above her head, too high for her to reach. She turned back to the men. The white horse was still bucking wildly, its hooves missing the man on the ground by inches. With a final disgruntled neigh, it bolted, galloping off down the hill and dragging its rider with it. The bearded giant roared ferociously at Bree and swung his sword above his head. Startled, his horse reared and stepped backwards. He slid the weapon back into its scabbard and tightened his grip on the reins. Bree's eyes were drawn to the yellow flames at the centre of the horse's breastplate. They seemed to come alive, twisting and writhing until they formed a word. Reinor.

Bree had no idea what this meant and no time to think about it, as the carpet whooshed up behind her.

'Jump on!' yelled Honey as the rug darted erratically above the ground.

'I will if you stop moving it!' said Bree as she ran after it.

'We're not controlling it!' cried Sandy, gripping one of the corners.

She threw herself at it but she was too slow. The rider on the red horse grabbed her hair and whipped her off her feet. The carpet dived off, its corners flapping like the wings of some prehistoric bird.

The horse skidded to a halt. Bree hung helplessly, pain stabbing her scalp as she felt the hair tearing from its roots. 'Let me go!' she screamed as she pounded her fists against the man's hand. Her scalp pulsed in time with the vibrations from the book in her pocket. She flailed around but it was no use; his grip was as strong as the roots of a well established tree.

A few feet away the carpet dropped to the ground. Sandy reached out and grabbed something before they rose up again. The carpet turned and flew straight at them.

'Duck!' screamed Sandy as they flew over the horse.

The axe cut past Bree's shoulder by an inch, the wooden handle striking the rider between his eyes with a loud crack. He yelped and let go of Bree. She jumped back up and ran after the carpet as it veered across the mountain path. It swooped and dived in low curves while Honey reached over the side to try and pull her up. Bree raced after it, faster and faster as it zigzagged past the boulders and sailed over the edge of the cliff.

'No!' she screamed, watching it fly off, over the valley through flowing swirls of cloud, until it was nothing more than a speck of dust in the distance. She felt her legs buckle but somehow managed to stay on her feet. Her mind was racing with thoughts of escape, even though in her heart she knew there would be no chance of getting away. When she turned to face the horseman cold fear wrapped itself around her. His dreadful gaze, intense and hungry, settled on her. He ran his tongue over his lips and fingered the handle of his sword. The horse's serpent tail whipped from side to side.

'What are you going to do?' she said.

'I'll give you a choice,' he smiled, the horse cantering towards her. 'Either you jump, or I take you prisoner. Which is it to be?'

The wind whistled in her ears. She clenched her

fists and tried to imagine what Sandy and Honey would tell her to do.

'Jump!' she imagined Sandy shouting.

'Jump!' she thought she heard Honey screaming.

She opened her eyes to see the smirk slip from the rider's face. Out of the corner of her eye she caught a glimpse of a red and orange blur speeding towards them like a firebolt.

'*Jump!*' Sandy and Honey shouted again.

She turned and ran. The rider raised his sword and let out a roar that sent his horse into a panic. With the sound of hooves thundering behind her, she ran as fast as her legs would carry her. She saw the carpet arc round over the precipice as she sped towards the sheer drop. Below was a thousand feet of empty air. When she closed her eyes she saw her mother, saw Annie Hooten, saw Sandy and Honey, saw even Bustopher her cat, and for a second before the ground fell away she realised her life would have been nothing at all without the trust she had in their love.

Bree spread her arms out and fell off the mountain into absolute silence.

Crash!

Fingers, arms, legs, blonde hair, and orange and red tufts of wool smashed in a blur before her eyes. In a dizzying moment Bree realised Sandy was grinning at her with tears in his eyes, Honey was embracing her, and Mimi was whooping with joy. The carpet spiralled through the air, rising up then swooping low through the clouds, brushing the tree tops.

'Are you all right, Bree?' asked Honey.

'Yes!' she laughed, clutching the side of the carpet tightly. 'I'm more than okay thanks to you guys.' Bree looked back to see the horseman galloping down the side of the mountain, his rust-coloured cloak flapping out behind him.

'And don't worry,' shouted Sandy, tilting his body left and right, 'I've worked out how to steer this thing!'

'Good,' said Honey, pointing towards the outline of Castle Zarcalat, 'because we don't want to end up back there!'

'I think it's had enough of us for now,' smiled Bree. 'Rockwell here we come!'

'We have a slight problem though,' Honey whispered in Bree's ear. 'I love my sister and I almost died trying to save her, but there is no way she'll be able to keep this a secret.'

'What are we going to do?' asked Bree.

'I already thought of that,' said Honey with a wink. She pulled a tissue from her satchel and unfolded it carefully.

'Sandy if you go any higher I'm going to tell your Gran!' complained Mimi, her face turning a strange shade of green.

'Come over here sis,' said Honey reassuringly. 'You hold onto me.' Mimi edged across and Honey put her arm around her, dropping a Slumber Bud down the collar of Mimi's T-shirt as she did. She squeezed her little sister close and there was a muffled crack. A wisp of smoke wreathed up into the air, surrounding Mimi's head with a halo of blue.

'What was—' Mimi tried to finish the sentence but the words seemed to turn to dust in her mouth. Bree watched for a reaction. Within two seconds Mimi's eyes were closed.

'Sweet dreams, little sis,' whispered Honey as she made Mimi comfortable.

'Do you think she'll be all right?' asked Sandy.

Honey pushed a loose strand of hair away from her face and stared down lovingly at her sister. 'Remember what Witch Hammamalis told us about the Slumber Buds?' she said.

A memory stirred at the back of Bree's mind.

'They make you sleep really deeply and wipe out the horrors in your mind,' she said.

'On waking,' Sandy quoted Hammamalis, 'bad memories evaporate like smoke on the breeze.'

'Exactly,' said Honey, 'so, hopefully when Mimi wakes up she will have forgotten everything.'

'I really hope so,' said Bree. 'There will be enough awkward questions just from finding her…'

Sandy tilted the carpet higher, and as Honey stroked Mimi's hair tenderly he flew them towards the door in the sky.

19.

Perfect Timing

The air pulsed with energy as they soared upwards, through clouds that seemed to flare and flicker with colour. Flashes of lightning and peals of thunder buffeted the carpet as it spiralled towards the blazing light.

'We're headed straight for the doorway,' yelled Sandy, pointing at it blazing bright white-blue against the concrete-coloured sky.

'Hold on tight to each other!' shrieked Bree. With Mimi between them, Bree, Honey and Sandy kneeled down and linked arms.

'I can't look into the light,' screamed Honey, shielding her face.

Bree was about to reply when the air around them exploded into a million shards, enveloping everything in a white radiance. A torrent of roars and crashes tangled Bree's senses and made it feel like there was a hurricane churning inside her head. Hot air blasted over her body sending a million tiny sparks to prickle her arms like electric currents.

Bree knew the locket was still pulsing but when she tried to reach for her pocket her limbs felt like they belonged to someone else. Her arms were heavy and loose and for a second she was terrified she was going to let go of the others. She clenched her eyes shut and tried to scream but the air was sucked from her mouth in a noiseless gasp. In an instant the air shimmered, the way it does in a dream, before it burst apart in an explosion of stars and for a sickening second Bree felt she was going to fall, or that she was already falling.

Before Bree could panic everything became calm. She felt a soft warm breeze blowing over her hair and a rush of scents: cut grass, flowers, and fresh air. She opened her eyes very slowly, the flash of colours still burning in her head. It took a couple of seconds for her to get her bearings.

'My head…' she groaned, rubbing her temples, 'I feel like I've been inside a washing machine.'

Honey, her ponytail blowing up in wisps around her face, shook Bree's shoulder. 'Snap out of it—we're flying over Rockwell. On an *actual magic flying carpet!* Can you believe this?'

Bree could not help but laugh. 'I know! Hello home!'

'Look, there's Auriel Forest down below!'

Sandy, straightening his skewed glasses, struggled into a sitting position and then sprang up excitedly. 'And there's the War Memorial clock where you met Adam.'

'It says it's only ten past three,' noted Bree. 'So, we've been away for just under four hours?'

'What? Is that all?' squealed Honey. 'It feels like it's been weeks since we were home!'

When Bree saw the towers of the Rockwell Estate loom up in the distance her heart swelled with relief. 'Coming in to land, people,' she smiled, resting her hand on the throbbing shape of the book. 'We *actually* made it!'

Honey scrabbled in her bag for her phone. 'This calls for one last holiday snap.' Instinctively, Bree, Honey and Sandy leaned their heads together and beamed as Honey held the phone at arm's length to get them and the distant horizon in shot.

'We're awesome,' she decided, looking at the photo on the screen. 'And I don't just mean in this picture.'

'Let's just get this thing landed before we go celebrating,' said Sandy, shifting his weight from left to right. The carpet responded to his movements, lifting and dipping, taking them home.

Bree looked over her shoulder to see the grey rectangle, stark against the perfect blue of the summer sky, shifting and shrinking. It was closing over like a zip being pulled.

'The door in the sky is disappearing,' she said, pulling the book from her pocket.

'Great,' said Honey, checking on Mimi. 'Let it stay that way.'

The locket throbbed bright and steady but the pages were already stuck back together, telling Bree that the end of their mission was near. She smiled down at Mimi, curled up in a ball, her hair half obscuring her face. She was breathing deeply and Bree was sure she could see the hint of a smile on her lips.

'That was one bumpy ride, sis,' whispered Honey, tucking a loose strand of Mimi's hair behind her ear. 'And I'm glad you slept through it.'

'I guess she'll sleep for a little while yet,' said Bree.

'I know this sounds silly, Bree,' Honey said with a sudden sadness creeping into her expression, 'but this is the first time I've really looked at Mimi properly.' Honey struggled to explain but Bree already thought she knew what she meant. 'I don't think I've ever really seen her properly before,' Honey continued. 'Her freckles, her sweet shyness, the way her nose wrinkles when she sleeps. I've been such a cow to her.'

'Look at it this way. At least you can make up for lost time,' said Bree, 'not everyone gets a second chance to put things right.'

Honey nodded gratefully and made to slip her phone back in her bag, but as she did she checked it again and thumbed a few buttons.

'We're back in signal range I guess. There's a text. No way. It's from *Adam!*'

'No it isn't. Is it? What does it say?' said Bree, trying not to smile.

Honey's mouth fell open and she giggled.

'Let me see!' laughed Bree, turning the phone to read it:

'Hey—did you remember to give Bree my number? Thx A'

'W-what is he saying?' said Sandy.

'*Someone* wants to hear from Miss McCready here,' replied Honey.

'Are you going to phone him?' he asked without taking his eyes off a distant spot on the horizon. Bree shifted under their scrutiny. She bit down on her bottom lip and shrugged shyly.

'You could just text him back?' Honey suggested gently.

'I guess he's probably going to Alice Renshaw's party anyway,' muttered Sandy, picking at a loose thread in the carpet.

'Yeah, he probably is…' agreed Bree, desperate for a change in the subject. 'Oh look, there's Rockwell Tower.'

'You can change the subject all you like, Bree McCready,' Honey whispered. 'But if you don't text him, I'm going to, and I'm going to pretend it's you.'

'You wouldn't!' laughed Bree.

'There's only one way to stop me. Do it yourself.'

'Guys, we're nearly home!' interrupted Sandy as they swooped over Ramthorpe Junior School. 'I'm going to try and land on the rooftop garden.'

'Can you imagine if Mr Flangelberry looked up right now?' giggled Honey. 'He'll think he's seeing things!'

'Bree, I hope your mum hasn't decided to do a spot of sunbathing on the roof,' Sandy said, half laughing.

'Boy, do we have a lot of explaining to do if she is…'

'Mum definitely won't be sunbathing,' said Bree. 'Not if she still thinks Mimi is missing. She'll be too busy making cups of tea and trying to keep everyone's spirits up.'

'That's a point. I hope there's some honey fruit cake left,' said Sandy. 'I'm running on empty.'

'Flying on empty more like,' giggled Honey.

The carpet slowed as they circled Guinessberry Heights. It dived and curved but the movements were so gentle that nobody worried about being thrown off. The flying rug seemed to know where it was going. At last they were hovering a few feet above the rooftop garden.

'There's Bustopher, fast asleep!' smiled Bree, happy to see a familiar friend.

The carpet glided to a soft bump, so gentle that Bustopher did not stir. Stretched out in a patch of sunlight, his paws twitched as he chased rabbits through the grass in a dream.

Between them they helped to lift Mimi off the carpet and onto the wooden bench that sat in the shade of a parasol. She did not stir. Bustopher opened one eye lazily and rolled onto his side, feigning disinterest. 'Hello handsome,' said Bree, stroking his head. He lifted his chin in response and started purring like a well-oiled motor.

'How the heck did he get up here anyway?' said Sandy.

'Remember?' said Bree with a smile and a wink.

'Cats are mysterious, independent and unfathomable.'

'That's for sure,' he said.

'Do you think we can keep this?' said Honey, kneeling down to roll up the carpet. As she did, a gust of wind unfurled it and whipped it from her hands. It was enough to tip her off balance and throw her backwards, to land on her bottom with an undignified whump. Bree and Sandy ran over and helped her up.

'What on earth is it doing?' Honey said, as the carpet flapped above their heads like a panicked bird. It shot into the air and spun around until all the individual colours blurred into one big windmill of red and orange. They watched it rise into the blue sky like a flaming ember from a dying fire. It floated over the city until it got so far away that it became almost impossible to see. Soon, it had disappeared altogether.

'Does that answer your question?' asked Sandy.

'Oh well, I suppose that means I'll be walking home then,' she chirped as she removed her satchel and tossed it to the ground.

The wind died to a secret whisper and the throbbing at Bree's hip stopped abruptly. Honey brushed the hair away from her face and shrugged questioningly. Bree pulled the book out of her pocket and looked down at the locket. 'It's over,' she said, feeling a rush of different emotions all at once.

'Well, thank goodness for that,' cried Sandy.

'We still need to take it back to Ramthorpe Junior though,' said Bree, gently prising the locket from the sunken hole. 'And put it back where it belongs.'

She laid the book down on the bench where Mimi continued to sleep peacefully. Snapping the two halves of the locket apart, she handed Honey hers and carefully threaded the other onto her chain.

'Could you help me fasten this please?' she asked Honey, lifting her hair away from her neck. Honey fastened the clip on Bree's necklace. The little gold half-heart fell neatly into the hollow of her neck, glinting in the sun.

'I hope Mimi has learned her lesson not to go rummaging around my stuff,' said Honey.

'With any luck she won't even remember seeing the locket,' said Bree, stroking her half-heart affectionately.

'I wonder how long she'll sleep?' asked Sandy, as if reading Bree's thoughts.

Honey shrugged loosely. 'Meems can sleep for days at the best of times,' she said, putting her half-heart into her trouser pocket, 'but I think we should let my folks know she's okay.'

'They're going to be so relieved,' Bree nodded.

'You can say that again!' laughed Honey, skipping over to the ladder.

Somewhere in the distance the sky grumbled ominously. Despite the clammy heat, Bree felt goose bumps rise all over her body.

'Bree, can you stay up here with Mimi?' said Honey, tugging Sandy's arm. 'And we'll go downstairs and tell everyone the good news.'

She agreed as Sandy started to climb down the ladder.

'I hope everyone's still there and they haven't all gone home,' said Bree.

'And risk missing your mum's honey fruit cake? Never!' smiled Honey, climbing after Sandy.

'Be quick,' Bree said, looking up into a sky full of fat purple clouds, 'it looks like it's going to rain.'

But Honey had already disappeared down the ladder.

• • •

Creeping from the horizon, dark clouds threw a veil over Rockwell, turning the air as thick and heavy as syrup. Shortly after Honey and Sandy left, Bustopher jumped to his feet, suddenly alert, and started pacing restlessly. 'Oh Bustopher,' smiled Bree, picking him up, 'always a bit slow to catch on.' She rubbed his head to soothe him. 'But Honey and Sandy will be back shortly,' she said as the first fat drops of rain blotched the floor with dark stains. It was warm rain, heated by the thunder that brought with it the smell of hot, damp concrete. Bree thought it tasted metallic.

It should have felt like a relief after the pressing heat but it made her shudder. Bree gathered up the cat and hurried over to the parasol as the sky opened and rain began to drum in the plant pots and gutters. Under it, on the bench, stretched Mimi peacefully, her chest rising and falling in steady breaths. Bustopher pressed himself into Bree, his soft fur studded with tiny raindrops that glistened like diamonds.

'What's taking your sister so long…?' Bree muttered to Mimi as she watched the rain bounce off the concrete. A violent gust of wind tossed the wind chimes against the walls in a shriek of jangled notes. With a hiss Bustopher leaped out of her arms and scurried under one of the picnic tables, trying to crouch as small as he could.

The rain stopped abruptly, as if someone had turned off a sprinkler, leaving the rooftop garden awash with puddles. The flowers bowed, too heavy to hold their heads up, and drips fell from the rim of the parasol. Bustopher glared up from the shadows, his face squashed into a grumpy expression.

'It is fine now,' Bree told the cat. 'You can come out from under there.' She stood up and wandered over, but Bustopher started to recoil. 'Come on,' she cooed. 'Out you come.' She unpeeled the reluctant cat from the floor and took him up in her arms. He wriggled and twisted. 'What's up with you?' Bree rubbed his ears. 'You're acting like something's coming to eat you…'

When she looked up, her heart slammed into her mouth. There, standing a few feet away was

Hallux Valgus. He grinned, revealing his gnarled teeth and black gums, his mismatched eyes boring through her.

Bustopher pounced to the floor and slunk away between the plant pots. Bree slapped a hand to her mouth to cover a shriek. The ground beneath her seemed to tilt. Bree glanced over to the top of the ladder and back to him again. 'What are you doing here?' she managed to say.

'Are you surprised? Did you think I had died in Castle Zarcalat?' He beamed. 'You know what I've come for,' he hissed.

Bree acted quickly, feeling too desperate even to be afraid. She ran over to the bench and grabbed the book, shielding Mimi with her arms. 'Stay away from her,' she spat, trying to stop her voice from wobbling. 'You've put her through enough already!'

He moved closer and Bree felt her hand starting to ache from the intensity with which she gripped the book. 'We should have thrown that little worm to the Cleptathorns. I'm not interested in her. And I haven't come to see you either…'

The wind chimes clanged in the breeze, making him whirl around. The skin from his nose to his ear and up over his forehead was an angry mottled mess of burns. Bree's skin crawled with revulsion. He spat a curse under his breath and turned back to her.

'You thought you could run away from what you did at Castle Zarcalat.'

'No! I didn't start the fire,' she cried, unable to take her eyes off the fiery patterns that seemed livid against his waxy pallor. 'I mean, I didn't mean to start it...'

Little pools of foaming spittle had gathered at the corners of his mouth. Bree's pulse beat so hard that her whole body seemed to shake. Behind her Mimi let out a soft moan. *Not now, Mimi!* Bree screamed inside her head. Hallux stared hungrily at the book.

'I think you know it's not the child I want!' he said angrily.

Rage bubbled under Bree's skin. 'I will never hand it over!' she said, thrusting it deep into her pocket.

Hallux Valgus seemed to swell up with fury. He started twisting his diamond ring, mumbling some low words. Bree glanced over her shoulder to see Mimi's forehead crinkle as she stirred from her sleep.

'Levo Exhumus,' Valgus chanted under his breath.

Bree scanned the rooftop garden, her mind racing. What if everyone came up now? Would he kill them or would they scare him off? She could make a bolt for the ladders but that would mean leaving Mimi on her own with one of the men who had taken her prisoner...

The mangled remains of Valgus's Flame tattoo changed from black to red and Bree suddenly felt pins and needles in her feet. She tried to run but she felt she was stuck to the concrete. The sinister chant got louder and as it did Bree felt herself rise up.

'Tabernus Occumbo!' Hallux bellowed as he pointed his ring at her feet.

Bree stared down in horror to see that she was floating about a foot above the ground. Hallux Valgus dragged his finger in a slow line through the air and Bree was unwillingly dragged with it. He pointed out over the wall around the rooftop garden. Bree realised she was being pulled nearer the edge. She tried to struggle but her feet were paralysed.

'No! Put me down!' she screamed, but Hallux Valgus laughed.

'How high is this castle?' he smirked.

'Eight floors,' she said, trying to kick her legs.

'That's a long way to fall without magic to save you.'

'Let me go.'

'You have one last chance to save yourself,' he sneered, his words spaced out to give them a sharp, lucid cruelty. 'Give me the book. If you do not, I will drop you over the edge and take it from your poor dead hand.'

Before Bree could answer the air jangled with Honey's ringtone. Despite being inside Honey's satchel, it was still shrill and sudden. And it was enough to startle Hallux Valgus. The grin slipped from his mutilated face and he looked alarmed as his eyes darted around wildly.

'What is that sound? What kind of creature makes noises like that?'

In a flash his tattoo changed back to black and Bree dropped like a stone. She scrambled to her feet and ran over to Honey's satchel where she felt around for the phone. She pulled it out and looked down at the tiny screen. Two words sprang out, illuminated in vivid green and pulsing intermittently:

BREE CALLING

For a moment she was confused. How could she be calling herself? This had never happened before. Then Bree realised that Honey must be using Bree's phone she had left downstairs in her bedroom.

'What is this weapon you have?' Hallux Valgus stammered, eyeing the block of pink plastic.

Bree used the opportunity to her favour. She held the phone out in front of her and waved it around threateningly.

'Don't come any closer,' she warned, suddenly feeling braver. 'You'll regret it! I'm warning you. I'm not afraid to use this.'

The tinny music pulsed in the air between them. Valgus covered his ears and cowered, fear shadowing his mismatched eyes. Bree willed Honey not to hang up as she thrust the phone out in front of her and walked forwards, forcing Valgus to stagger back, close to the gap in the perimeter wall where the ladder began.

And then the ringing stopped. Horrified, Bree glanced at the phone.

1 MISSED CALL

it said on the little screen.

In the silence, all she could hear was Valgus's heavy breathing and her own thumping heart. She fumbled with the buttons on the phone to see if she could make it ring again, but it was no use. Valgus's lip curled with malicious triumph as he took a step towards her. His expression changed, the bewilderment evaporating into something much more sinister. The flicker of a grin turned Bree's blood cold. Before she saw him lift his hand he had smacked the phone out of her fingers, sending it skidding across the floor.

'It's not a weapon at all. You have nothing to protect yourself with,' he said. 'Give me the book.'

Suddenly, something flew over Bree's shoulder in a single dark streak. It was so fast and unexpected that she did not have time to work out what it was. For a second it looked like a blur of fur and muscle. Bustopher landed on Hallux Valgus's chest, making a solid thud which knocked the sour breath from his lungs.

'Arrgh!' he screamed, frantically flapping his arms around his head. Bustopher had turned into a ferocious ball of fur, spittle and claws flying in all directions. He hung there, digging his claws in and tearing through Valgus's cloak. Bree had never seen her cat like this. He was wild and angry, ears flat and tail bushed out. Valgus looked petrified. He took hold of the cat and tried to tear him off, but Bustopher hissed and spat. Valgus staggered backwards, then stumbled, and flipped over the wall. Bree shrieked. For a moment it looked like Bustopher might jump off in time but he went over with him and disappeared.

'No!' she screamed, running over, her hand automatically searching her pocket for the last of the magnetic dust. She blew hard, sending it into the air to hang there and merge into a fat wobbling bubble. Looking over the wall she saw Hallux Valgus falling backwards towards the pavement, his cloak flapping around him like a faulty parachute. Bustopher was still clinging to him but it was too late, they were both going to slam into the ground any second.

A flare of blue light blotted out everything in front of Bree's eyes. When she could see again she expected to see Hallux Valgus on the ground in a broken heap, limbs twisted and bent. But there was no sign of him – or the cat.

'Oh Bustopher…' Bree sobbed, her legs buckling from under her. She pulled away from the wall with tears pouring down her cheeks. Then she stopped abruptly and laughed with relief. Hanging by his collar from the magnetic bubble was Bustopher, looking even more cross-eyed than usual. He swivelled his head at a funny angle and licked his lips at her.

'You're safe!' she squealed, reaching out and pulling him to safety. She cuddled him tightly, pushing her nose deep into his fur until he was wet with her tears. He purred ferociously as she tickled him under the chin. 'My brave boy,' she laughed, 'what would I do without you?'

Honey and Sandy's laughter rose up from the balcony outside the bathroom window. Bree had never been so happy to hear their voices! She turned to see Sandy's head popping over the top of the ladder. 'Bree?'

'I'm over here!' she said, smiling.

Sandy eyed her and then the floating globule just as it turned to powder and floated away on the breeze. He raised his eyebrows, making his glasses ride up his nose. 'What did you need that for? Are you okay?' he asked.

'I am now you're here,' she smiled, kissing Bustopher gently on the head. He jumped out of her arms and stretched nonchalantly.

'What's my phone doing down there?' Honey picked her phone up from the ground and wiped off the dirt with her sleeve. 'Didn't you hear it ringing? I called you to let you know we were on our way back up,' she said with a questioning frown, 'but you didn't answer.'

Bree sighed and laughed at the same time. 'Honey Pizazz,' she grinned, putting her arm around her friend's shoulder, 'as always, you had perfect timing!'

Honey looked puzzled but there was no time to explain, because in that moment Mimi stretched and opened a bleary eye.

'Mimi!' squealed Honey, running over to the bench and throwing herself at her, 'you're awake!'

Mimi rubbed her eyes and squinted up, her face a picture of bewilderment.

'Did you sleep well sweetie?'

'Mmm-hmm,' she yawned, then furrowed her brow. 'I had a funny dream, and I think you were in it…'

Just then Bree's mother appeared at the top of the ladders. 'She is up here, Saffie!' she shouted over her shoulder before hauling herself up onto the rooftop. Madeleine leaned over and helped Saffron up the last few rungs. She was clearly struggling to pull herself over the top but she looked determined.

'Over here, Mum!' called Honey, 'she's fine!'

'Mimi? Is it really you? I don't believe it!' Saffron wailed. 'You had us so worried!'

Saffron's bones seemed to melt with relief as she waddled over to Mimi and grabbed her, pulling her close to her chest and showering her with kisses. Her voice was just a sudden soft rush of inflections and tender lilts. 'My baby, my baby,' she kept saying, holding Mimi out at arm's length and checking her over.

'What's up? What's all the fuss about?' frowned Mimi, her eyes flitting between her mum and her sister.

'We didn't know where you were. We've had everyone out looking for you,' said Saffron. 'Did you tell Mrs McCready or anyone else that you were coming up here?'

Mimi shook her head slowly, her face screwed up with the fuzz of sleep. 'I don't remember. I don't remember coming up here…' she sighed.

'It was all my fault, Mum,' said Honey. 'I was really mean and –'

Saffron shook her head, her earrings swinging. 'It doesn't matter now,' she said gently. 'Mimi is safe, that's all I care about.'

'I know, I mean you're right,' said Honey, 'but I'm still really sorry.'

Mimi pulled away from Honey and stared up at her suspiciously. 'Why are you being so nice to me?' she asked.

'Because sisters are special,' smiled Honey.

Mimi grinned, wide enough to show the gap in her front teeth. In that moment the sun broke free from a smouldering cloud, giving way to rinsed blue skies. Steam rose up from the concrete making misty rainbows in the bright light and the world seemed to come back to life. Madeleine put her arm around Bree and hugged her tightly.

'Ouch!' yelped Bree, pulling away and throwing her hand up to her shoulder. Madeleine's eyes flared in concern when she noticed the angry red patch.

'Sweetheart,' she sighed, somewhere between concern and annoyance, 'what have I told you?

You really must wear sun block in this heat.'

Bree waved her hand dismissively. 'I know, Mum,' she mumbled, relieved that the burn would need no further explanation, 'I won't forget next time.'

'Erm, is there any lemonade left, Mrs M?' asked Sandy. 'My mouth is as dry as an astronaut's slipper!'

Madeleine giggled but the smile slipped from her face when she spotted the bump on his forehead. 'What's this?' She cupped his chin and tilted his face to the light.

'I can't leave you two for a second, can I?' she sighed, her voice filled with motherly concern. 'Bree's been burned and you've got a bump on your head. What next?'

Sandy gave the bump a rub. 'It's nothing, honestly,' he said, brushing off her concern, 'we just got caught up in stuff, that's all.'

Madeleine ruffled his hair. 'Come on then, let's go and get some lemonade and cake,' she grinned. 'Your gran and Mr Pizazz are waiting downstairs for us.'

Hunger pangs roiled through Bree's stomach and she felt she had not eaten for weeks.

'Wait!' said Bree. 'We'll come in a second, Mum. But there's something me, Honey and Sandy need to do first.'

•••

Bree wiggled Don's magic key around in the library door.

'Hurry up,' whispered Honey, her eyes darting up and down the corridor, 'I think I can hear Mr Flangelberry coming.'

With a click the door sprung open. Bree, Honey and Sandy crept into the library, closing the door quietly behind them. The air inside felt soupy warm and stuffy.

'It's like an oven in here,' groaned Sandy, flapping his collar to let some air in.

'We're not hanging around. Let's just be quick,' said Bree, glancing cautiously at the door. 'Mr Flangelberry could come in at any moment.'

The sun shone in through the window and cast criss-cross patterns across the carpet. In aisle 142 shadows lay thick across the floor but everything looked pretty normal. To the inexperienced eye this looked like an ordinary aisle of books in an ordinary library.

'Someone has been tidying up in here,' said Sandy, noticing the clean floor and organised shelves.

'Or something…' said Honey with a shudder.

Sandy peered closely at the shelf along the back wall. 'The crack is almost invisible,' he said, running his finger over the thin scar that ran down the entire length of the bookcase.

'It is weird thinking about what's behind that wall,' said Honey, her mouth curling under at the corners.

Bree shuddered and rubbed her bare arms. 'I'd

rather not think about it.' she grimaced.

Honey flicked her ponytail over her shoulder and surveyed the rows of books. 'Weird though, don't you think?' she continued, tracing the faint crack. 'That every day pupils and teachers wander around this library without the slightest clue that there's more to this place than just bricks, mortar and all these dusty, dog-eared books.'

'They think it's just a boring old school library,' sighed Sandy. 'It's probably for the best they don't know.'

'And they're never going to know either,' said Bree, pulling the book from her pocket, 'because we are going to put this back and forget all about it.'

'I'll go and get the ladders,' said Sandy, disappearing around the corner.

Honey put a hand on Bree's shoulder and gave it a gentle squeeze. 'You know, I think your dad would be so proud of what you've done,' she said.

Bree brushed the cover of the book and smiled. 'Who knows. I hope so. I mean, I like to think that somewhere...'

The stepladders arrived with a creak and a groan. 'I'm going to give Mrs M some oil for these rusty wheels,' said Sandy, positioning the ladder in exactly the right spot. He took a step back and looked at Bree. 'Would you like me to go up?' he asked.

Bree shook her head and put her foot on the first

rung. 'No thanks, I'd like to do it this time.'

Standing on her tiptoes at the top of the stepladders, Bree pulled out *Origami: A Beginners Guide* from the shelf, and pushed the magic book as far back into the dark space as she could. She peered into the void one last time. The book lay resting in its rightful place. Hidden, protected, and safe again.

The afternoon sun slanted in through the windows, the shaft of light capturing a dancing swirl of dust motes. Bree let out a breath she hadn't realised she had been holding. Bree felt she was rolling a rock across the entrance to a tomb when she slid *Origami: A Beginners Guide* back into the gap.

She jumped off the last couple of steps, landing on the carpet with a soft thump. Honey smiled, her sapphire eyes glinting in the ray of sunlight. 'Job well done,' she said, patting Bree on the back.

'No offence,' said Sandy, pushing his glasses up his nose, 'but I hope it's a long time before we see that book again.'

Bree smiled, but secretly she hoped he was right.

20.

FALLING...

The night seemed to swallow his tumbling body, the earth pulling and sucking him down. The inky darkness told him that he had somehow ripped back through the fabric between worlds. Cold rain lanced his skin. He reached out for something to grab onto but his fingers found only air.

Falling...

As he plummeted through a torrent of wind and rain that girl's voice echoed in his ears, the image of her face burned into his mind's eye. He knew it would never fade.

The wind tore past, whipping and buffeting him as his cloak billowed around his head. A sudden flash of lightening allowed him to see the slash in his robe where the furry creature had clung to him.

Still falling...

He allowed his limbs to go limp and let the wind carry him downwards. He felt the prickle of blood running through his veins. Something swelled in his stomach, a feeling of fierce exhilaration.

This was not the end of him.

With the wave of euphoria came the absolute certainty that this was only the beginning.

A laugh erupted from deep within his being, exploding from his mouth and mingling with the sound of rushing air. His mismatched eyes burned.

21.

EVERY END IS A NEW BEGINNING

A lingering sunset heralded the end of a long summer's day in Rockwell. The sun had started to drift behind the horizon, turning the sky a deep and wonderful pink. The heat still loitered in the rooftop garden, warming the stone under Bree's bare feet.

Her mother had worked without a break to make everything look magical for Annie Hooten's birthday party that evening. She had decorated the perimeter wall with balloons and streamers, and hung multi-coloured lanterns that swung in the balmy breeze. She had scattered rugs and large plump cushions across the floor and lined flickering candles along the wall like an army of winking stars.

On the table there was a banquet of delicious things to eat and drink, including fairy cakes with buttercream icing, sausage rolls, apple punch and homemade lemonade by the gallon. Taking pride of place was the birthday cake that Madeleine had baked for Annie. It was beautifully decorated in swirls with white icing. In the centre a tiny figure had been painstakingly crafted from icing; a flame-haired lady in shades, standing on a skateboard. Madeleine had told Bree she thought it was not a bad likeness of Annie. Completely covering the cake however, was a forest of orange and yellow birthday candles, so many that Annie had joked about having a fire extinguisher close at hand in case she needed help to blow them out.

A compilation of Annie's favourite songs drifted out from two speakers perched on the wall, but not so loud that they drowned out the chatter and laughter from the guests.

Saffron's smile was as warm as the evening air as she stood arm in arm with Mort. Saffron had twisted her hair up in a loose coil but it fell down in strands around her bare shoulders, and with the complexion of a white peach, it was not difficult to see how Honey had been blessed with such beauty, inside and out. Saffron's pregnant belly poked out from under her long, wraparound skirt. Mort stroked it absentmindedly as he smiled lovingly at her. They looked just like the photo of Bree's parents, taken just before she was born. Bree felt a twinge of sadness as she remembered their faces full of happiness and excited anticipation. But although her father was gone, her mother was still here and so was she. The more she thought about how much she really did love her mother in spite of her occasional irritation, the more she felt a gentle contentment wrap around her heart. Everyone that she cared about was up here on this tiny improvised garden, eight floors above the ground.

Annie stood, resplendent and only slightly

wobbly in her platform shoes. She smiled as Mort poured wine into her glass from a height while she gestured wildly in conversation with the other hand. Honey and Mimi roared with laughter as they tried to synchronise their ambitious dance moves. Honey had painted their toenails to match their shocking pink skirts. She danced confidently, her loose hair a silky shimmer in the dusk. Annie spun Sandy around to the music and he joined in until she planted a big kiss on his cheek, leaving behind a huge rose-coloured smudge. He grumbled bashfully under his breath and wiped it off leaving a lavish smear.

Bree watched her mother sip a glass of something fizzy, a contented smile lifting the corners of her lips. Her eyes seemed to catch and hold the soft lights perfectly. It seemed to Bree that her mother was radiant, bubbling over with some secret happiness. Bustopher weaved his way in and out of her legs and she chuckled as she tried to keep her balance. She picked him up and put him across her shoulders and he curled round her neck like a furry boa.

'Now, attention please everyone. It's present giving time!' announced Annie in a sing-song voice. She teetered over to the buffet table on her impossibly high shoes and lifted the checked cloth to reveal a bag full of gift boxes. Mimi whooped excitedly and skipped over to take a closer look.

'Surely we should be giving *you* the presents, Annie?' laughed Saffron, 'It is your birthday after all.'

Annie hiccupped behind her hand and burped loudly. 'Excuse I! Dear, when you get to be my age it's much more fun to give than to receive,' she said with a dramatic flick of the wrist. 'And all of you are my presents anyway!'

There was a collective sigh of sweetness and a small ripple of applause. Madeleine placed Bustopher down on one of the cushions, and lowered the music as everyone gathered around the table. Annie lifted the bag but almost lost her balance.

'Now, you must excuse me,' she giggled, holding on to the corner of the table as she swayed, 'I may have had a little too much apple bobbing punch!' She drew in a deep, steadying breath and began to rummage around inside the bag. Picking out a pale green box she glanced at the label and smiled.

'Mimi, you gave us all a big fright today,' she said. 'So we are very glad you turned up safe and happy.'

Mort squeezed Saffron a little tighter and Honey flashed Bree a small, secret smile.

'I have something for you,' continued Annie, 'a gift that embodies your spirit.' She held out the box and Mimi stared at it with wide, expectant eyes.

'What is it Granny Annie?' she asked, her freckled face wreathed in smiles.

'Open it and see!'

Mimi pulled off the lid and there, nestled amongst some black tissue shreds and pieces of glittering heart confetti was a wooden swan. She stroked the yellow beak tenderly and smiled up at Annie. 'It's lovely, thank you!'

'Now, the swan symbolises the awakening of beauty,' said Annie, with a tender smile. 'It is sensitive, emotional – a bit of a dreamer – she represents innocence and love.'

On the last word Mimi giggled and hid behind her hair. She glanced over at Sandy who, this time, nodded back and smiled. She smiled bashfully, her cheeks soft pink beneath the freckles.

Annie hiccupped and giggled at the same time making everyone laugh. She plucked out a chocolate-coloured box from the bag, her face bright with the joy that giving presents always gave her.

'For Honey I have the most mystical creature ever to roam the earth!' she announced, handing the box to Honey. She lifted the lid and eagerly removed her wooden animal from its nest of white shredded tissue.

'A ginger cat!' she squealed, holding it up for everyone to see.

'The cat is the strong protector,' smiled Annie. 'Fiercely independent and self-assured, she represents balance and wisdom. But above all the ability to fight back when cornered.'

Bree smiled at that and heard Honey's father whisper, 'Remind you of anyone?' Saffron nudged him playfully.

'Now, Miss McCready. For you,' said Annie, her voice choked with emotion. For a moment, she looked at Bree the way she sometimes did, as if she saw something beyond what other people could see. When Annie smiled a thousand tiny lines appeared on her face like cracks in an oil painting. She pulled out another pastel green box and handed it to her.

Bree, who was struggling to contain her excitement, bit down on her bottom lip and willed herself to enjoy this short-lived moment of ticklish, quivering anticipation. Nothing ever matched this feeling. When she lifted the lid there inside was a painted wooden badger with a white-tipped tail and a knowing smile staring up at her.

'I love it,' sighed Bree, stroking it tenderly. It felt smooth and warm, almost alive.

'Well my dear, you should. Because the badger is the keeper of stories,' Annie beamed. 'She is best known for wisdom, passion and perseverance, the badger is renowned for showing inventive action in a crisis.'

Madeleine put a motherly arm around Bree and gave her the gentlest pat. 'It's perfect. Just like you, darling,' she whispered, making Bree blush with pride.

The last box from the bag was dark blue and slightly bigger than the others. Annie's eyes rested on her Grandson.

'And finally. This one is for Sandy,' she said proudly. He took the box from his Gran and slowly removed the lid. Everyone waited eagerly to see which animal Annie had chosen for him. He grinned and held aloft a large brown bear for everyone to admire.

'The creature of dreams,' mused Annie, 'best known for his intelligence and introspection; he represents transformation, thoughtfulness and quiet, natural strength.'

Bree and Honey nodded together in agreement and gave Sandy the thumbs up. He puffed out his chest, savouring the moment as the wooden bear was passed around for everyone to take a closer look. As always, Annie had chosen the perfect gift for everyone.

'Oh! We have something for you too, Mrs Hooten,' smiled Bree, giving Honey a wink. Honey skipped over to the corner of the rooftop garden and started rummaging around inside her satchel.

Annie wrapped an arm around Bree and kissed her on the cheek. 'What's this with *Mrs Hooten?* You make me sound like my old mother-in-law! When are you going to start calling me Annie?' she scolded jokingly. 'After all, you're growing up and soon we'll be practically the same age.'

Bree giggled as Annie clapped her hands together impatiently like an excited school girl. Honey pulled out bits and pieces from her satchel before she found what she was looking for.

'Goodness knows what she keeps in that grotty old bag,' laughed Saffron, 'it's not like she'll ever need any of it.'

Grinning, Bree and Sandy gave each other a knowing look as Honey skipped back over holding a present, wrapped in pretty turquoise paper and tied with a white ribbon. She presented it to Annie and gestured for her to open it.

'Happy Birthday,' she grinned widely, a tiny piece of heart confetti glinting on her cheek.

With an excited squeal Annie ripped off the paper to reveal a silver picture frame, which housed the photograph that Honey had carried around with her all day. It was slightly crumpled and water stained, but Honey had managed to jazz up the worst parts with stickers and smiley faces and flowers drawn on with silver pen. Bree, Honey, Mimi and Sandy had signed their names beside themselves in the picture.

'It's perfect! I love it!' gushed Annie as she gave each of them a tight hug.

'We hoped you would,' smiled Bree.

Honey skipped over to the stereo and turned a knob until a lively jazz number came floating over the speakers. Annie placed the frame down on the table and raised her glass high.

'A toast to all my wonderful children!' she said over the music.

Everyone raised their glasses and joined in.

'Let's light the candles on your cake, Granny Annie!' squealed Mimi. Madeleine stepped forward and lit them one by one until flames bobbed merrily on the warm breeze and lit Annie's face in a hue to match her hair.

'Make a wish!' Mimi clapped excitedly.

'And I'll take your birthday picture,' said Honey holding up her phone.

Annie closed her eyes, took a deep breath and blew. It took another two breaths to blow out all the candles. Everyone clapped and cheered. In the twilight Annie's eyes looked watery as she leaned over and planted her painted mouth on Sandy's cheek again, leaving behind a bright red pucker.

This time he didn't wipe it off.

• • •

Sitting alone at the edge of the roof garden, Bree looked out across the city. The sun was now a melting ball of fire that flashed across the sky and licked a golden paste over everything in its path. She could see the black rectangle of Guinessberry Heights opposite, the pink halo of the sky softening its edges. The balconies bulged with drying clothes, pushchairs and children's bikes. Rockwell looked like a toy town from up here, a patchwork of grey roofs, green gardens and glinting glass.

She was about to turn around when a flicker of red caught her eye. A butterfly had landed on the perimeter wall, the evening sun capturing the colour of its satin wings, turning them crimson and gold. She remembered what Dunubas had told her about butterflies being the souls of the dead coming back to visit those they loved. She felt a warm blush travel through her body. She gently lifted it with cupped hands and immediately the butterfly panicked, its wings beating wildly against her palms. So much strength and power for such a delicate little creature, thought Bree as she carefully uncurled her fingers and let it fly free. She watched it flutter and disappear into the evening sky, her heart soaring with it.

When she turned around she saw that Annie's platform shoes had been tossed aside and she now danced barefoot with her arms above her head. Mort was spinning round in circles with Mimi on his hip until she was all dizzy and giggling. Bree was surprised to see that Harry Montague had turned up. He stood with her mum in the far corner of the garden, deep in conversation. Harry looked much fresher than he had when they had seen him this morning; his shirt was crisp and his hair was neat and shiny. He was carrying a bottle in one hand and a bunch of flowers in the other. Her mum had her head tilted to one side and was smoothing her hair, the way she did when she was feeling self-conscious.

And then it was her turn to feel the same way. Her heart gave an odd little flutter when she clapped eyes on Adam Eastbough talking with Saffron and Honey. How on earth had he known where to come? She stood up and straightened her clothes while he wasn't looking, combed her thatch of unruly hair with her fingers and took a deep breath. Bree felt her mouth dry up as she saw him making his way over to her. Every muscle, every cell in her body seemed suddenly to vibrate, to come alive. She swallowed hard and took a slow, blundering step forward.

'Hey. Your furry friend is causing havoc,' Adam laughed, pointing at Bustopher trying to run away with one of the cheese scones off the buffet table. Madeleine was trying to gently shoo him away and her antics were the source of much hilarity. Bree cringed with embarrassment and tried to distract Adam.

'So, how was Alice's party then?' she said.

'Oh, I dunno. It's not really my scene to be honest.'

'Great,' Bree said with more delight in her voice than she had intended. 'Well, I know what you mean. That's not really my scene either.'

'Cool. And besides,' Adam shrugged, his ebony eyes looking out from behind his black, tousled fringe. 'The view is much better up here.' His eyes seemed to bore through Bree's skin and she felt herself blush.

'How did you know where to come?' she asked, desperate to fill the pressing silence.

Adam gave her a puzzled look. 'Because I got the note you wrote me,' he replied, pulling something out of his shirt pocket.

Bree searched her memory. She could not recall giving Adam a note when they met outside Ramthorpe Junior. But it had been a long day and to be honest nothing would surprise her anymore.

'Honey gave it to me at lunchtime,' he continued, handing her a piece of bubble gum wrapper. 'She said you were too busy to give it to me yourself.'

Bree looked down at the flattened strip of foil and suddenly everything made sense. On the white side of the wrapper there was a hastily scribbled message in Honey's distinctive handwriting:

Flat 8B, Rockwell Tower Block. Front door will be open, make your way up to the roof. See you around 8pm. Bree x

Bree did not know whether to be angry or grateful, whether to stamp her feet or whoop for joy. All she knew was that firstly she had the best friends anyone could ever wish for and secondly this was quite possibly the best night of her life so far. She handed the little scrap of paper back to Adam but couldn't think of a single thing to say to him.

'I'm glad you came,' she eventually managed to stammer. His eyes fixed on hers for what felt like an eternity and Bree was relieved when Honey skipped over and threw her arms around her neck and kissed her cheek.

'You can thank me later, hotstuff,' she whispered out the side of her mouth.

Bree tried to look cross but eventually her face broke into a beam which rivalled the rays from the moon that hung over Rockwell Tower.

Sandy tried to look casual as he stopped next to Adam. He gave him a sideways glance, eyeing him like he was some new and previously undiscovered animal.

'Oh wow, look!' Honey cried, wriggling her fingers under Bree's nose. 'My mood ring has turned purple.'

Adam laughed a soft, easy laugh. 'And that's good?'

'And that's what I asked too,' said Sandy with a roll of his eyes. 'You can't get better than purple. Apparently *everybody* knows that.'

'Except for us, eh?' laughed Adam.

'Maybe you should slip it on, Sandy,' smiled Honey, ruffling his hair affectionately. 'Who knows what it would tell us about you…?'

Sandy wiped his mouth with a napkin and looked at Adam nervously.

'Why don't you show Adam where he can get a drink?' Bree said to Sandy, giving him an encouraging look.

Sandy's face reddened and he shifted awkwardly. He eyed Adam hesitantly and then nodded towards the buffet table. As they walked away Honey took Bree's hand and rested her head on her shoulder.

Bree said, 'Honey, I hope there won't be any jealousy.'

'Oh boy,' replied Honey. 'Me too…'

'Do you think it is obvious?'

'That Sandy likes Adam? I think so. But it's not obvious to Sandy.'

'What are you talking about?'

'I've been watching them. You cannot hide anything from Honey Pizazz! I think Sandy has a boy crush going on.'

'No – I meant is it obvious that *I* like Adam?'

'Well, Sandy can tell. But that's because he's a good friend. To the rest of Rockwell, nope. You're always playing it too cool, missus.'

They watched as the two boys stacked their paper plates with party food. They were as different as night and day; Adam was relaxed and confident, whereas Sandy was painfully aware of every move he made. They were talking animatedly and laughing together.

'I hope they can get on with each other,' Bree sighed.

'Absolutely. Maybe they'll end up being good friends,' Honey said hopefully.

• • •

Harry offered Madeleine a huge bunch of sweet peas. The ends had been wrapped in wet tissue paper to stop them from drying out. She stared down at the ruffled blossoms and put both hands over her chest as though she were trying to stop something from escaping her heart.

'My favourite!' she swooned. 'I can't believe you remembered.'

Harry looked pleased as Madeleine took the flowers from him and inhaled their heady scent. 'Oh, and I have something else for you,' he said, digging around in his pocket. He held up a small envelope with a pretty watercolour picture of the same flowers on the front.

'Lathyrus Latifolius,' Harry said with a grin. 'Everlasting Sweet Peas.

'Madeleine frowned and then a sprinkling of understanding crossed her face.

'If you look after them you should get a good show of blossom right up until the first frost…' He tapped the envelope gently. 'This kind doesn't have much of a fragrance, but then you can't have everything, can you?'

As she took the sachet of seeds from him, she shook her head gently, trying to chase away wisps of unwanted emotion.

'I'm sorry, Harry. I'm getting emotional,' she said, dabbing mascara from beneath her eyes. 'It's…it's just such a lovely gesture.'

'You should sow them between February and May,' he continued, shrugging boyishly. 'I can help you, if you like?'

Madeleine studied his face for a moment and a look of uncertainty creased her brow. A gentle breeze wafted over the garden stirring the petals of the sweet peas in her hand like butterfly wings. She smiled softly and looked up at Harry. After she had blinked away her tears she said with a smile, 'Yes. Yes, I'd like that very much.'

• • •

As dusk fell, the world beyond the roof garden became a vast concrete forest, the roads a network of grey rivers. Bustopher sauntered over to where Bree was standing dreaming. He arched his back around Bree's legs and she scooped him up and sunk her face into his soft fur. He responded by padding her cheek with the plump pads of his feet.

'How's my hero?' she whispered into his ear and his entire body vibrated with delight. She turned back to look out over Rockwell. The rooftops were gilded in the last light of the setting sun, the rays touching paint and stone with pure fire.

She was suddenly filled with the feeling that she might be standing at the edge of something wonderful. A touch on her arm startled her, chasing the thought away and she wheeled round. Adam was standing there.

'Would you like to dance?'

Somehow, in those five words, there was a promise of *something,* the chance for an entire life to be lived if only she took the chance.

Adam's eyebrows lifted in silent enquiry, his neat white teeth hesitantly nibbled on his lip. Bree could feel the hot beginnings of a blush so took a moment to compose herself. She looked away, up at the faint bloom of the moon that hung in the darkening sky where traces of clouds shifted to reveal an indescribable density of stars. They seemed to hang over her, silent, kindly and watchful.

It was as though they were privy to the secrets of the world, always listening, winking knowingly. Who knew what those stars had in store for her?

Bree looked back at Adam. His dark eyes seemed to flicker magically in the candlelight.

'I would. Yes. I'd like that very much,' Bree McCready said with a smile.

THE END

Bree McCready and the Half-Heart Locket
ISBN 978-1-905537-11-2 (paperback, RRP £6.99)

Twelve-year-old Bree McCready has a mission: she has just one night to save the world!

It starts when a clue inscribed on a Half-Heart Locket leads Bree and her best friends Sandy and Honey to an ancient magical book. With it they can freeze time, fly and shrink to the size of ants.

But they soon discover the book has a long history of destruction and death. And it's being sought by the monstrous Thalofedril, who will stop at nothing to get it.

Using its incredible powers, he could turn the world into a wasteland.

Bree, Sandy and Honey go on the run—hurtling off city rooftops, down neck-breaking ravines, and through night-black underground tunnels—to keep the book out of his lethal hands. Little do they know that the greatest danger of all lies ahead, in the heart of his deadly lair…

Can Bree find the courage to face this terrifying evil, and to confront the secrets of her tragic past?

DarkIsle

ISBN 978-1-905537-04-4 (paperback, RRP £6.99)

For 10-year-old Morag, there's nothing magical about the cellar of her cruel foster parents' home. But that's where she meets Aldiss, a talking rat, and his resourceful companion, Bertie the dodo. She jumps at the chance to run away and join them on their race against time to save their homeland from the evil warlock Devlish, who is intent on destroying it. But first, Bertie and Aldiss will need to stop bickering long enough to free the only guide who knows where to find Devlish: Shona, a dragon who's been turned to stone.

Together, these four friends begin their journey to a mysterious dark island beyond the horizon, where danger and glory await—along with clues to the disappearance of Morag's parents, whose destiny seems somehow linked to her own...

DarkIsle: Resurrection
ISBN 978-1-905537-18-1 (paperback, RRP £6.99)

Two months after she saved The Eye of Lornish, Morag is adjusting to life in the secret northern kingdom of Marnoch Mor. But dark dreams are troubling her and a spate of unexplained events prove that even with the protection of her friends—Shona the dragon, Bertie the dodo and Aldiss the rat—Morag is still not safe from harm…

Lee and the Consul Mutants
ISBN 978-1-905537-01-3 (paperback, RRP £6.99)

It's not every day that a part of your body explodes, but Lee's appendix does exactly that, landing him in hospital.

Soon after his operation, Lee is shocked to discover that evil Consul Mutants are trying to take over the world. Worse still, the hospital he is stuck in contains the portal they are using to invade Earth.

Other kids might quake in their boots at this news, but not Lee. He's determined to save the world and comes up with a cunning plan to stop the aliens.

This is the story of a young boy battling against intergalactic odds for the sake of humankind. Lee's only weapon is his intelligence…which is a pity.

Lee Goes for Gold

ISBN 978-1-905537-00-6 (paperback, RRP £6.99)

Meeting his dad's multizillionaire employer inspires ten-year-old Lee to come up with a brilliant get-rich-quick scheme of his own.

But not everyone is keen for Lee to succeed. Local shop-keeper Panface certainly isn't, and it seems that he has sneaky spies out there, trying to ruin Lee's plans.

Will Lee overcome those out to stop him making his fortune? Or will he spend the whole time daydreaming about how many houses he'll be able to own and how many of them will have swimming pools and butlers?

Lee will need to rely on his common sense and financial genius if he's to succeed...so it could be an uphill struggle.

Lee's Holiday Showdown
ISBN 978-1-905537-02-0 (paperback, RRP £6.99)

Nothing is ever straightforward when Lee is around. Not even a summer holiday in Spain. It ought to be a case of lazing by the pool, but Lee is soon spying on dodgy men in shiny suits and sunglasses, battling with a family that seems determined to ruin everyone's holiday, and haranguing horrendous holiday reps.

With so much going on, how will Lee ever get a tan?

Lee on the Dark Side of the Moon
ISBN 978-1-905537-13-6 (paperback, RRP £6.99)

Lee has won the chance to be The First Child In Space. It's amazing what you can win these days by filling in a form on the back of a cereal packet!

Under the command of Captain Slogg, and with Sports Bob at the controls, Lee blasts off for the Moon on the trip of a lifetime. However, he and his fellow astronauts are not the only ones with their eyes on the big lump of cheese in the sky.

When disaster strikes, Lee faces the most important challenge of his life. If he succeeds he will return to Earth a hero. If he fails, he may not return at all.

The Comet's Child
ISBN 978-1-905537-12-9 (paperback, RRP £7.99)

For as long as anyone can remember there have been rumours about the return of a chosen one. When Fin discovers the prophecies point to him he is scared, at first. He resolves to learn the truth about his origins and uncover the secrets surrounding his birth; only then can he embrace his true destiny.

The journey ahead is exciting and full of danger, but others must stop him before he learns the truth…

The Cat Kin
ISBN 978-1-905537-16-7 (paperback, RRP £6.99)

Everyone who came to the strange gym class was looking for something else. What they found was the mysterious Mrs Powell and Pashki, a lost art from an age when cats were worshipped as gods.

Ben and Tiffany wonder: who is their eccentric old teacher? What does she really want with them? And why are they suddenly able to see in the dark?

Meanwhile, in London's gloomy streets, human vermin are stirring. Ben and Tiffany may soon be glad of their new gifts. But against men whose cunning is matched only by their unspeakable cruelty, will even nine lives be enough?